Fall in love with all the **BABYMOUSE** books!

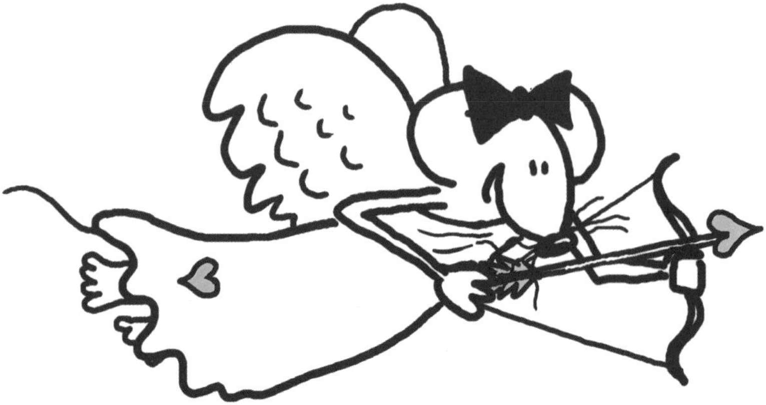

#1 BABYMOUSE: Queen of the World!
#2 BABYMOUSE: Our Hero
#3 BABYMOUSE: Beach Babe
#4 BABYMOUSE: Rock Star
#5 BABYMOUSE: Heartbreaker

472184

1/14

BABYMOUSE
HEARTBREAKER

BY JENNIFER L. HOLM & MATTHEW HOLM

RANDOM HOUSE NEW YORK

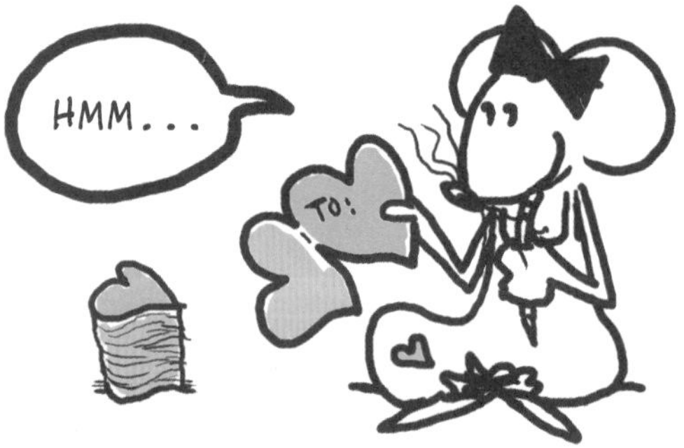
HMM...
TO:

This is a work of fiction. Names, characters, places, and incidents either are the product of the authors' imagination or are used fictitiously. Any resemblance to actual persons, living or dead, events, or locales is entirely coincidental.

Published in the United States by Random House Children's Books, a division of Random House, Inc., New York.

www.randomhouse.com/kids
www.babymouse.com

Educators and librarians, for a variety of teaching tools, visit us at
www.randomhouse.com/teachers

Library of Congress Cataloging-in-Publication Data
Holm, Jennifer L.
Babymouse : Heartbreaker / Jennifer L. Holm and Matthew Holm.
p. cm.
ISBN-13: 978-0-375-83798-2 (trade) — ISBN-13: 978-0-375-93798-9 (lib. bdg.)
I. Graphic novels. I. Holm, Matthew. II. Title.
PN6727.H592B27 2006
741.5'973—dc22
2006045418

PRINTED IN MALAYSIA 10 9 8 7 6 5 4 3 2 1 First Edition

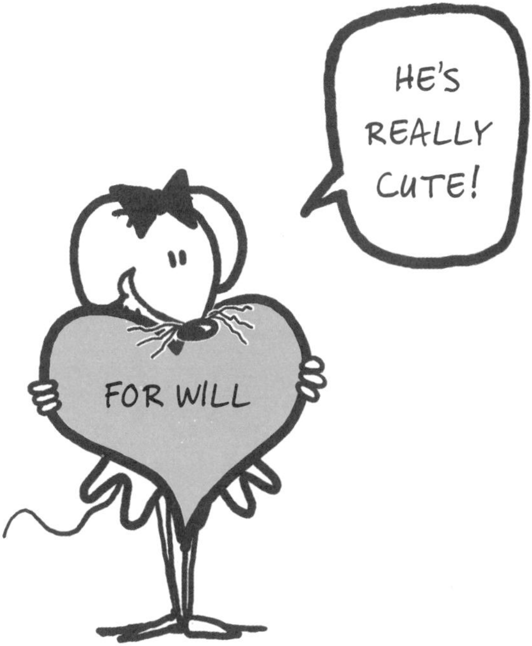
HE'S REALLY CUTE!
FOR WILL

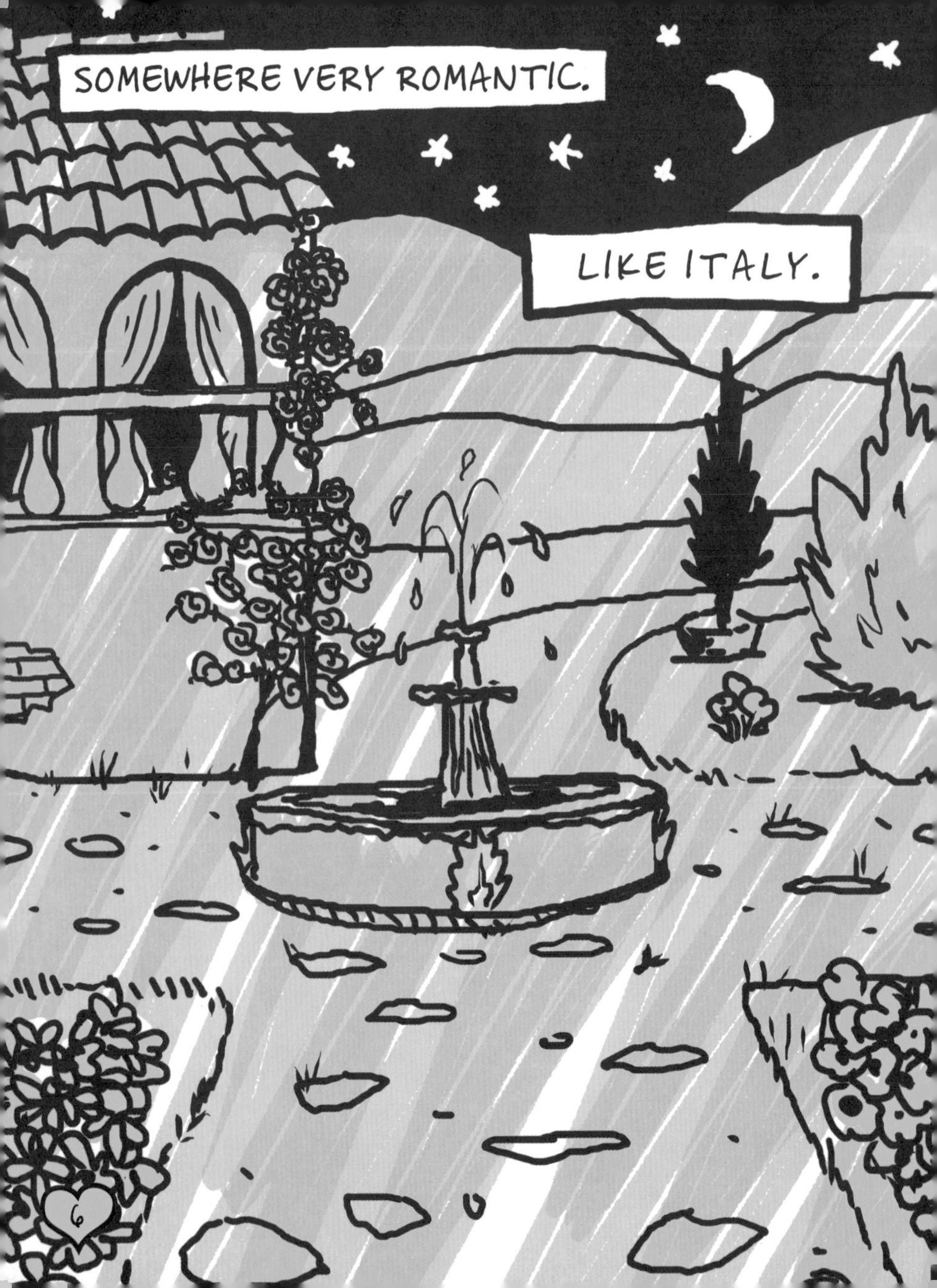
SOMEWHERE VERY ROMANTIC.
LIKE ITALY.

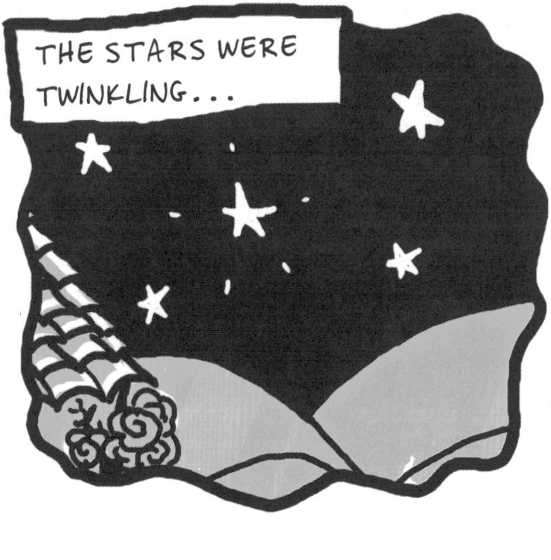
THE STARS WERE TWINKLING...

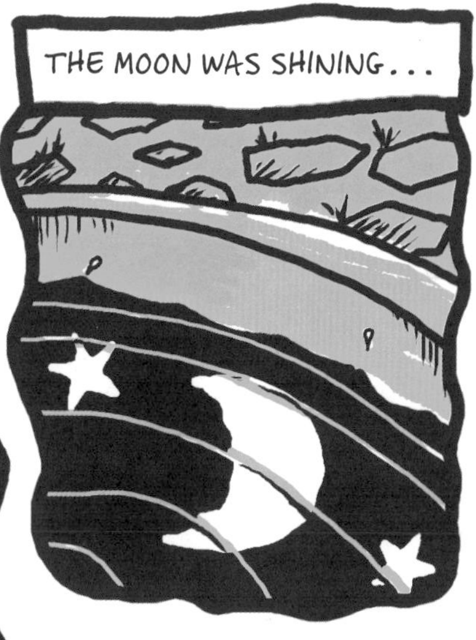
THE MOON WAS SHINING...

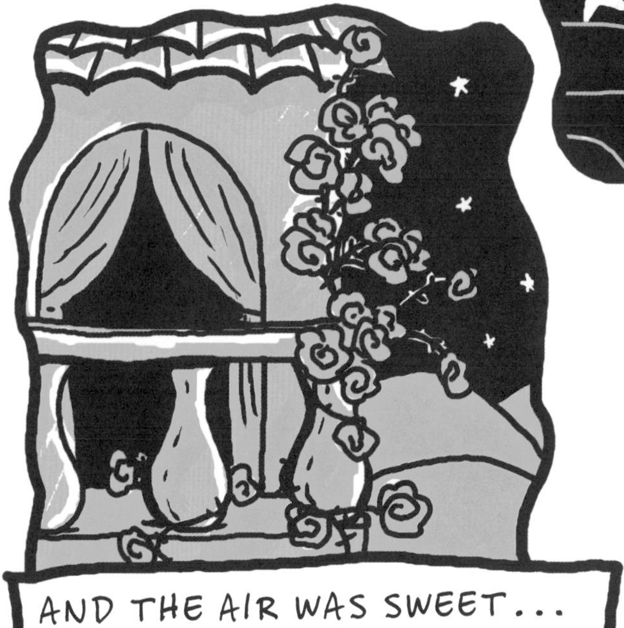
AND THE AIR WAS SWEET...

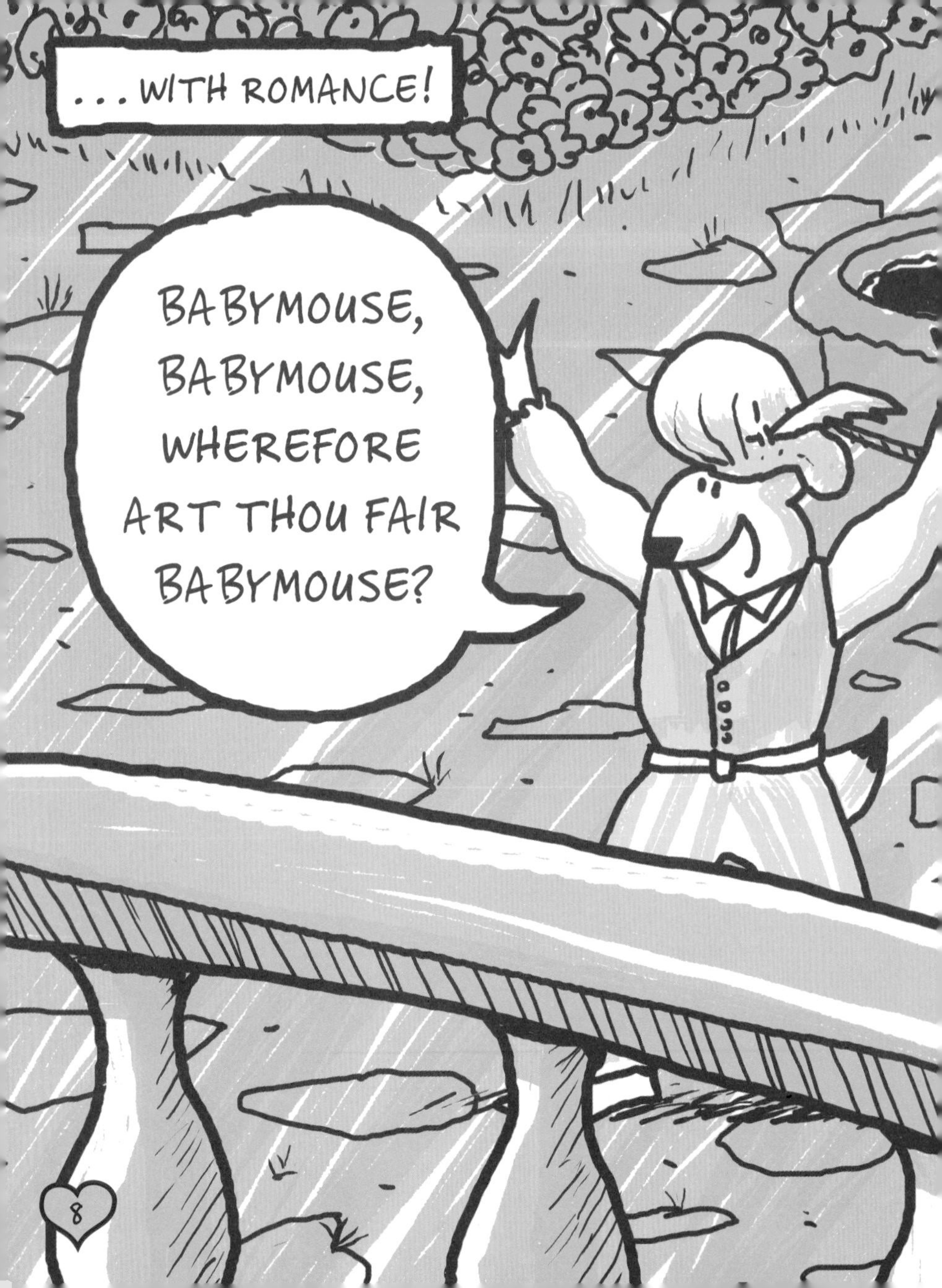
. . . WITH ROMANCE!
BABYMOUSE, BABYMOUSE, WHEREFORE ART THOU FAIR BABYMOUSE?

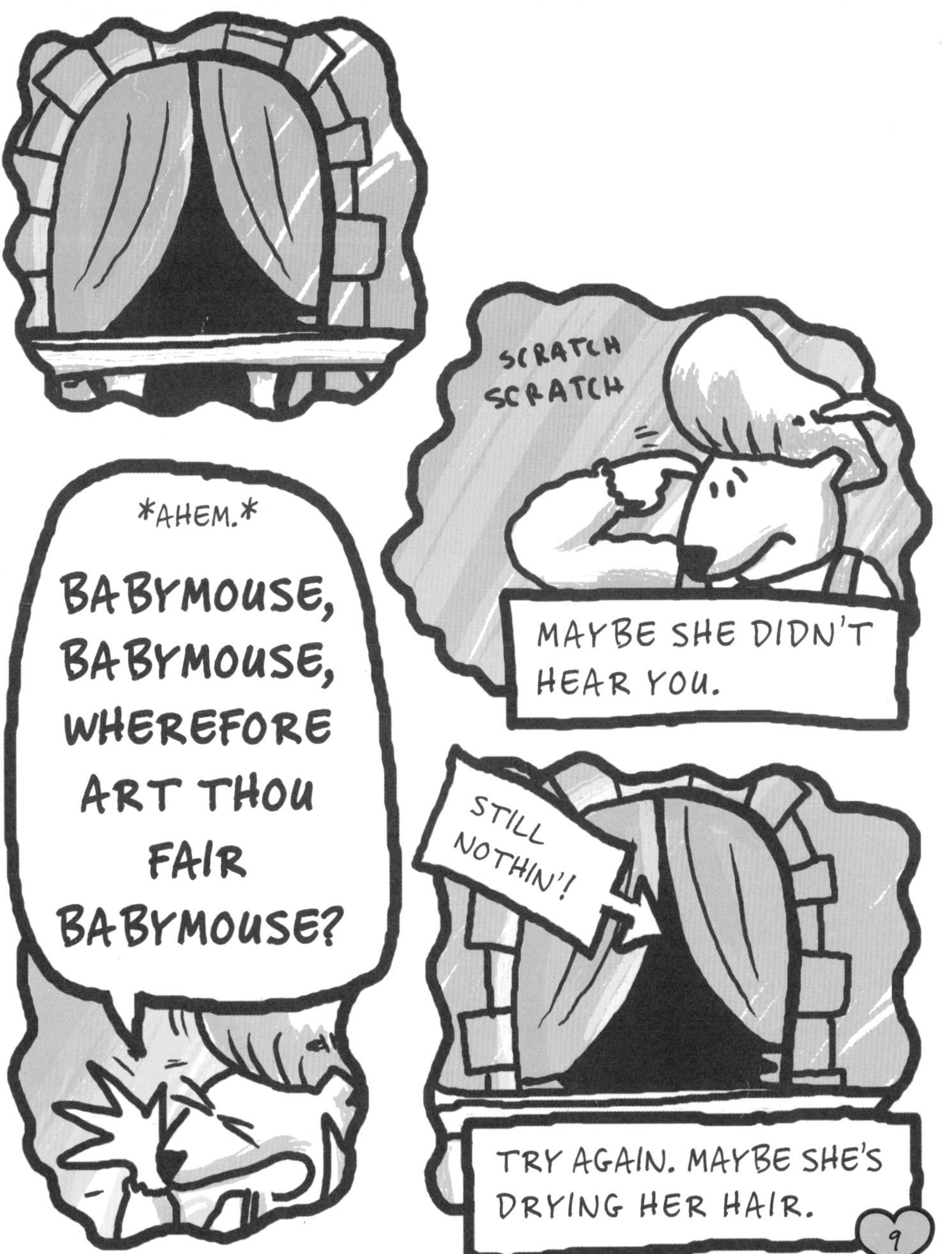
SCRATCH
SCRATCH
MAYBE SHE DIDN'T HEAR YOU.
AHEM.
BABYMOUSE, BABYMOUSE, WHEREFORE ART THOU FAIR BABYMOUSE?
STILL NOTHIN'!
TRY AGAIN. MAYBE SHE'S DRYING HER HAIR.

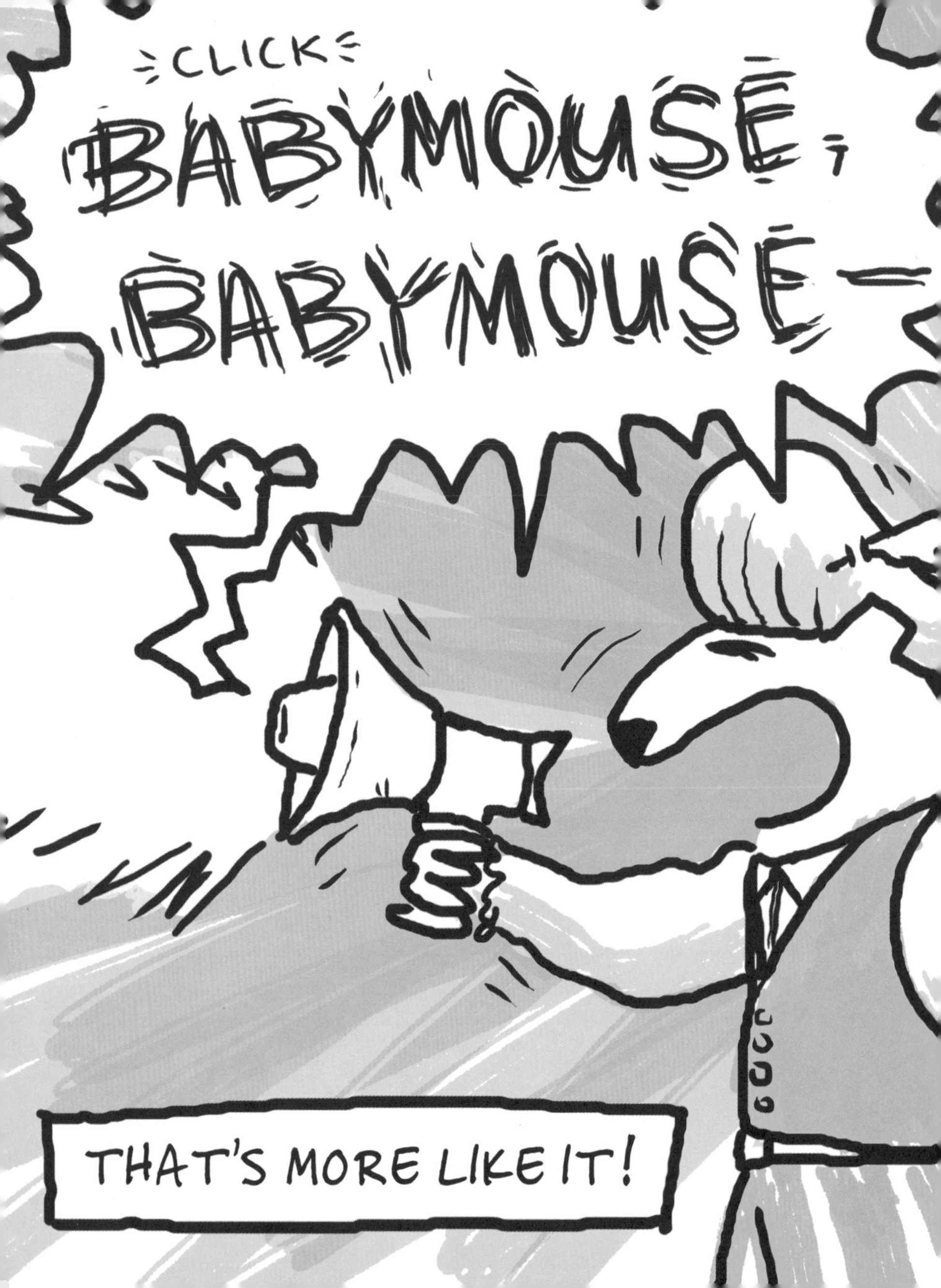
CLICK
BABYMOUSE, BABYMOUSE, BABYMOUSE—
THAT'S MORE LIKE IT!

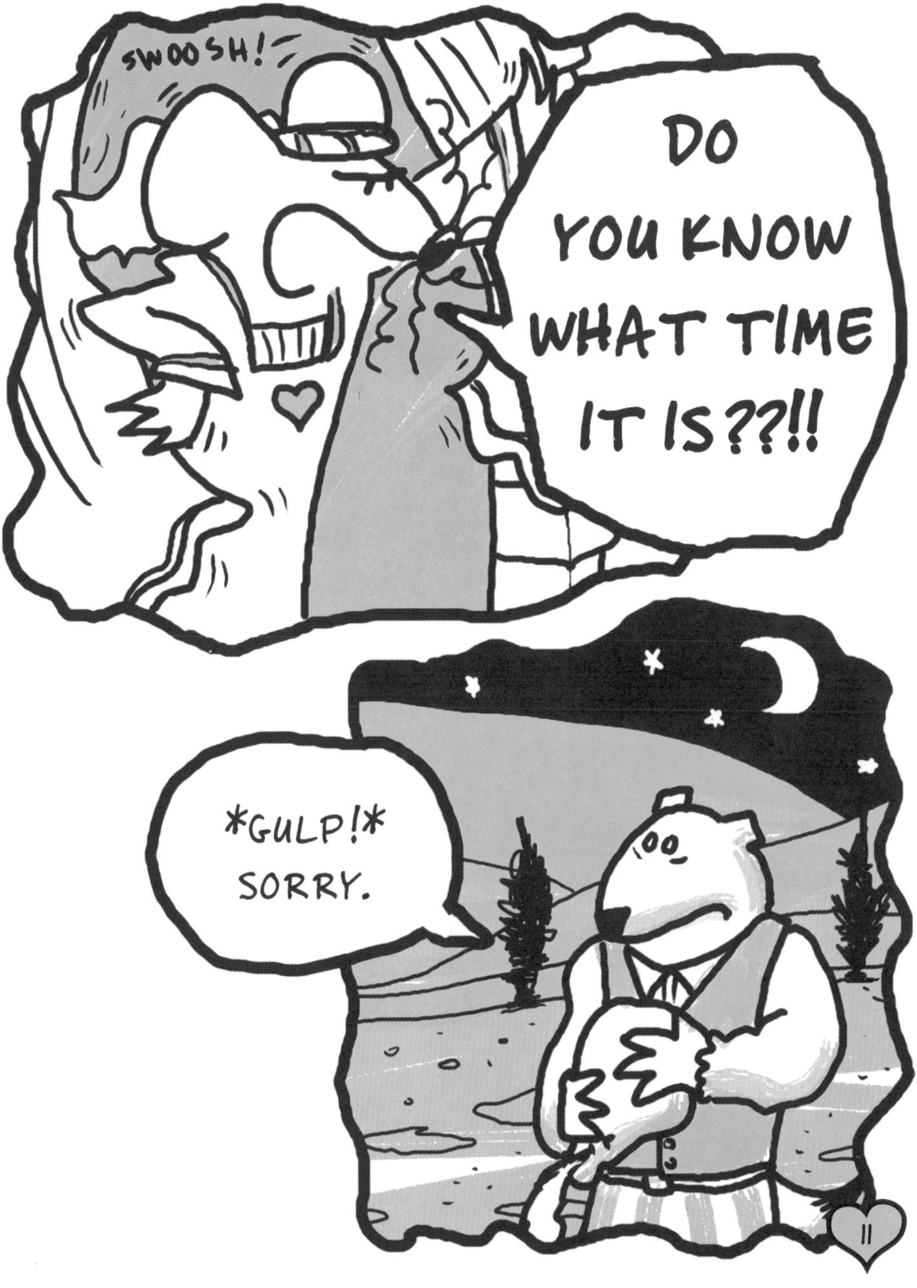
SWOOSH!
DO YOU KNOW WHAT TIME IT IS??!!
GULP! SORRY.

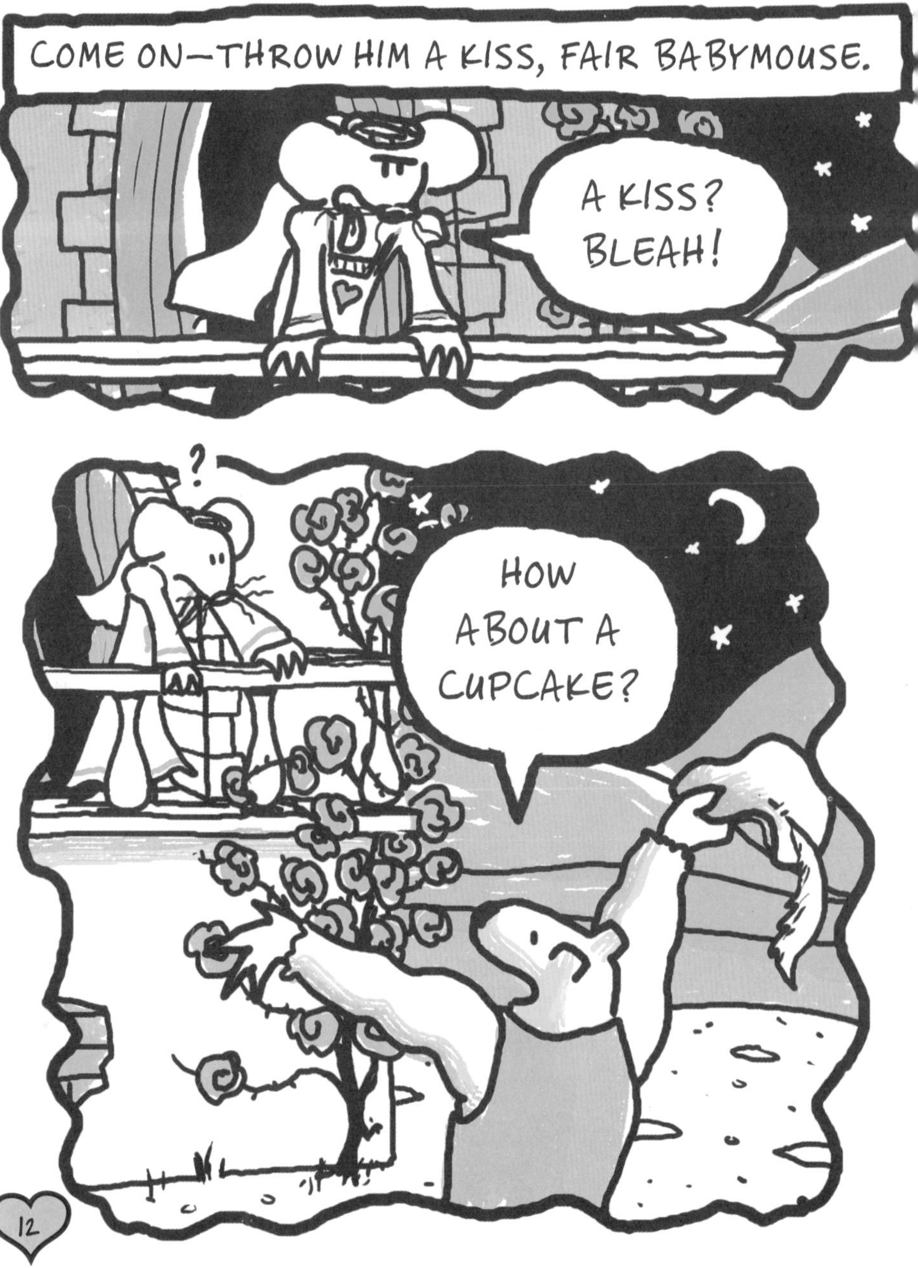
COME ON—THROW HIM A KISS, FAIR BABYMOUSE.
A KISS? BLEAH!
HOW ABOUT A CUPCAKE?

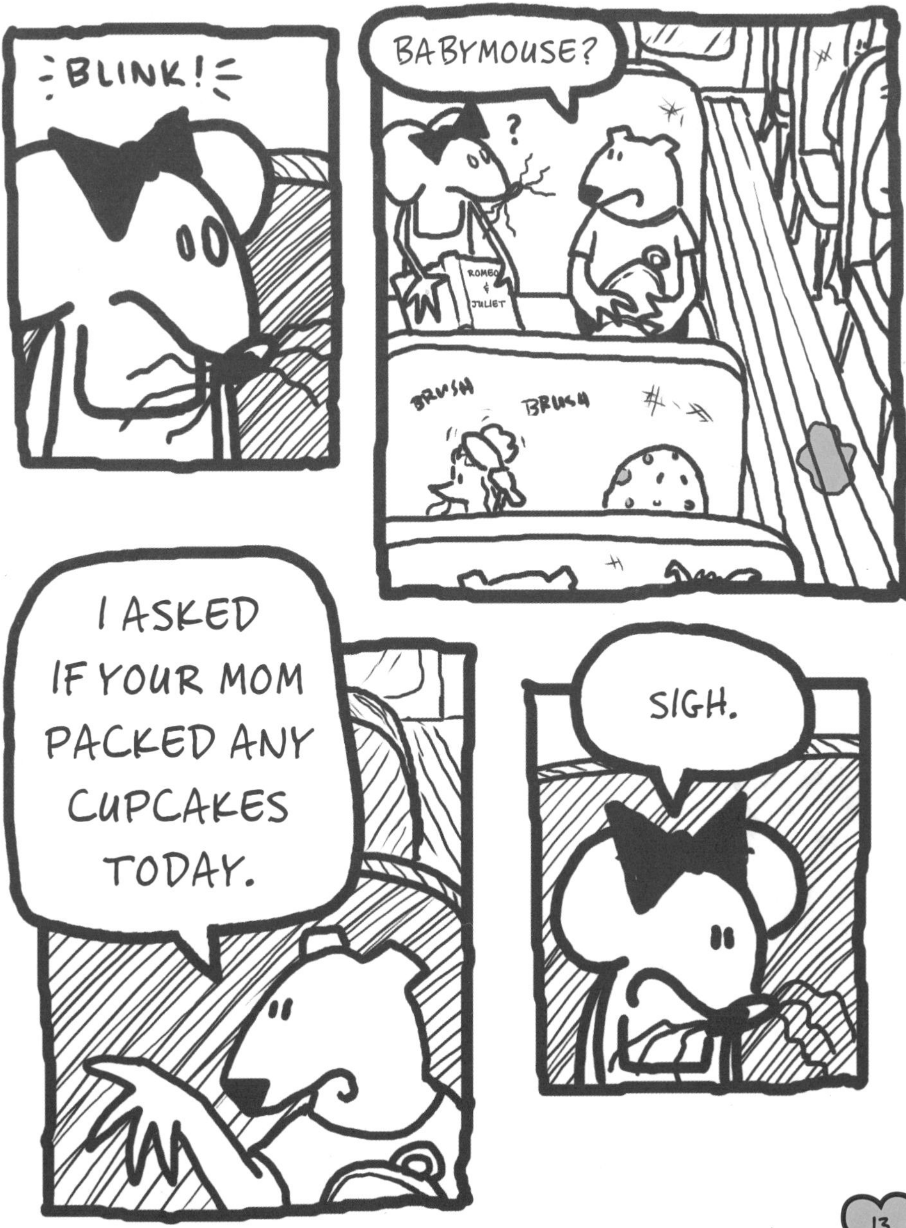
BLINK!
BABYMOUSE?
?
ROMEO & JULIET
BRUSH
BRUSH
I ASKED IF YOUR MOM PACKED ANY CUPCAKES TODAY.
SIGH.

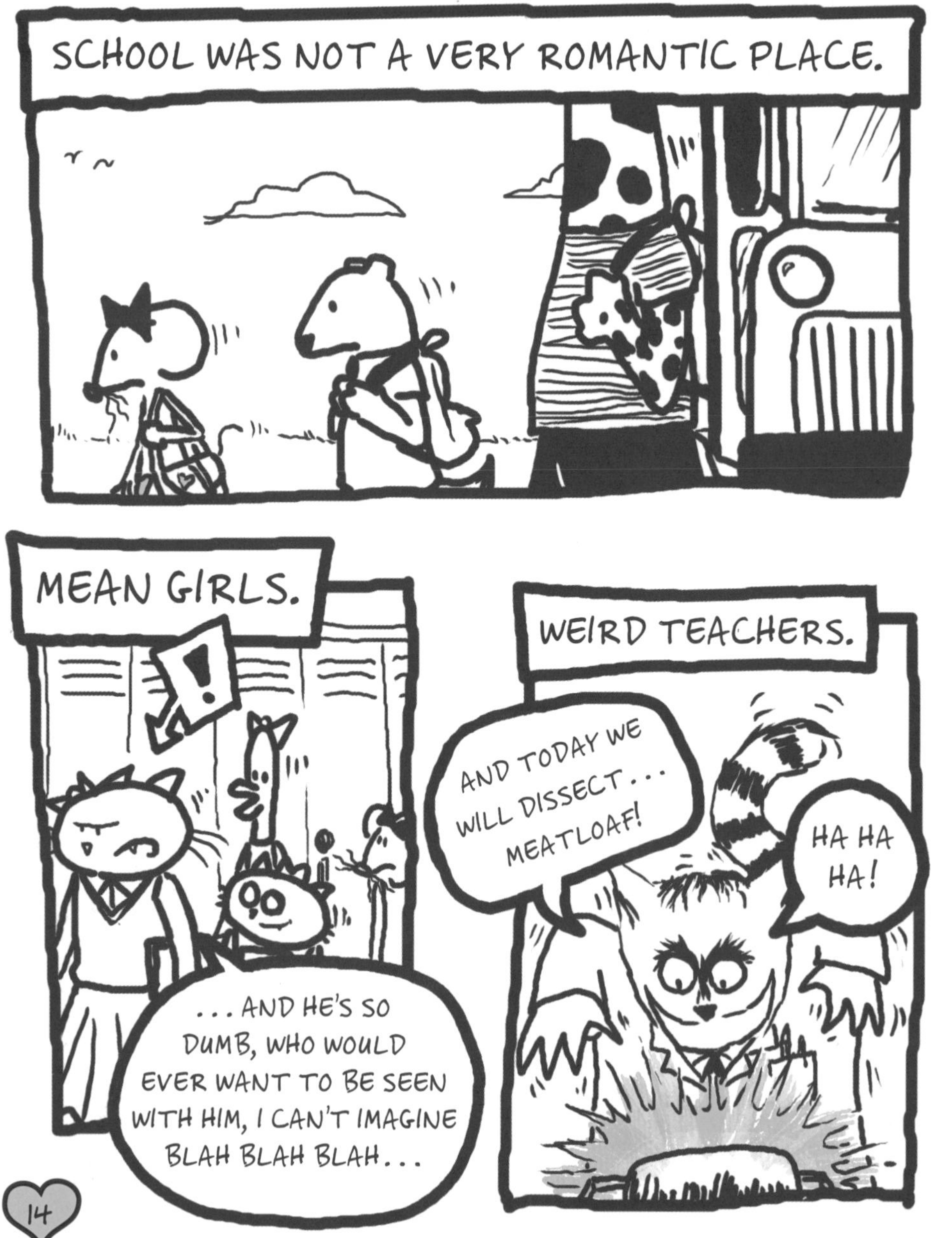
SCHOOL WAS NOT A VERY ROMANTIC PLACE.
MEAN GIRLS.
. . . AND HE'S SO DUMB, WHO WOULD EVER WANT TO BE SEEN WITH HIM, I CAN'T IMAGINE BLAH BLAH BLAH . . .
WEIRD TEACHERS.
AND TODAY WE WILL DISSECT . . . MEATLOAF!
HA HA HA!

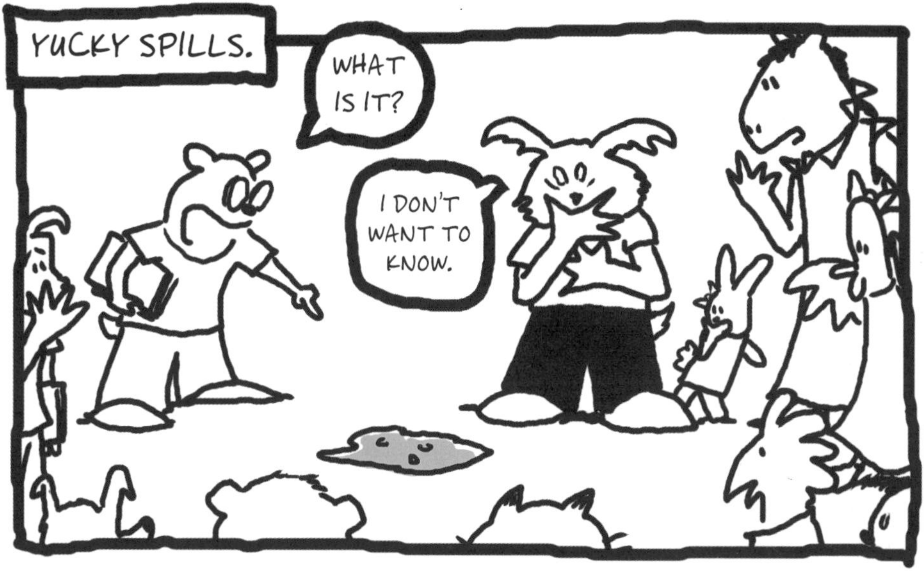
YUCKY SPILLS.
WHAT IS IT?
I DON'T WANT TO KNOW.

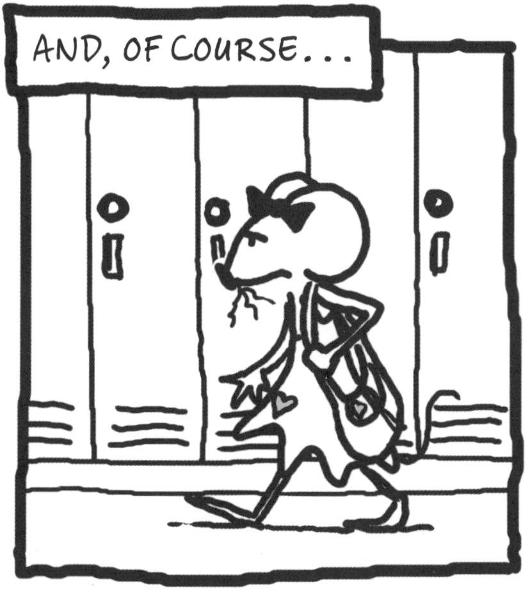
AND, OF COURSE...

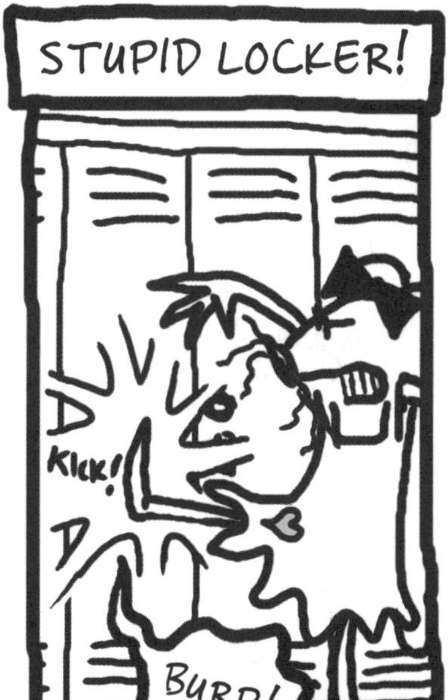
STUPID LOCKER!
KICK!
BURP!

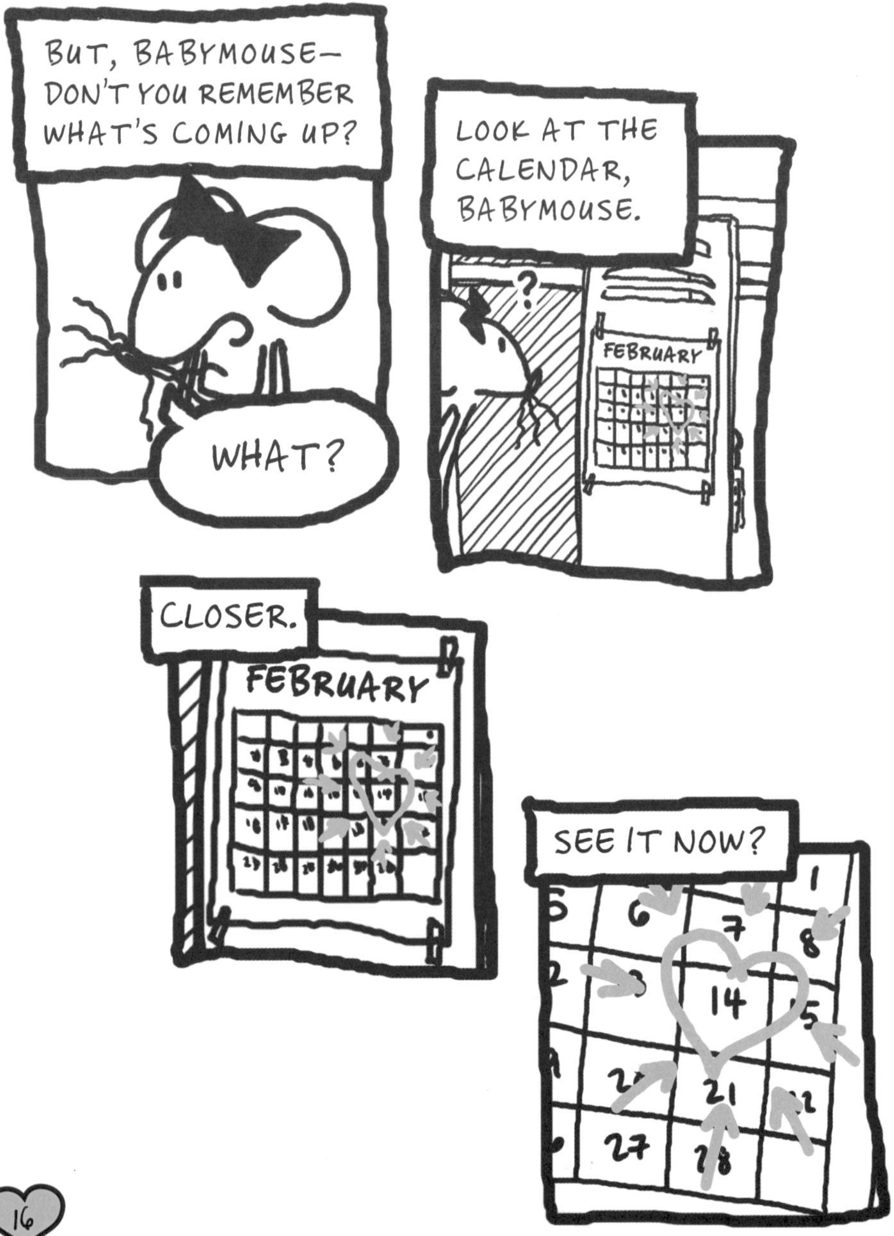
BUT, BABYMOUSE—
DON'T YOU REMEMBER
WHAT'S COMING UP?
WHAT?
LOOK AT THE
CALENDAR,
BABYMOUSE.
?
FEBRUARY
CLOSER.
FEBRUARY
SEE IT NOW?
14

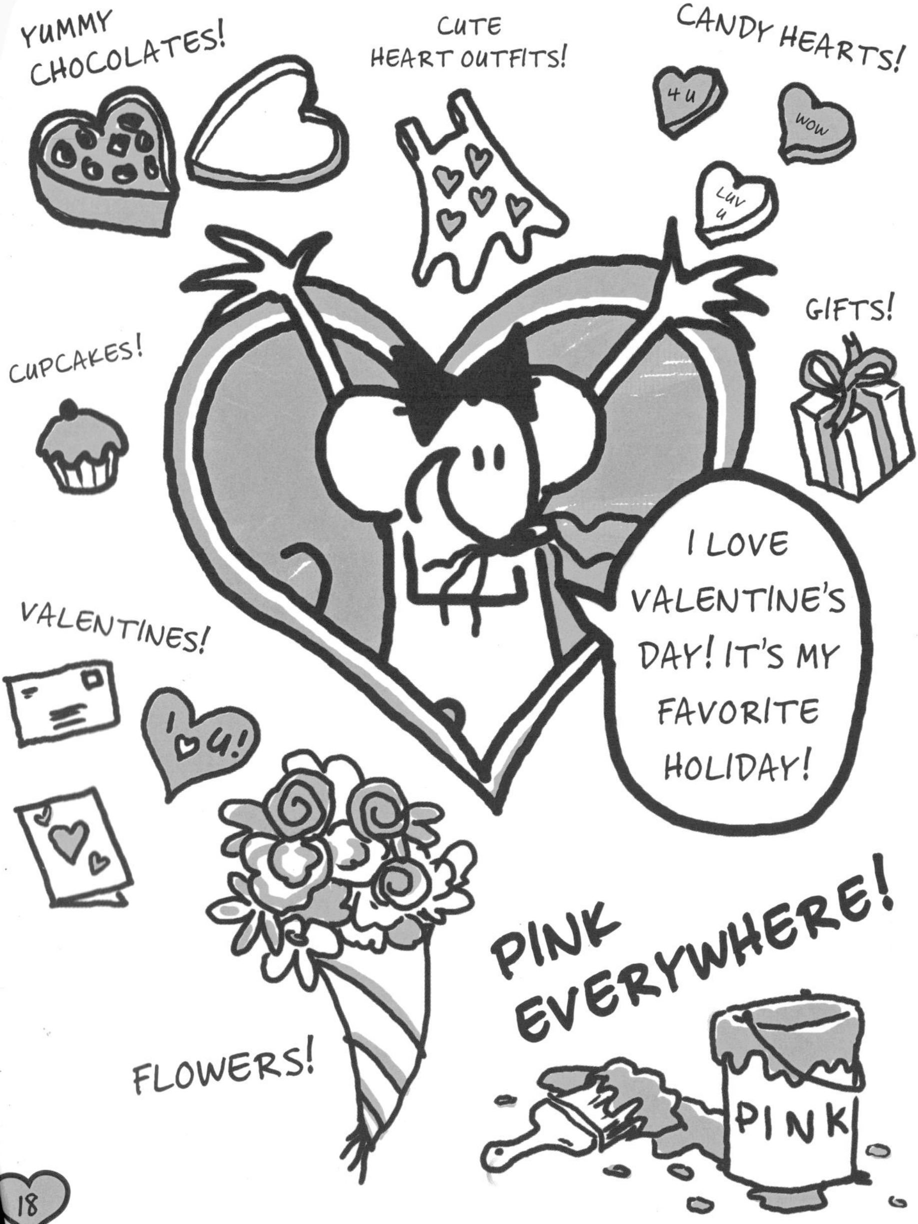
YUMMY CHOCOLATES!
CUTE HEART OUTFITS!
CANDY HEARTS!
4 U
WOW
LUV U
GIFTS!
CUPCAKES!
I LOVE VALENTINE'S DAY! IT'S MY FAVORITE HOLIDAY!
VALENTINES!
I ♡ U!
PINK EVERYWHERE!
FLOWERS!
PINK

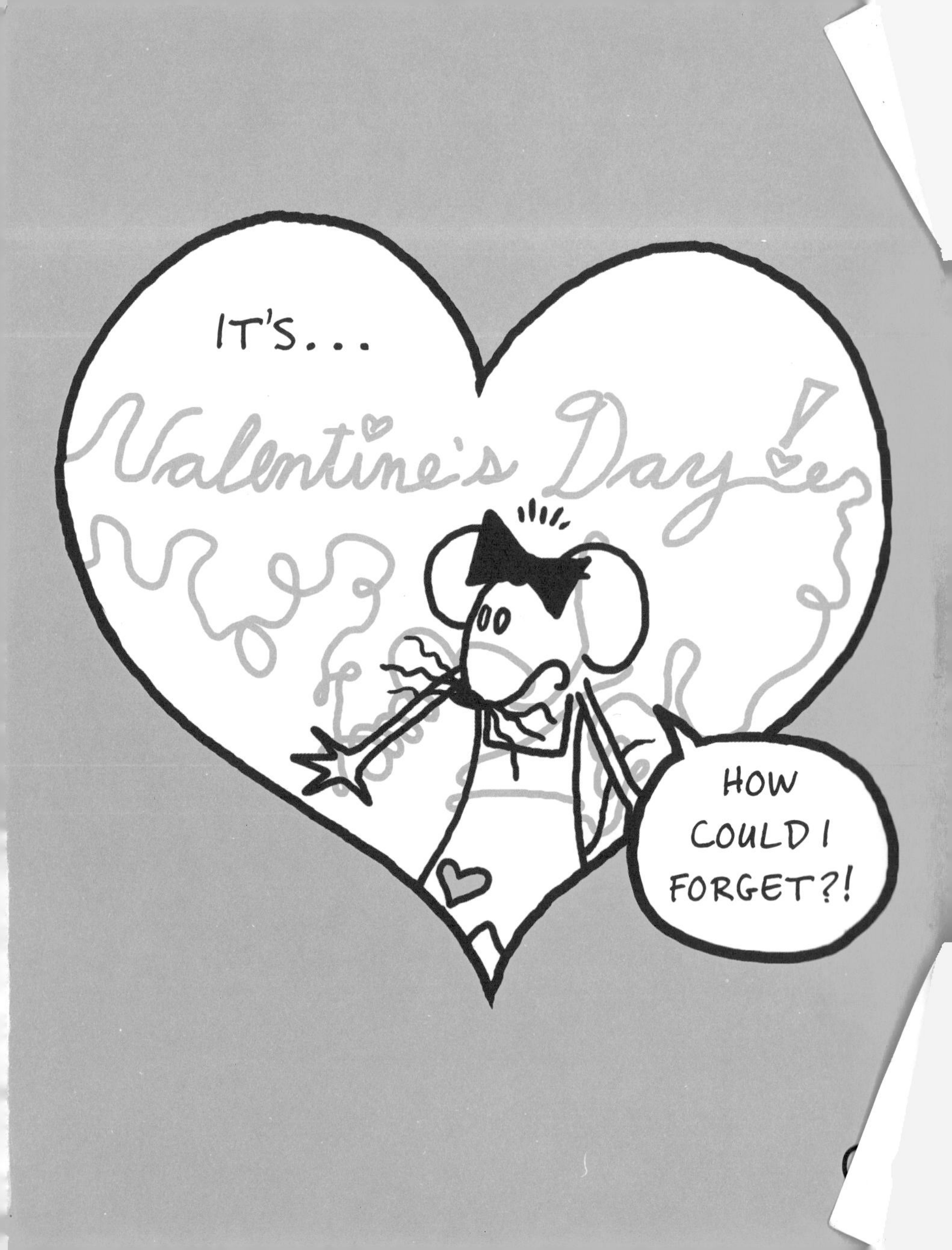
IT'S...
Valentine's Day!
HOW COULD I FORGET?!

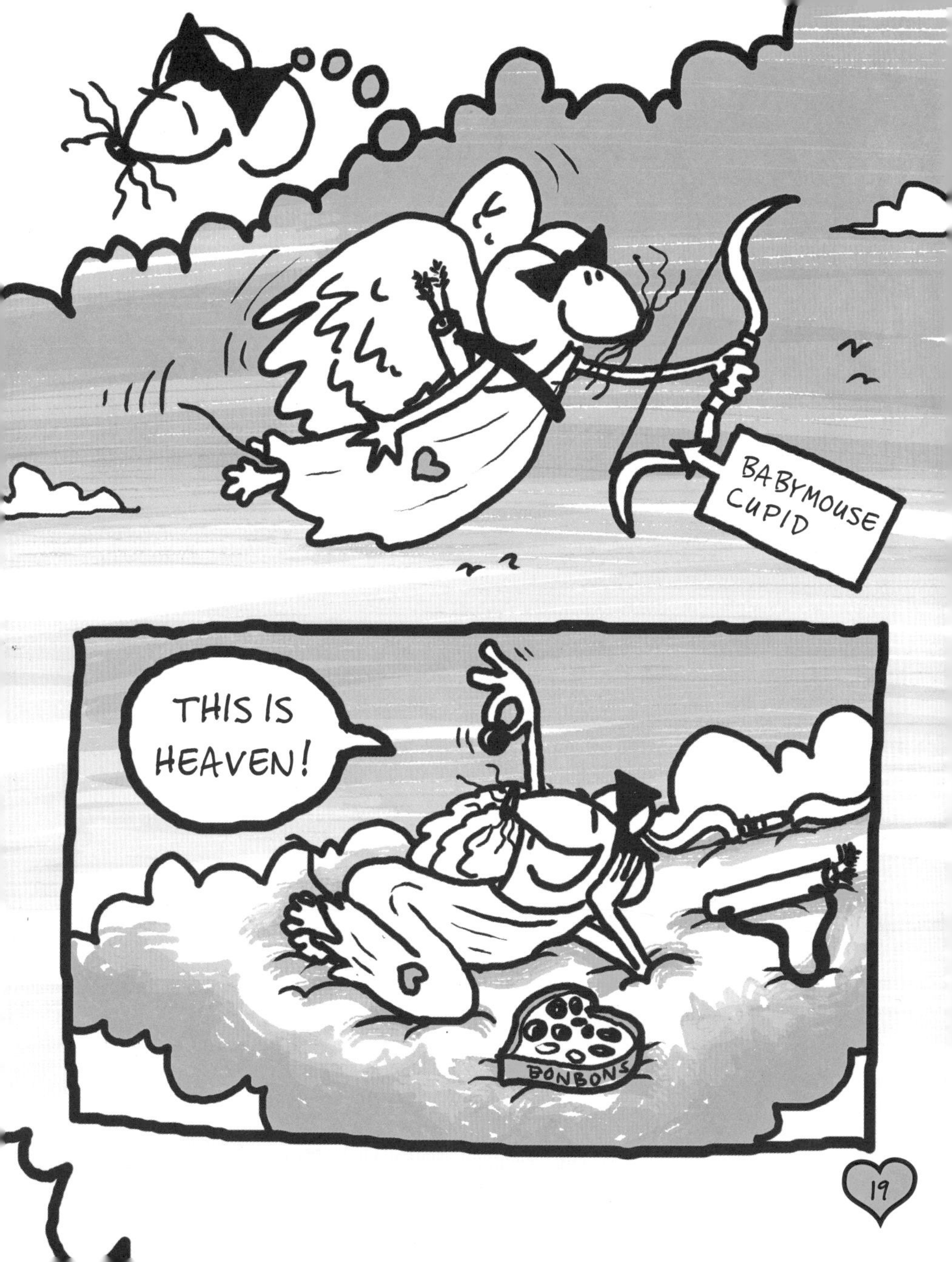
BABYMOUSE CUPID
THIS IS HEAVEN!
BONBONS

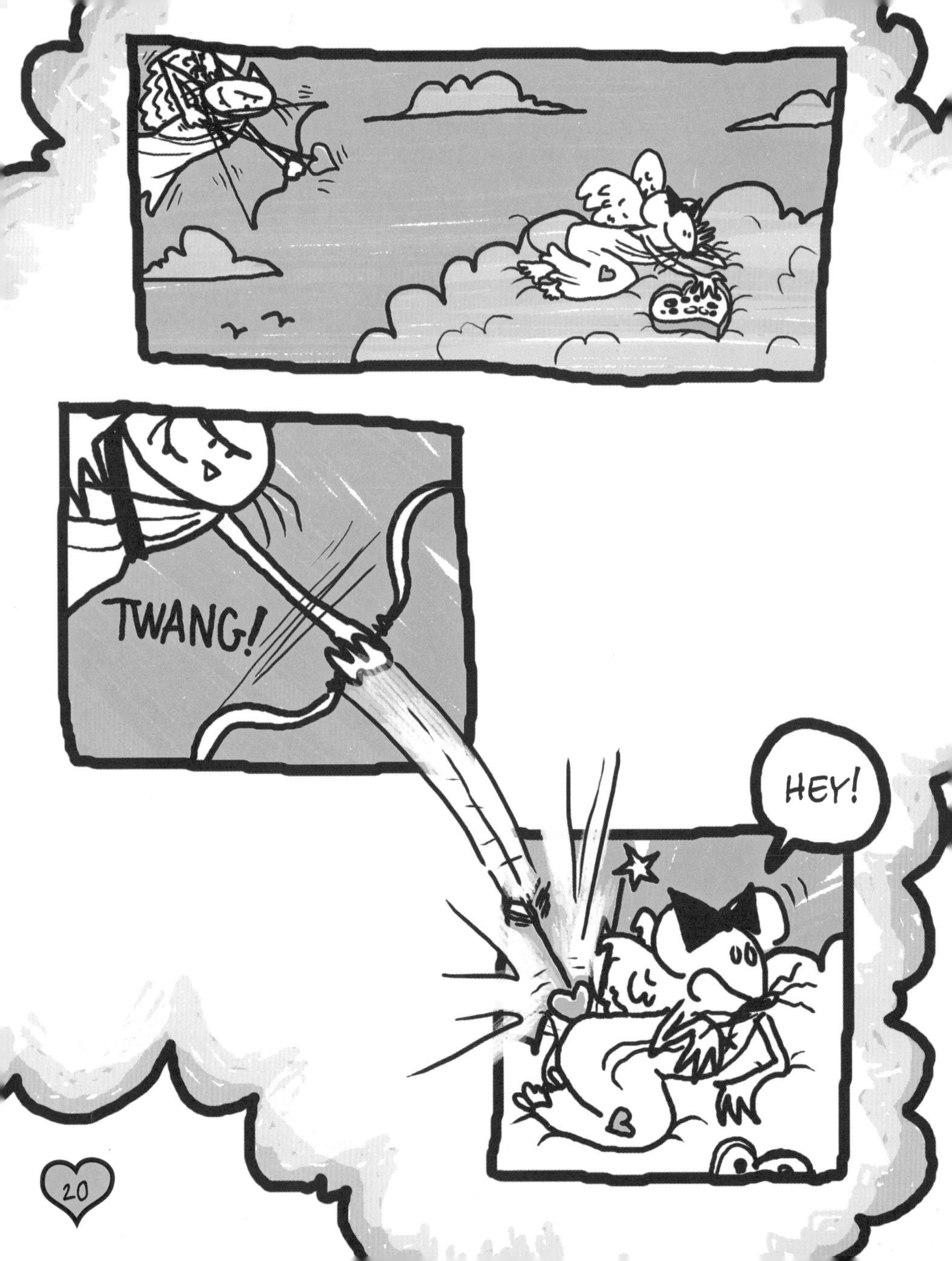
TWANG!
HEY!

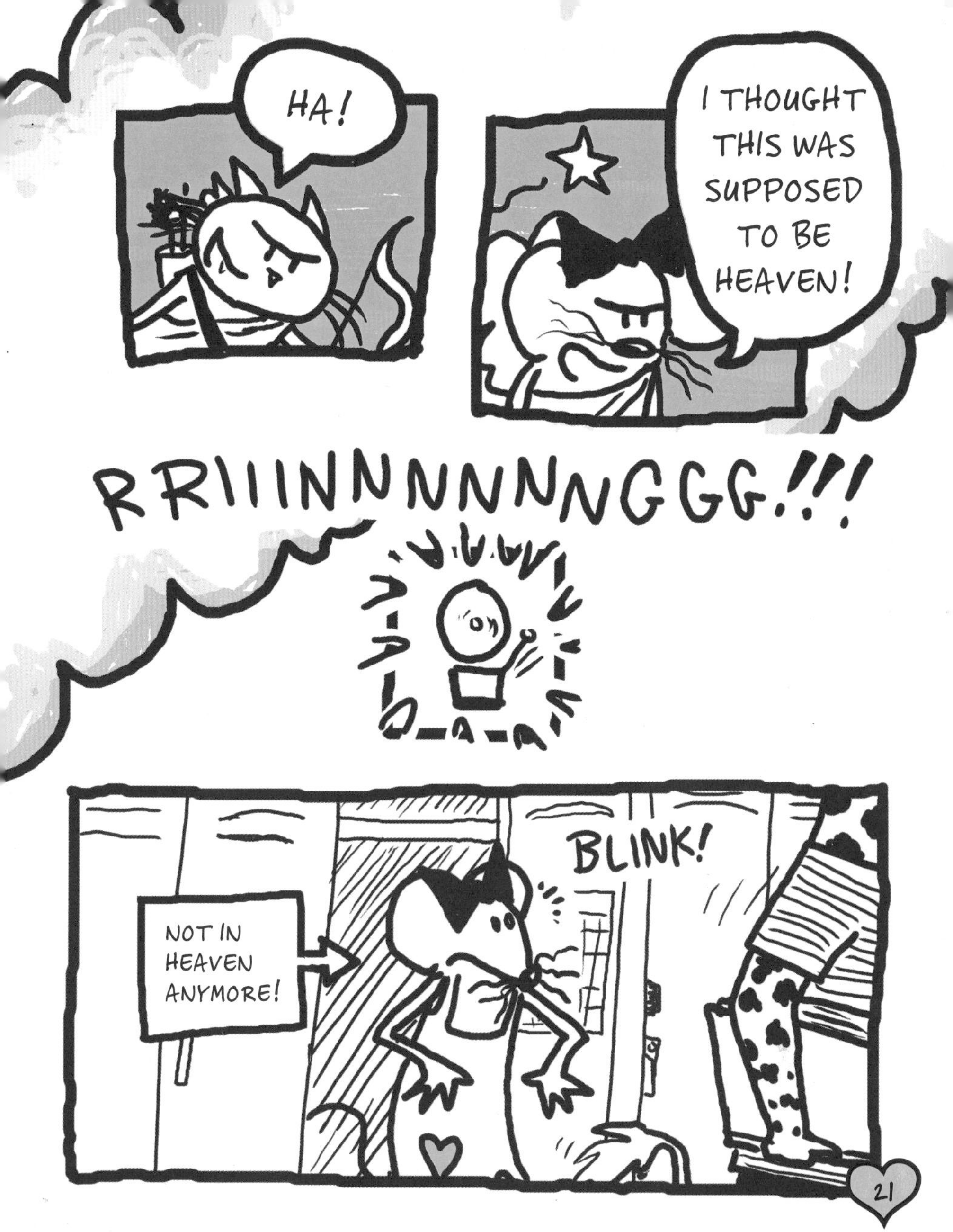
HA!
I THOUGHT THIS WAS SUPPOSED TO BE HEAVEN!
RRIIINNNNNNGGG!!!
BLINK!
NOT IN HEAVEN ANYMORE!

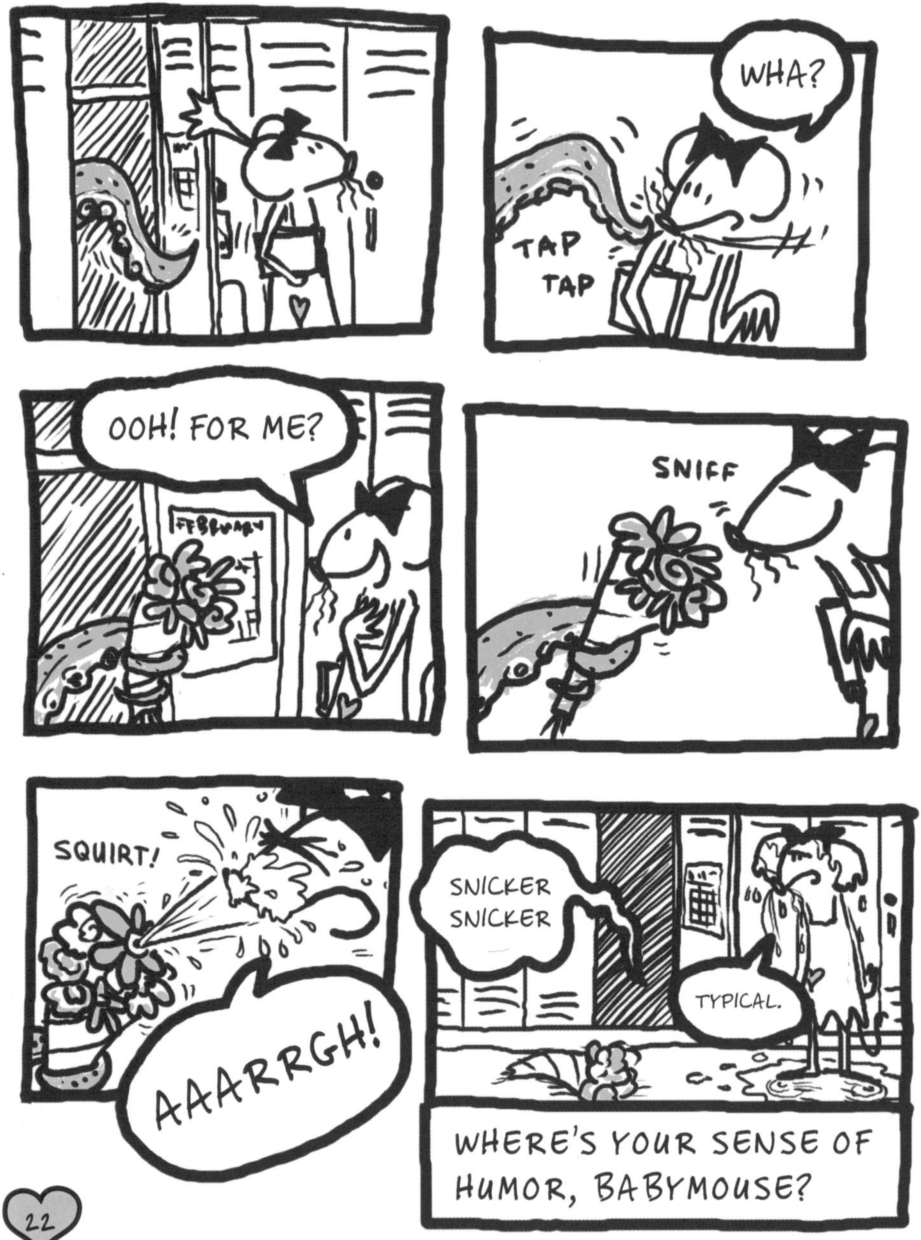
WHA?
TAP
TAP
OOH! FOR ME?
SNIFF
SQUIRT!
AAARRGH!
SNICKER
SNICKER
TYPICAL.
WHERE'S YOUR SENSE OF HUMOR, BABYMOUSE?

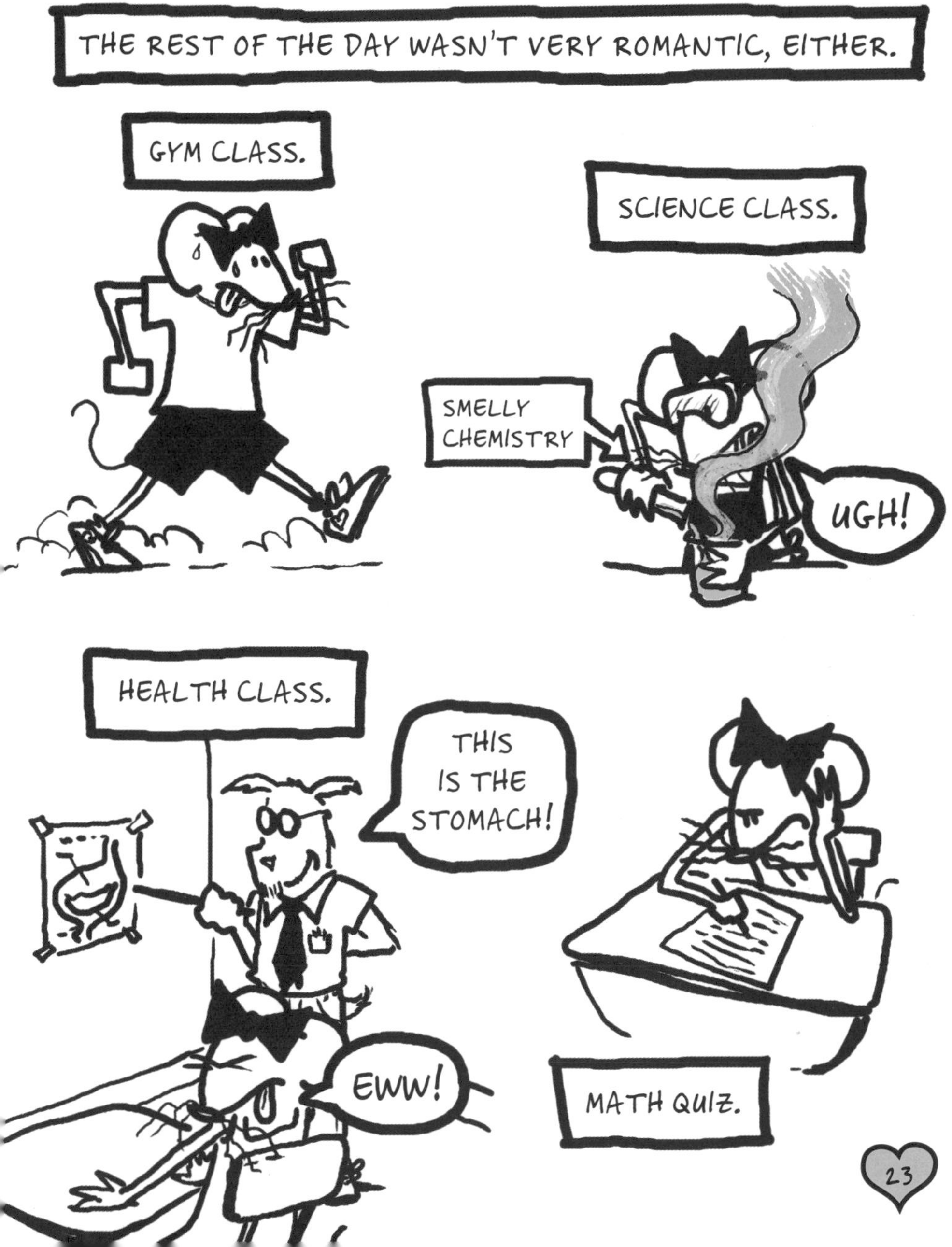
THE REST OF THE DAY WASN'T VERY ROMANTIC, EITHER.
GYM CLASS.
SCIENCE CLASS.
SMELLY CHEMISTRY
UGH!
HEALTH CLASS.
THIS IS THE STOMACH!
EWW!
MATH QUIZ.

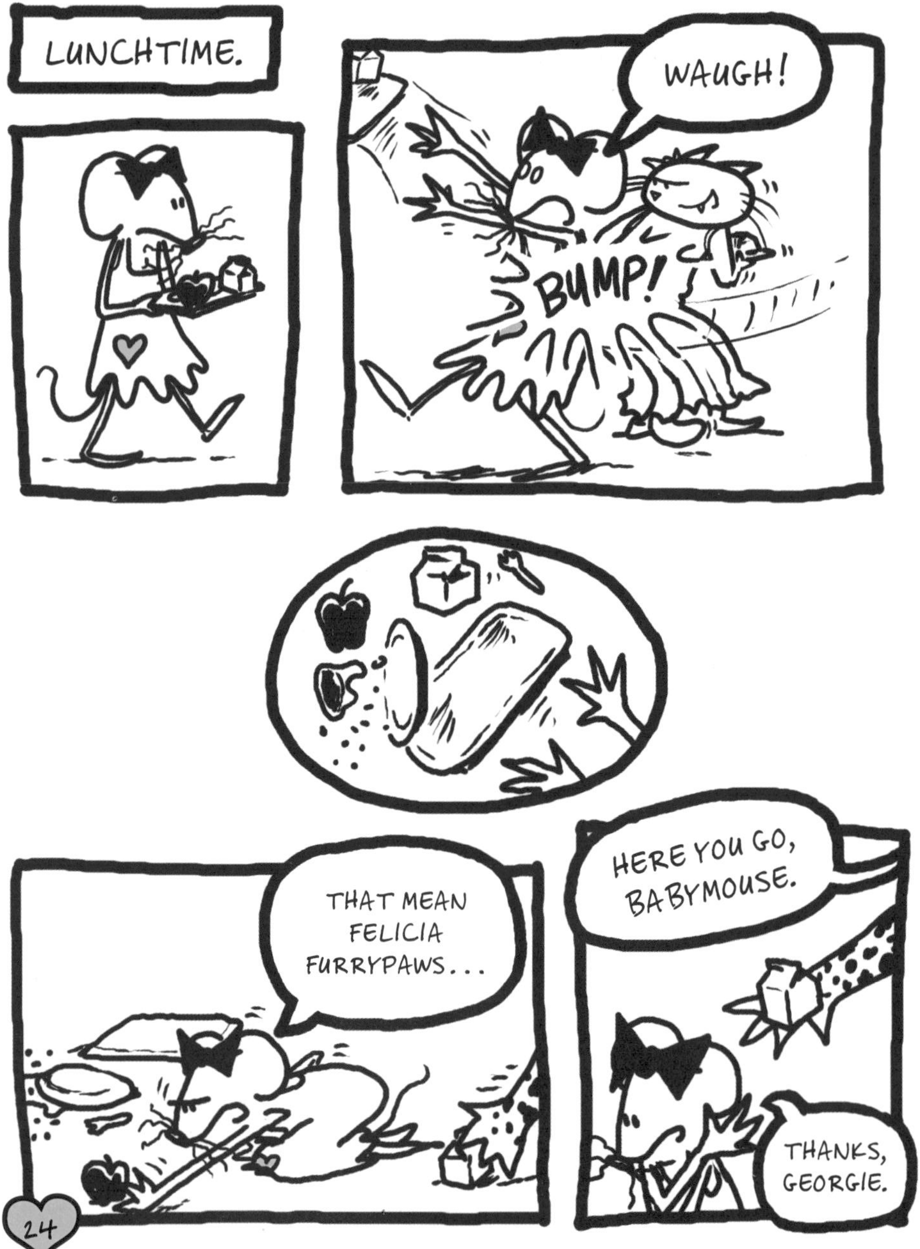
LUNCHTIME.
WAUGH!
BUMP!
THAT MEAN FELICIA FURRYPAWS . . .
HERE YOU GO, BABYMOUSE.
THANKS, GEORGIE.

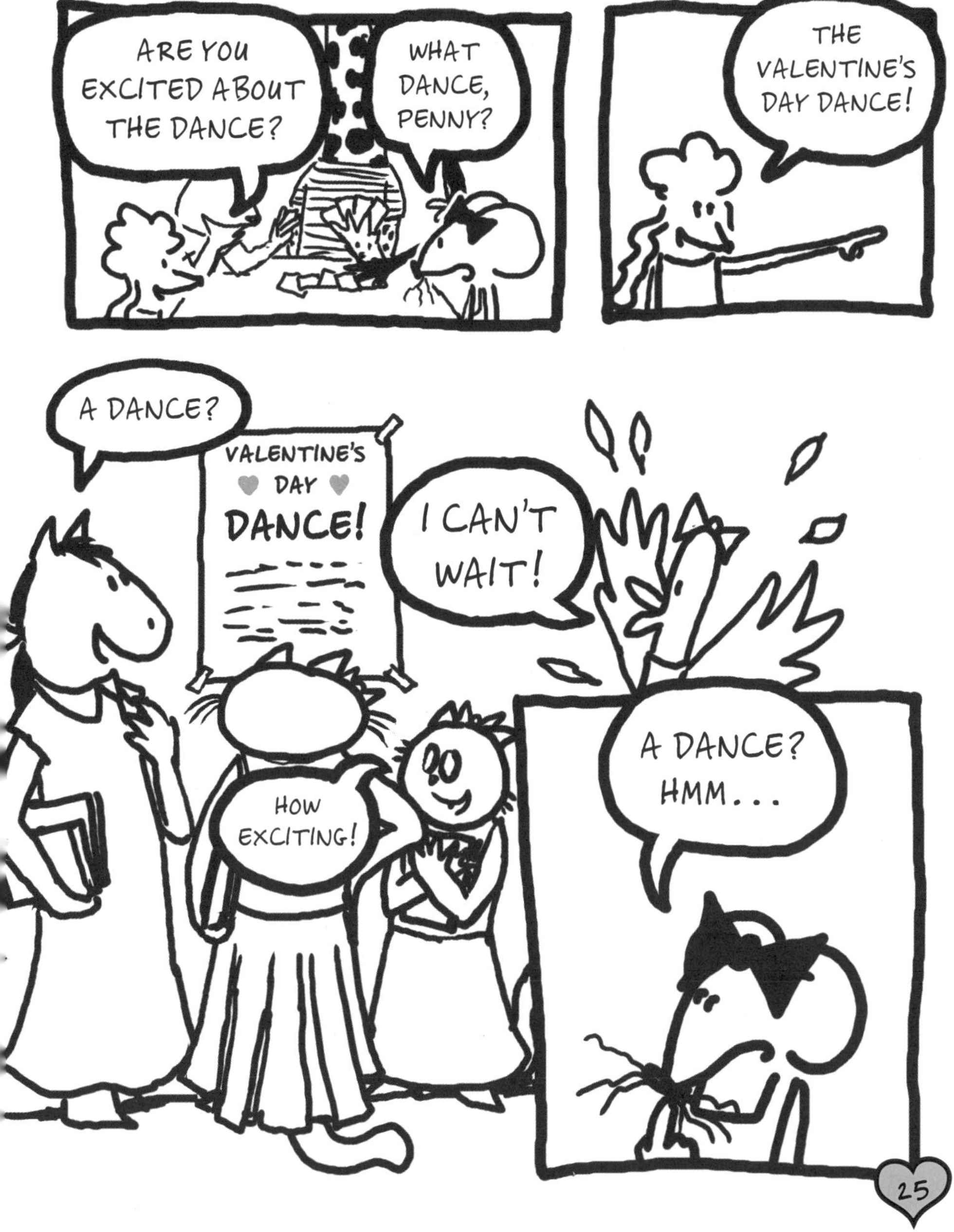
ARE YOU EXCITED ABOUT THE DANCE?
WHAT DANCE, PENNY?
THE VALENTINE'S DAY DANCE!
A DANCE?
VALENTINE'S DAY DANCE!
I CAN'T WAIT!
HOW EXCITING!
A DANCE? HMM...

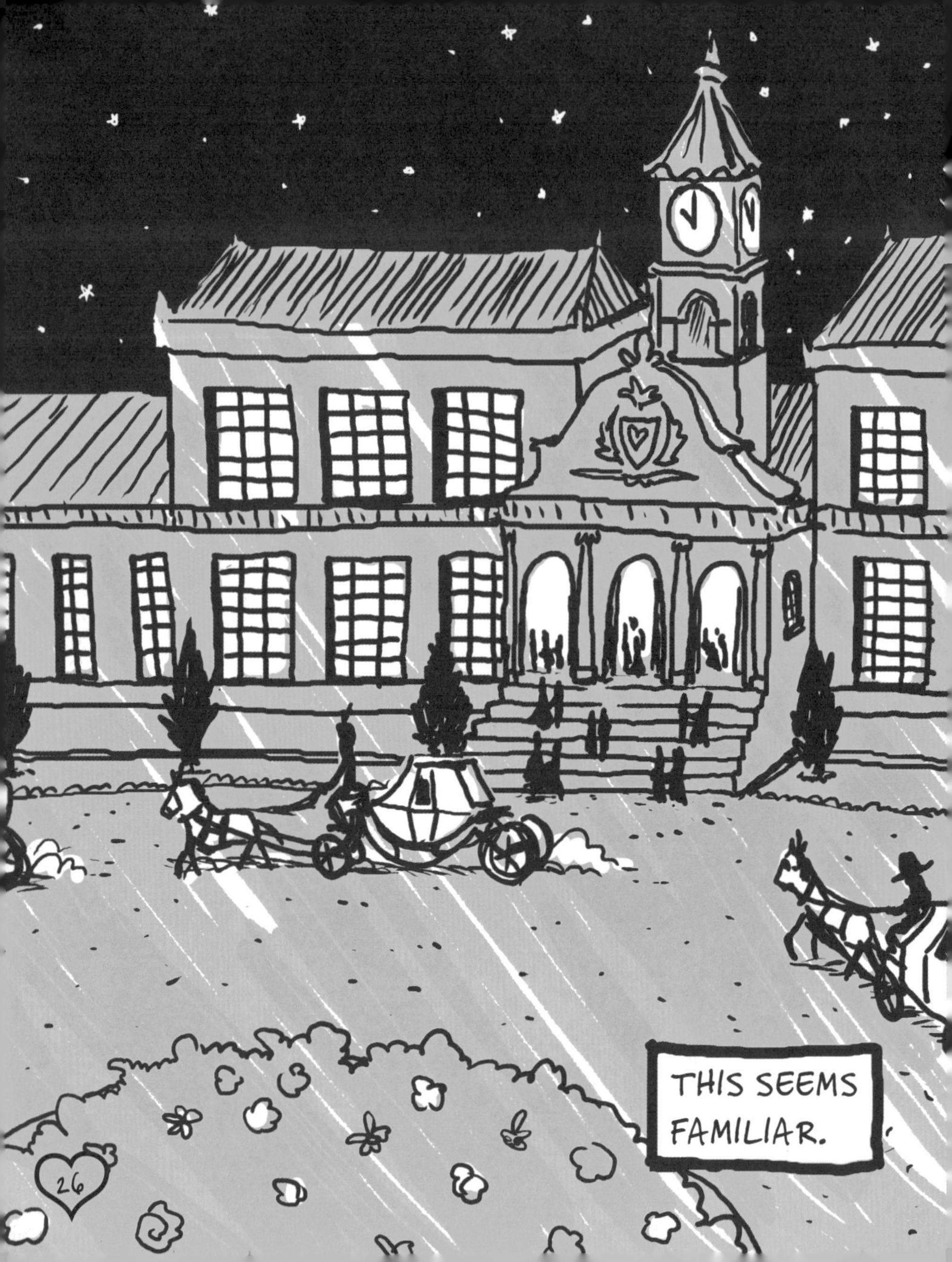
THIS SEEMS FAMILIAR.

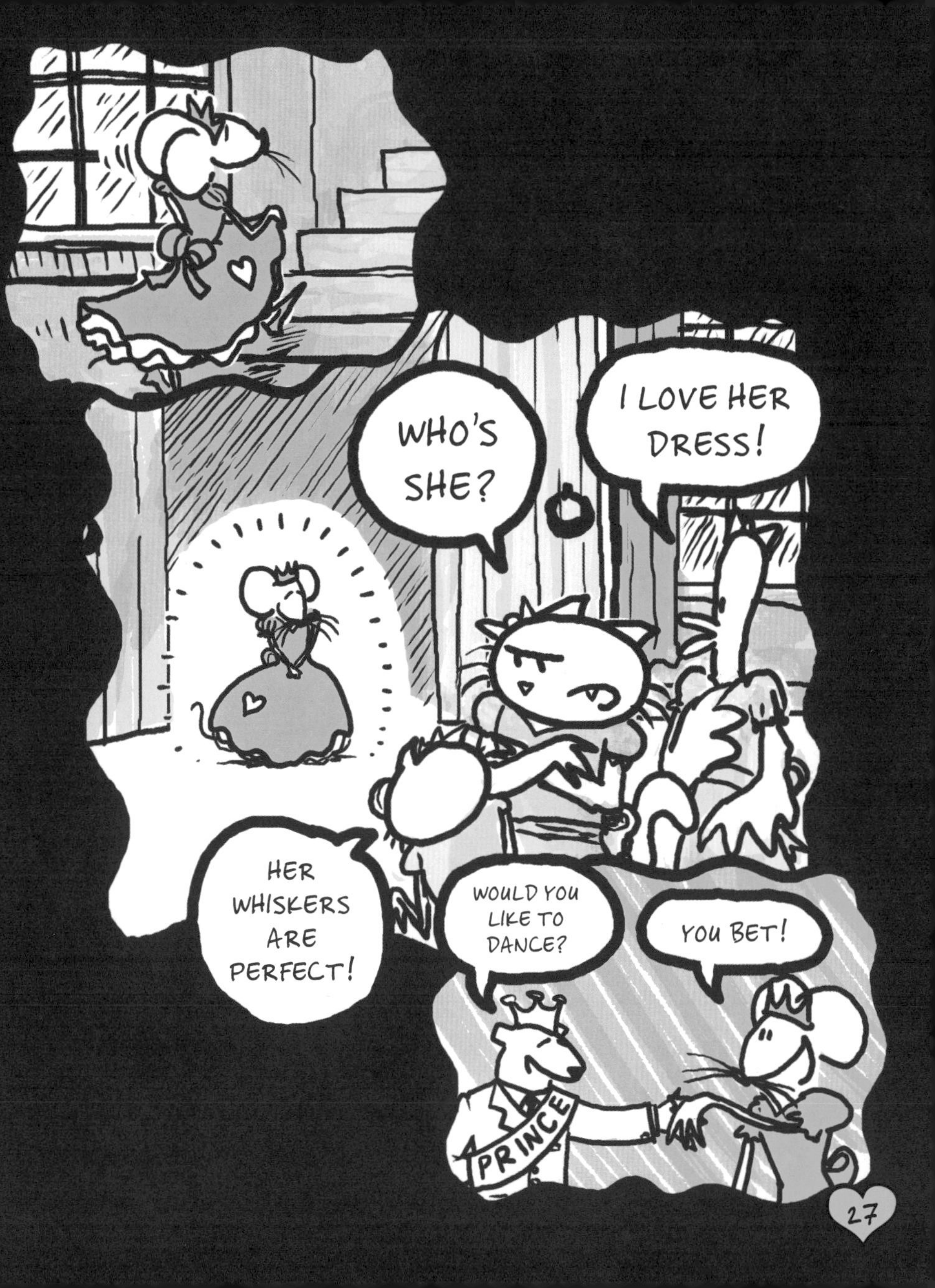
WHO'S SHE?
I LOVE HER DRESS!
HER WHISKERS ARE PERFECT!
WOULD YOU LIKE TO DANCE?
YOU BET!
PRINCE

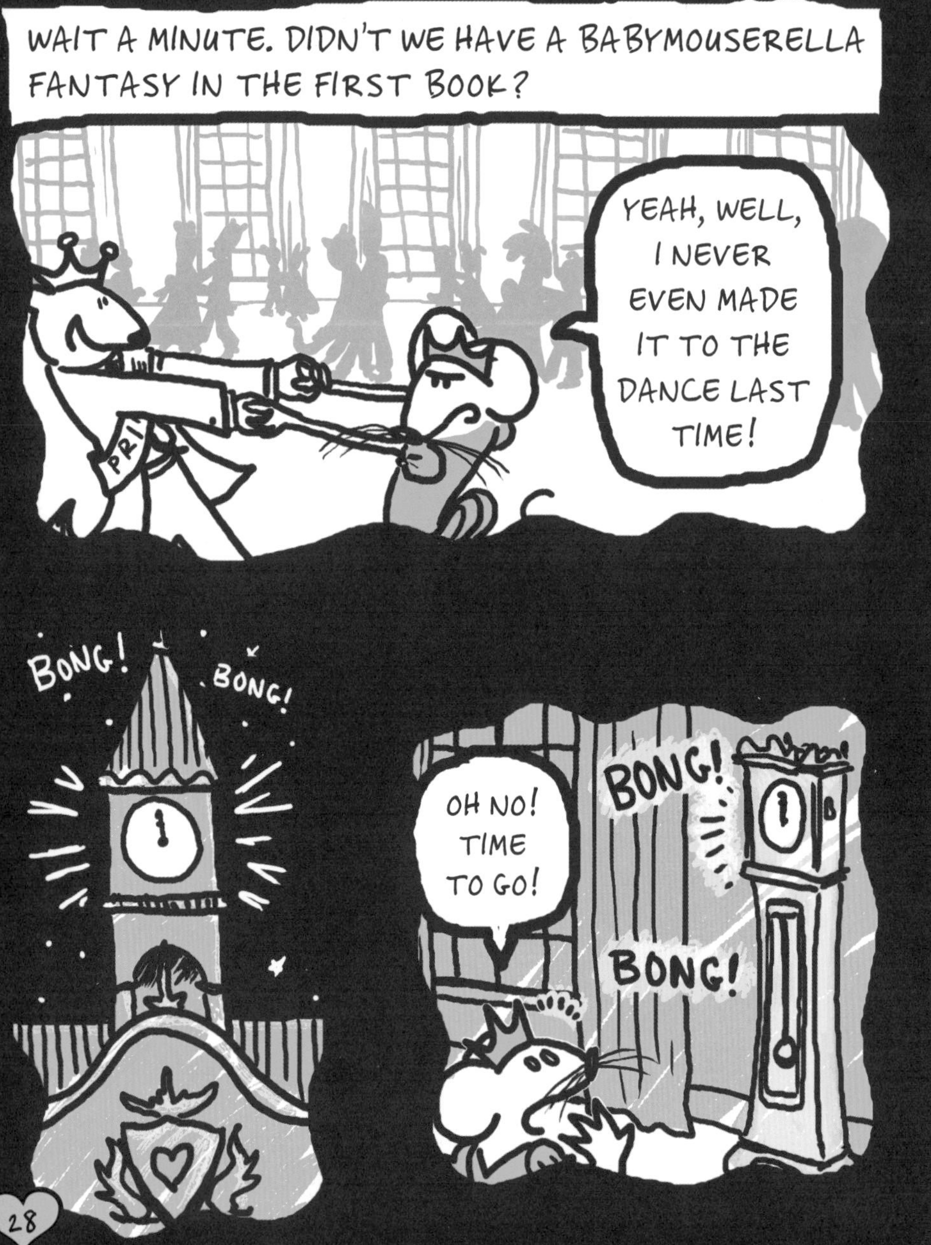
WAIT A MINUTE. DIDN'T WE HAVE A BABYMOUSERELLA FANTASY IN THE FIRST BOOK?
YEAH, WELL, I NEVER EVEN MADE IT TO THE DANCE LAST TIME!
PRI
BONG!
BONG!
OH NO! TIME TO GO!
BONG!
BONG!

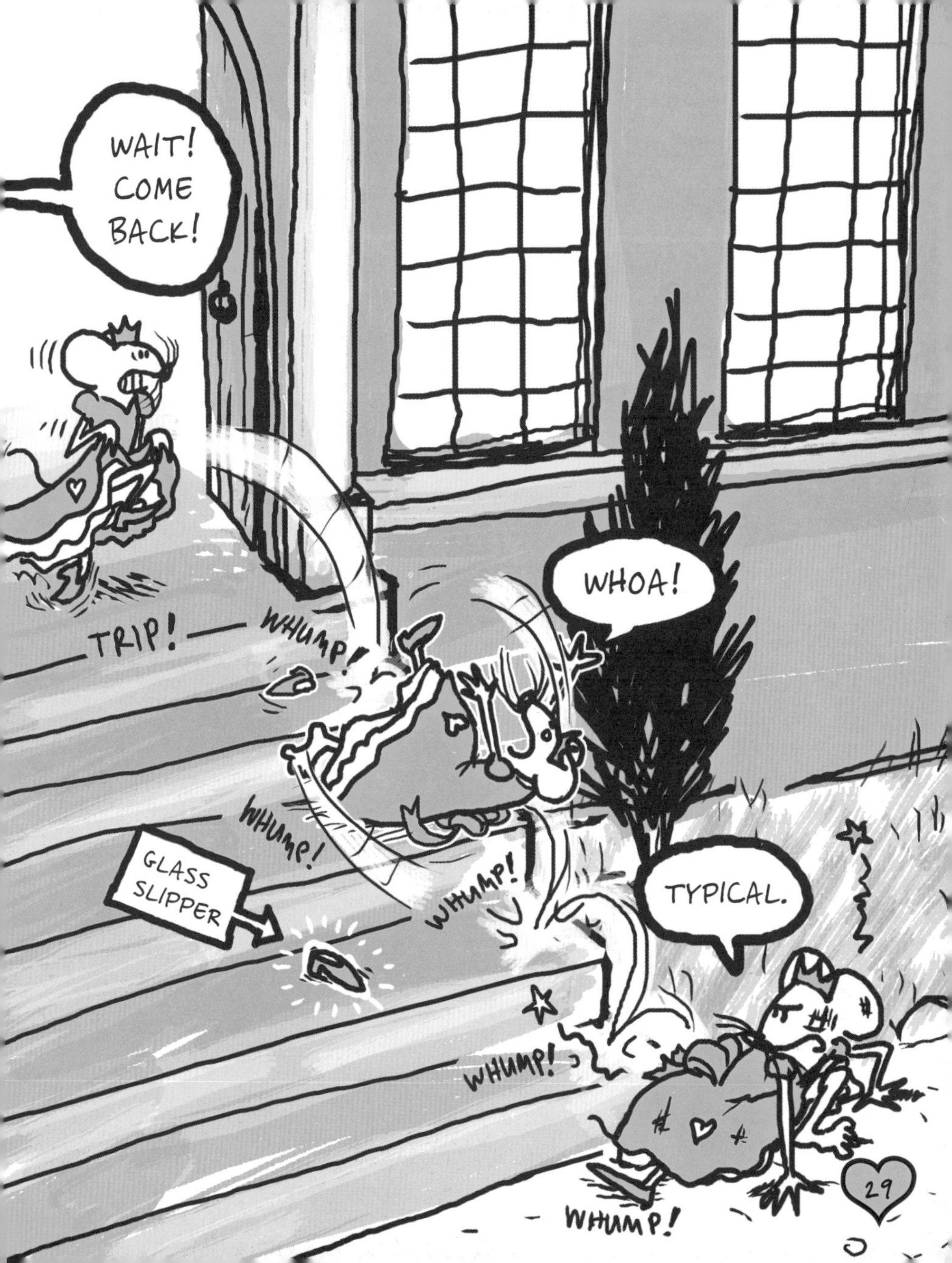
WAIT! COME BACK!
TRIP!
WHUMP!
WHOA!
WHUMP!
GLASS SLIPPER
WHUMP!
TYPICAL.
WHUMP!
WHUMP!

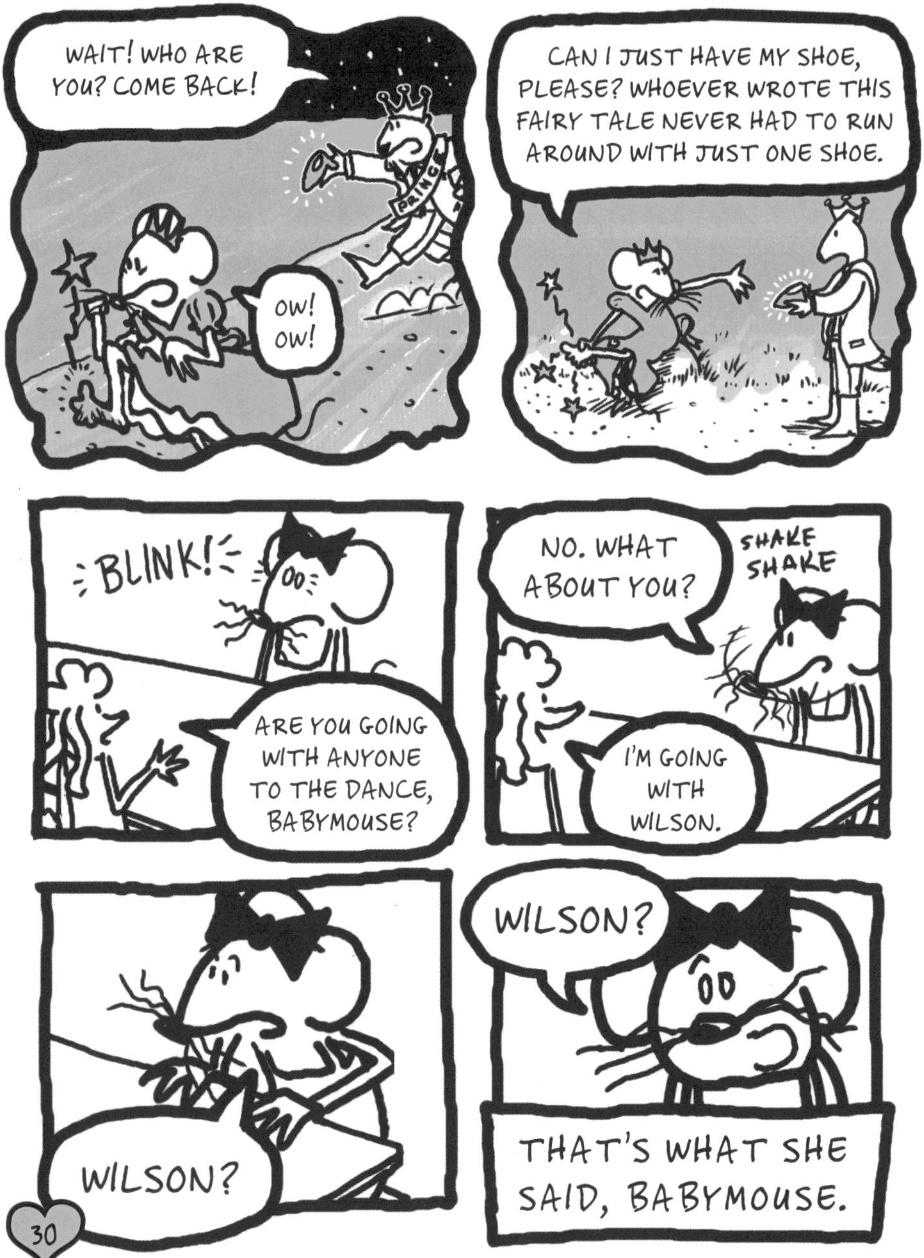

WAIT! WHO ARE YOU? COME BACK!
PRINCE
OW! OW!
CAN I JUST HAVE MY SHOE, PLEASE? WHOEVER WROTE THIS FAIRY TALE NEVER HAD TO RUN AROUND WITH JUST ONE SHOE.
BLINK!
ARE YOU GOING WITH ANYONE TO THE DANCE, BABYMOUSE?
NO. WHAT ABOUT YOU?
SHAKE SHAKE
I'M GOING WITH WILSON.
WILSON?
WILSON?
THAT'S WHAT SHE SAID, BABYMOUSE.

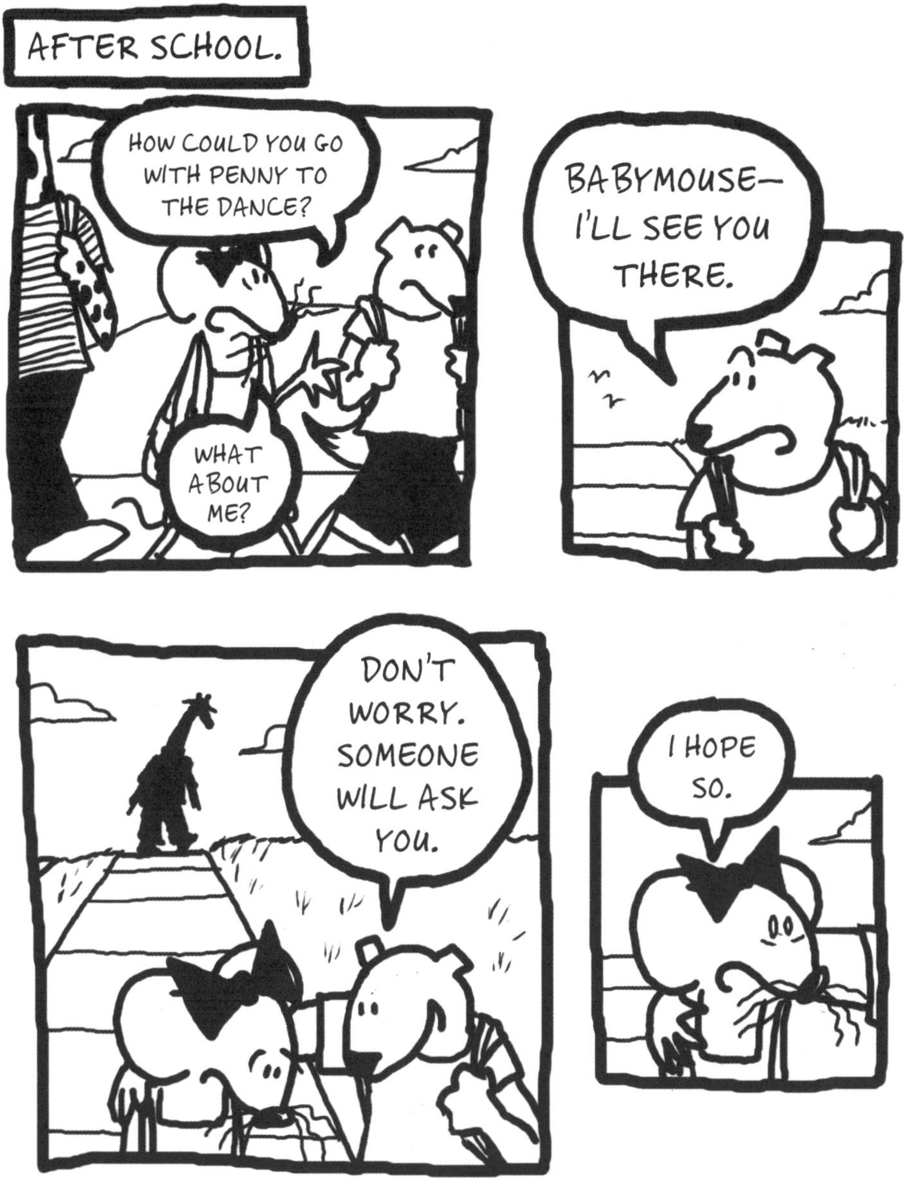
AFTER SCHOOL.
HOW COULD YOU GO WITH PENNY TO THE DANCE?
WHAT ABOUT ME?
BABYMOUSE— I'LL SEE YOU THERE.
DON'T WORRY. SOMEONE WILL ASK YOU.
I HOPE SO.

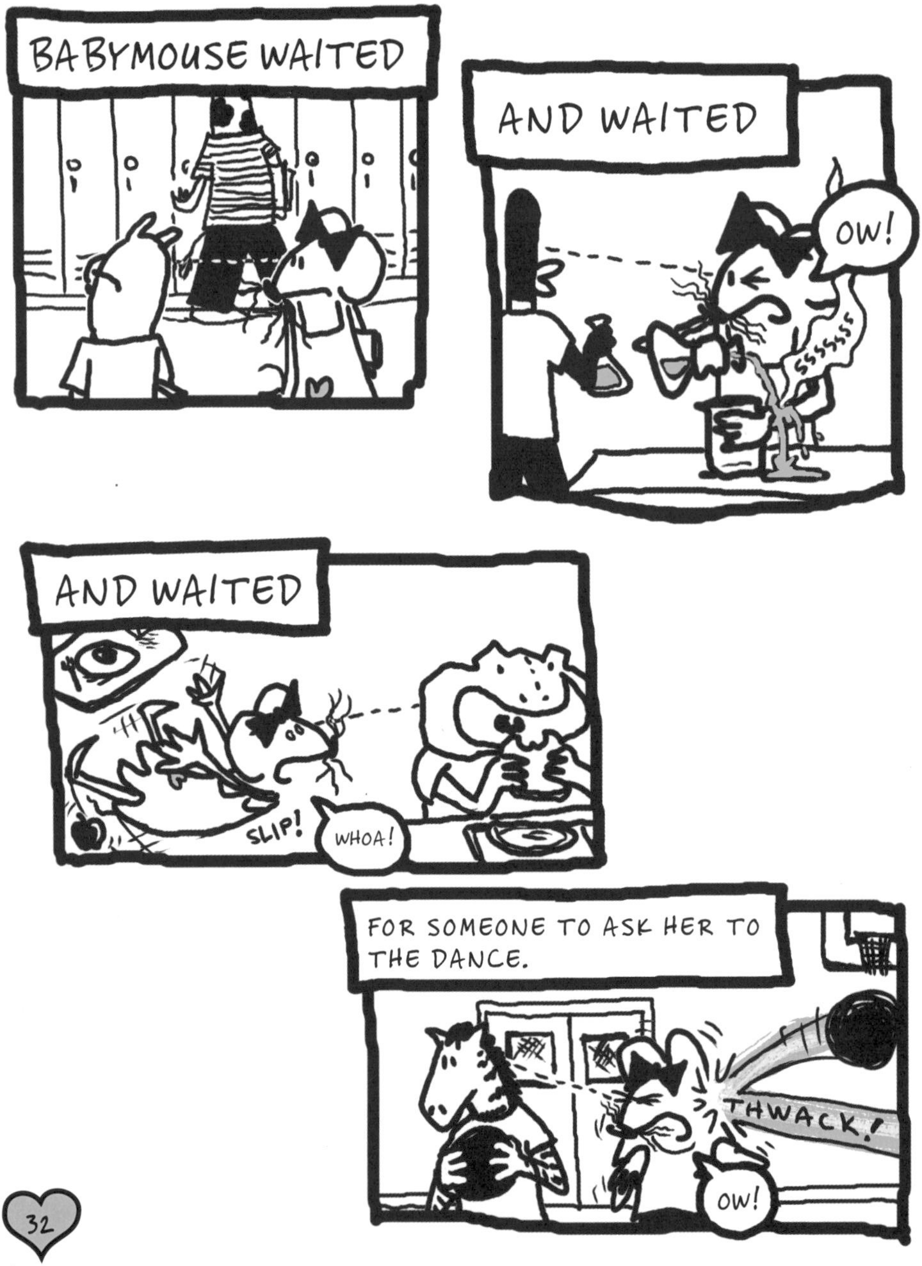
BABYMOUSE WAITED
AND WAITED
OW!
SSSSSSS
AND WAITED
SLIP!
WHOA!
FOR SOMEONE TO ASK HER TO THE DANCE.
THWACK!
OW!

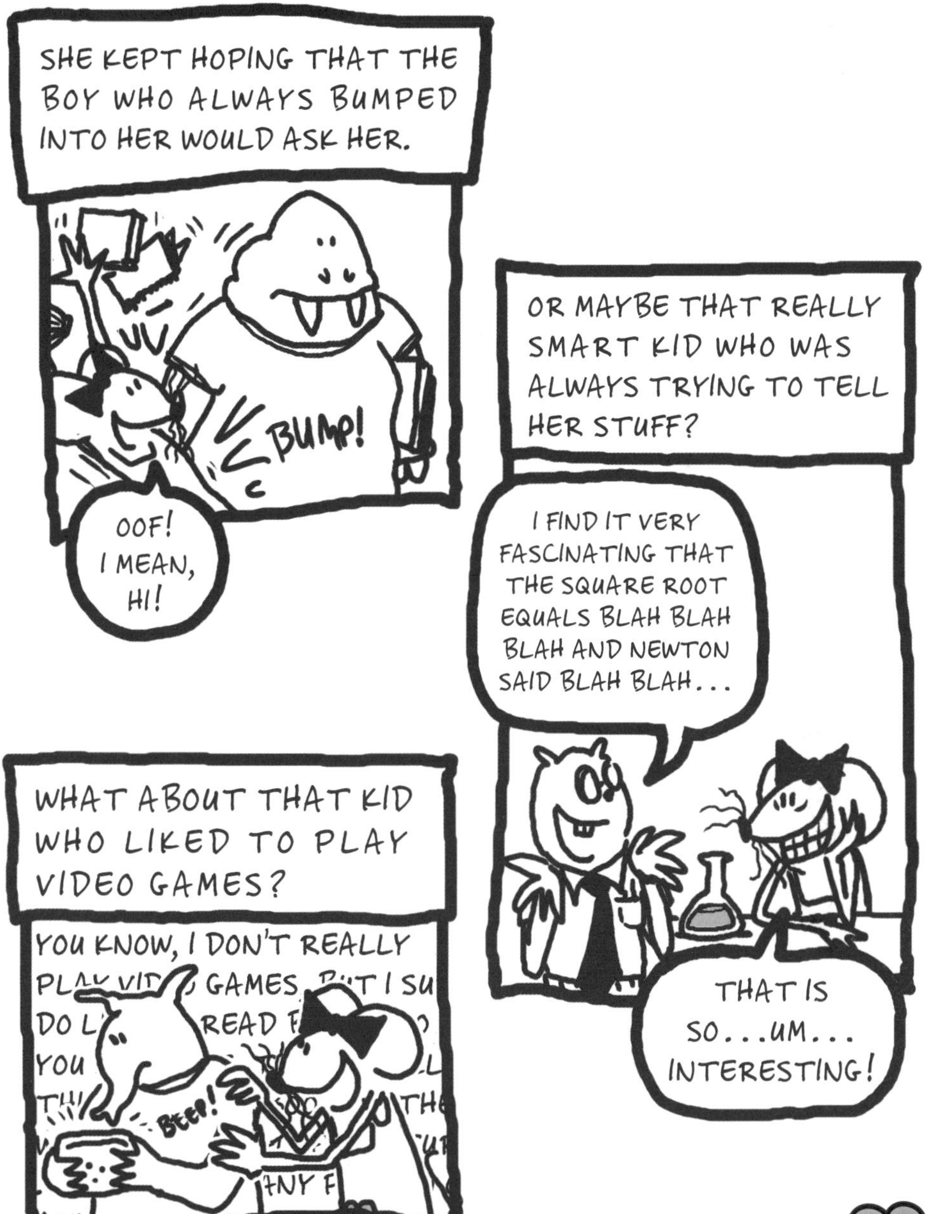
SHE KEPT HOPING THAT THE BOY WHO ALWAYS BUMPED INTO HER WOULD ASK HER.
BUMP!
OOF! I MEAN, HI!
OR MAYBE THAT REALLY SMART KID WHO WAS ALWAYS TRYING TO TELL HER STUFF?
I FIND IT VERY FASCINATING THAT THE SQUARE ROOT EQUALS BLAH BLAH BLAH AND NEWTON SAID BLAH BLAH...
THAT IS SO...UM... INTERESTING!
WHAT ABOUT THAT KID WHO LIKED TO PLAY VIDEO GAMES?
YOU KNOW, I DON'T REALLY
BEEP!

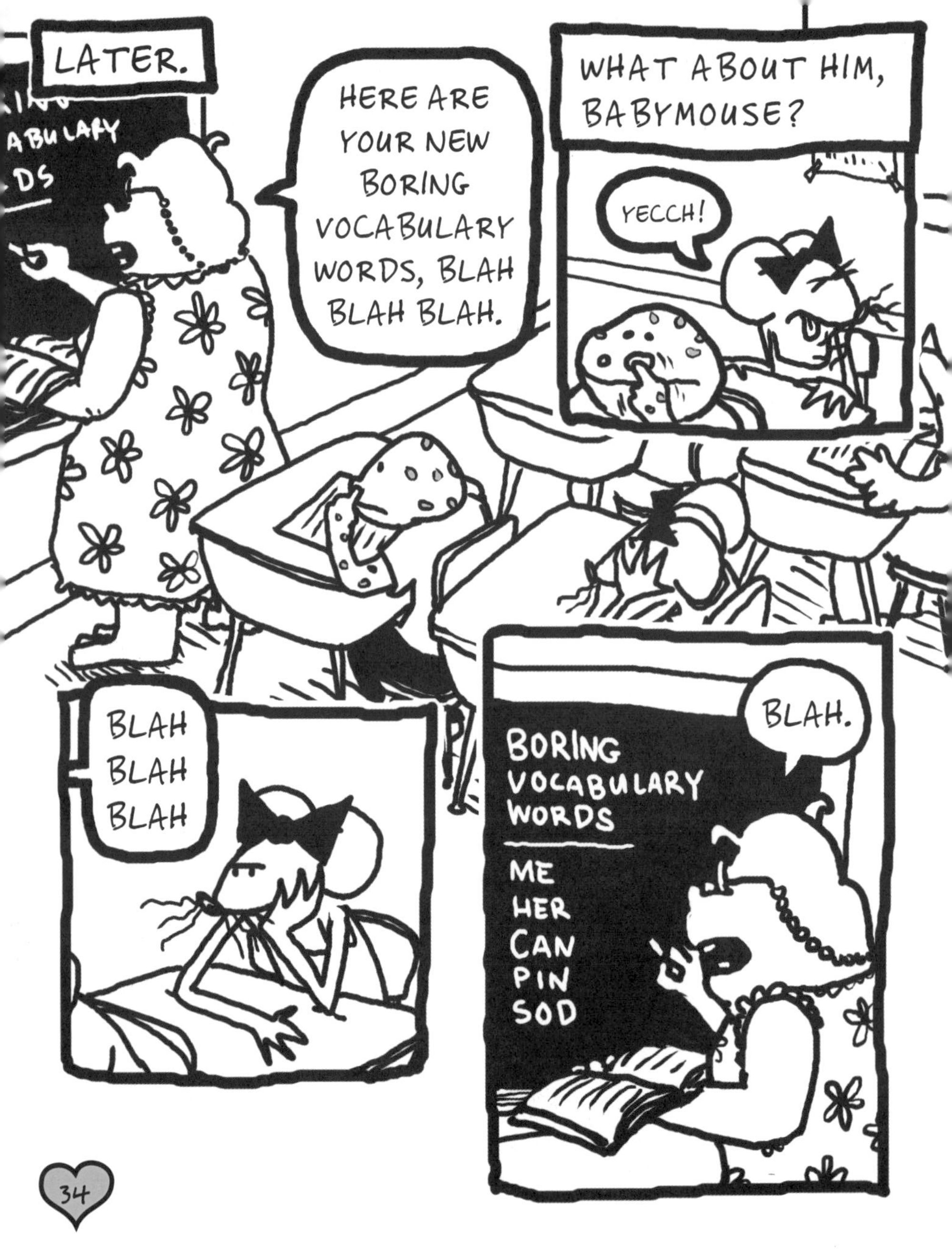
LATER.
HERE ARE YOUR NEW BORING VOCABULARY WORDS, BLAH BLAH BLAH.
WHAT ABOUT HIM, BABYMOUSE?
YECCH!
BLAH BLAH BLAH
BLAH.
BORING VOCABULARY WORDS
ME
HER
CAN
PIN
SOD

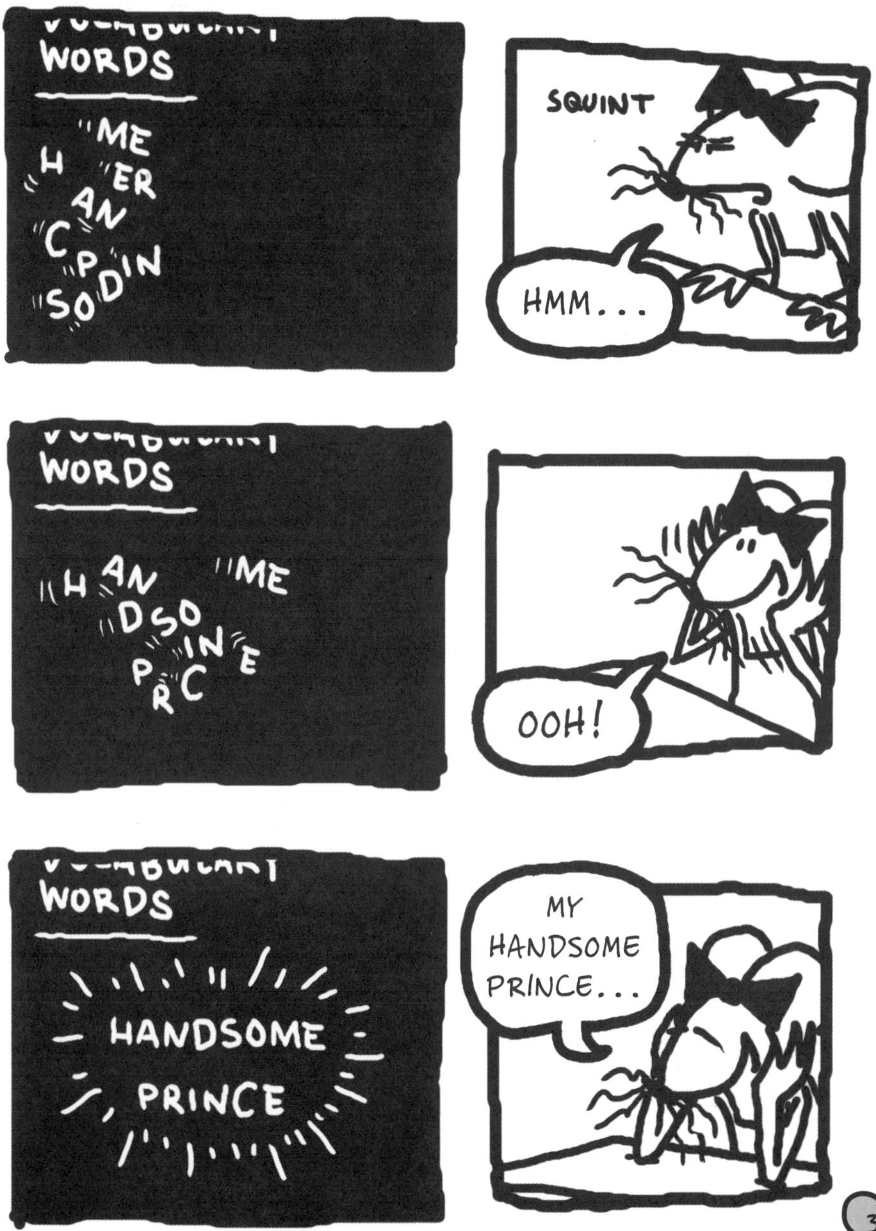
WORDS
SQUINT
HMM...
WORDS
OOH!
WORDS
HANDSOME PRINCE
MY HANDSOME PRINCE...

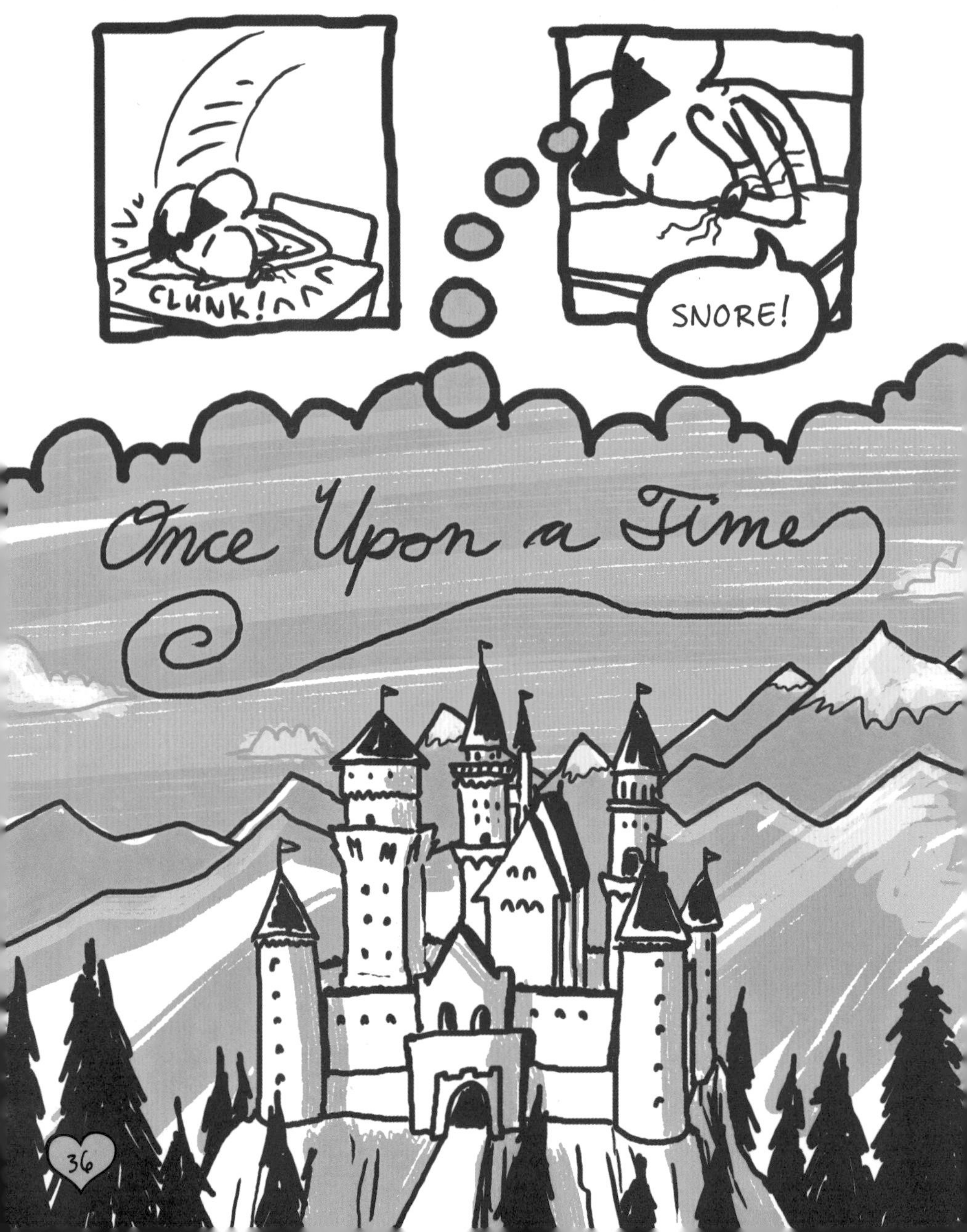
CLUNK!
SNORE!
Once Upon a Time

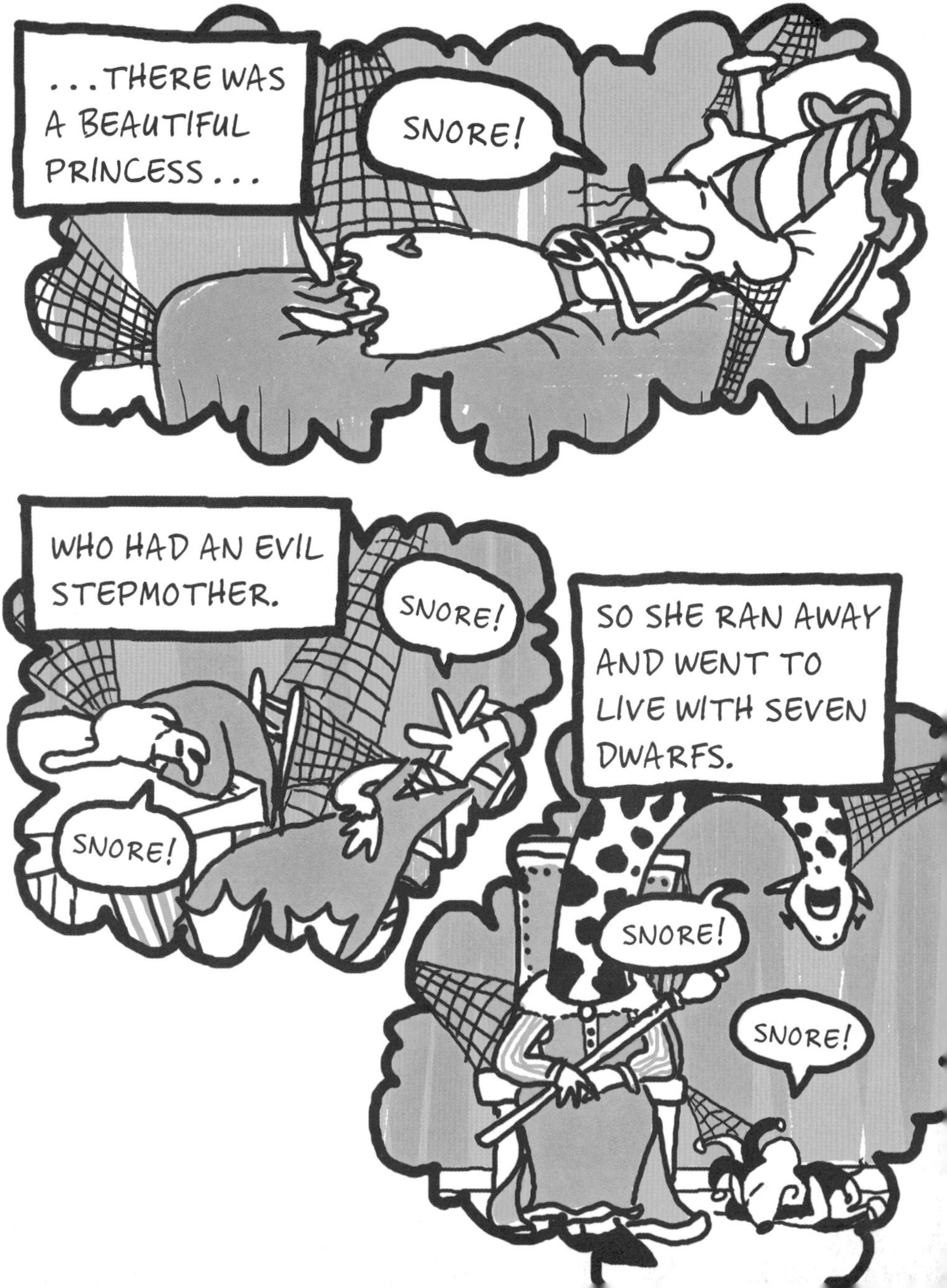

. . . THERE WAS A BEAUTIFUL PRINCESS . . .
SNORE!
WHO HAD AN EVIL STEPMOTHER.
SNORE!
SNORE!
SO SHE RAN AWAY AND WENT TO LIVE WITH SEVEN DWARFS.
SNORE!
SNORE!

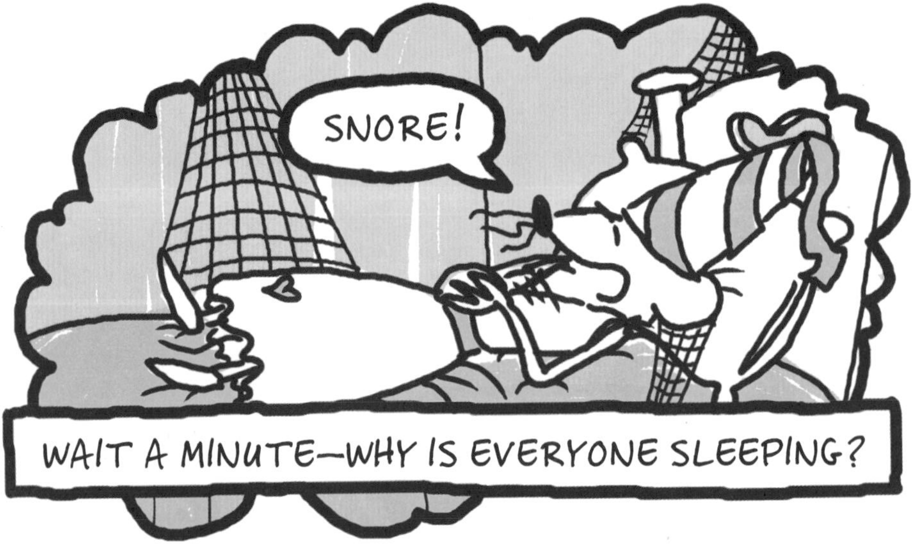
SNORE!
WAIT A MINUTE—WHY IS EVERYONE SLEEPING?

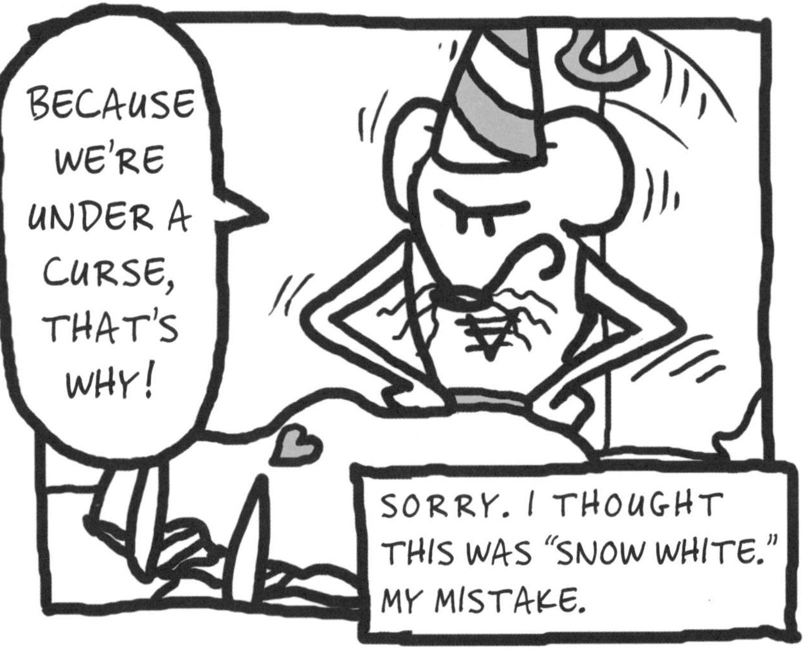
BECAUSE WE'RE UNDER A CURSE, THAT'S WHY!
SORRY. I THOUGHT THIS WAS "SNOW WHITE." MY MISTAKE.

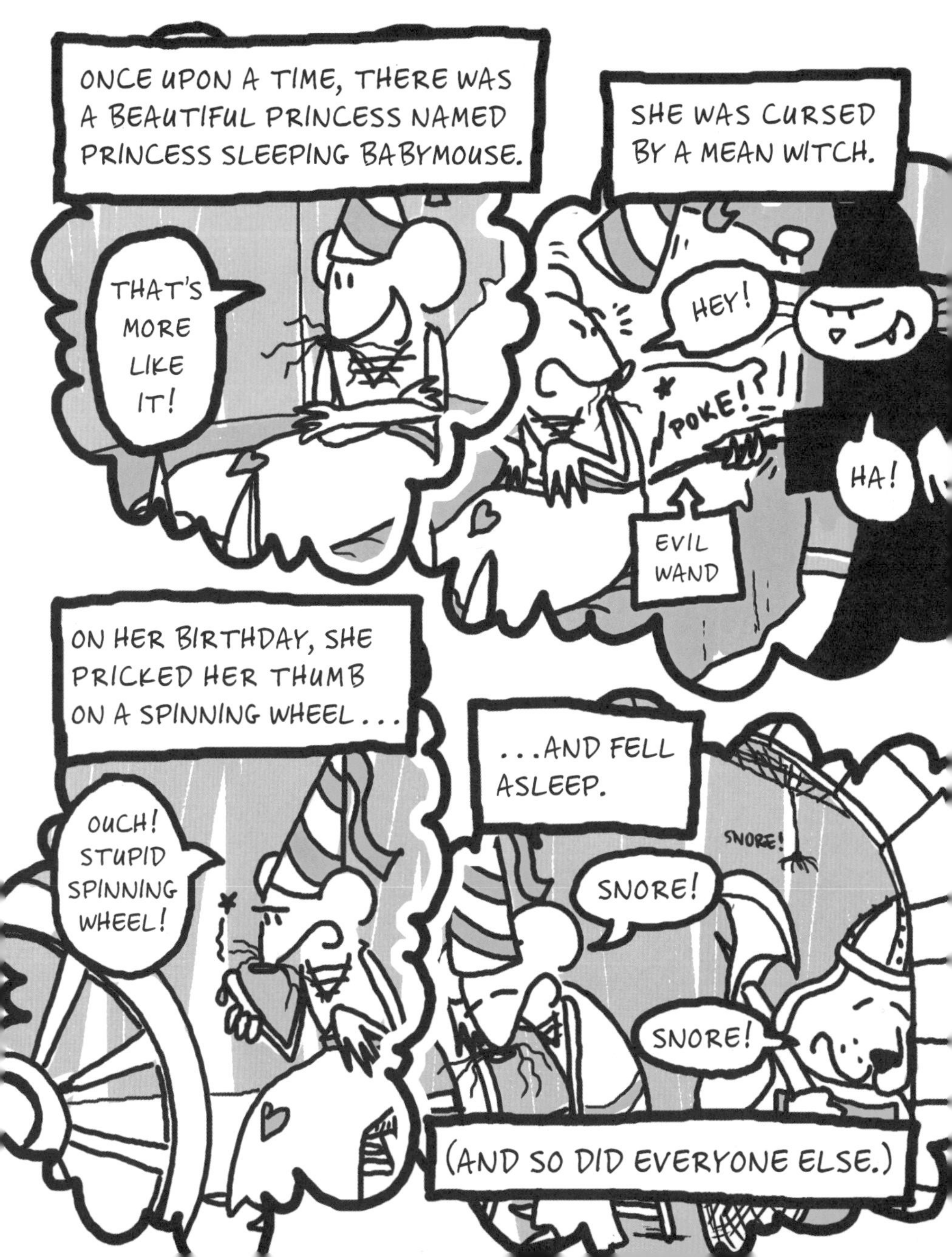
ONCE UPON A TIME, THERE WAS A BEAUTIFUL PRINCESS NAMED PRINCESS SLEEPING BABYMOUSE.
THAT'S MORE LIKE IT!
SHE WAS CURSED BY A MEAN WITCH.
HEY!
POKE!
HA!
EVIL WAND
ON HER BIRTHDAY, SHE PRICKED HER THUMB ON A SPINNING WHEEL . . .
OUCH! STUPID SPINNING WHEEL!
. . . AND FELL ASLEEP.
SNORE!
SNORE!
SNORE!
(AND SO DID EVERYONE ELSE.)

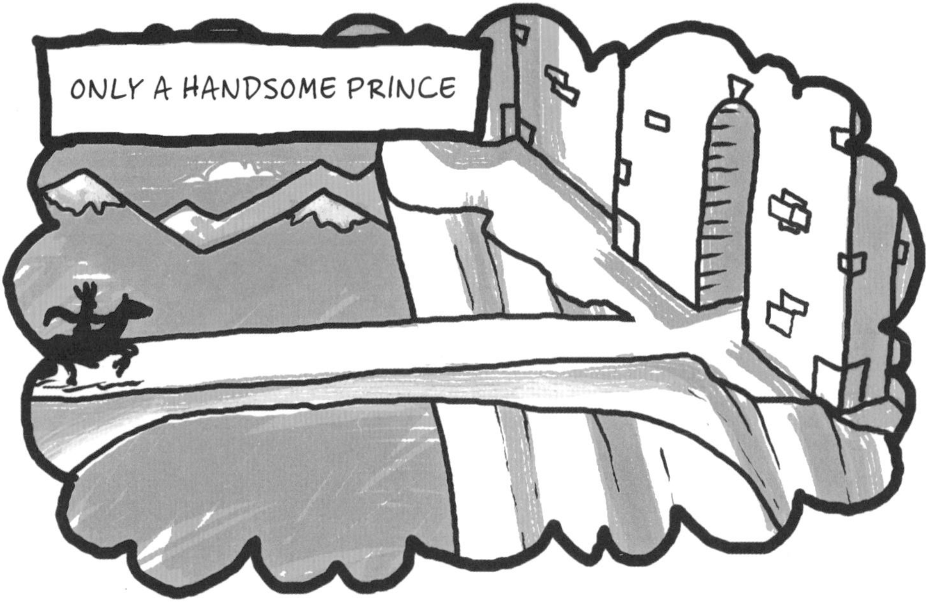
ONLY A HANDSOME PRINCE

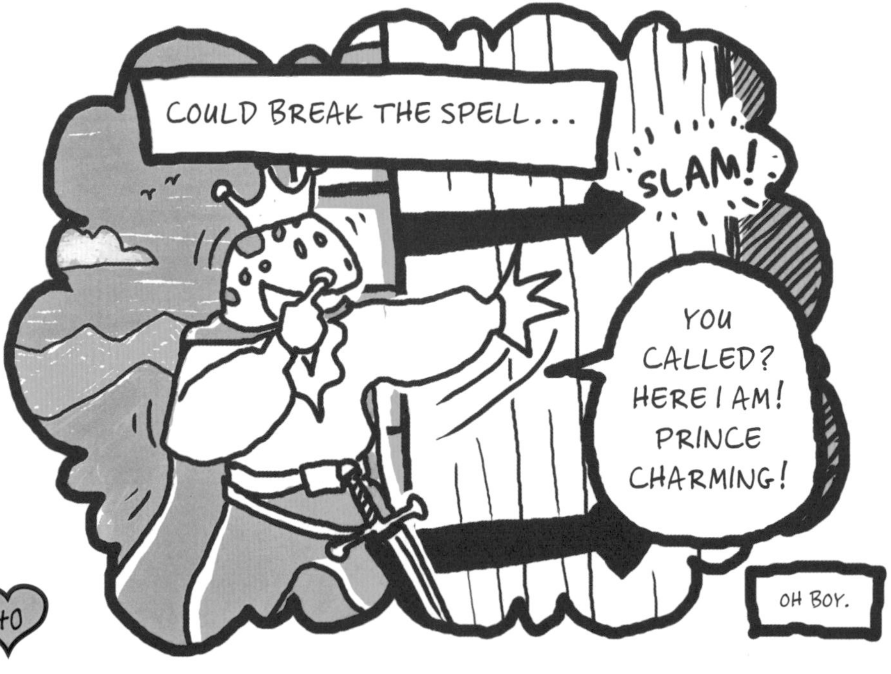
COULD BREAK THE SPELL...
SLAM!
YOU CALLED? HERE I AM! PRINCE CHARMING!

OH BOY.

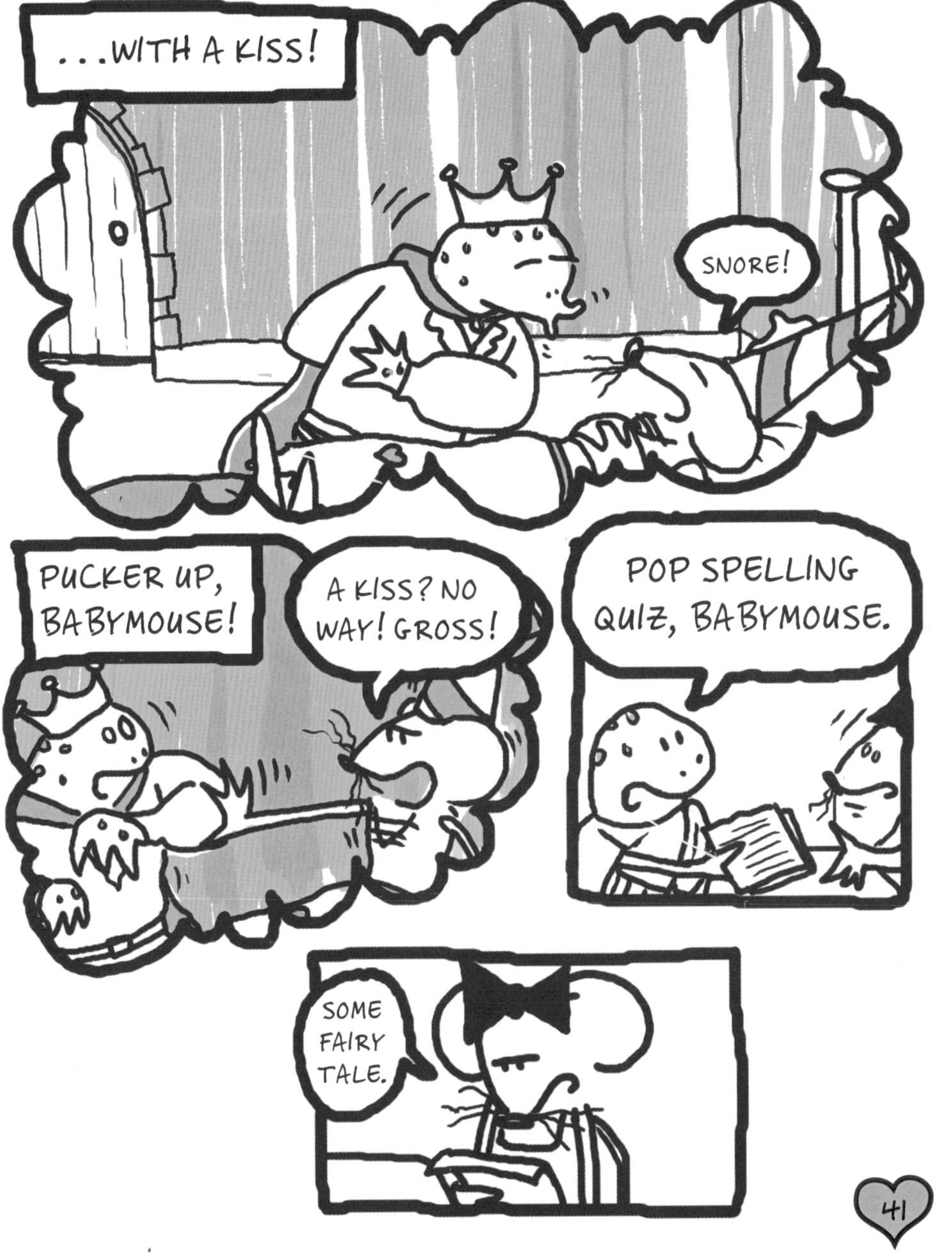
...WITH A KISS!
SNORE!
PUCKER UP, BABYMOUSE!
A KISS? NO WAY! GROSS!
POP SPELLING QUIZ, BABYMOUSE.
SOME FAIRY TALE.

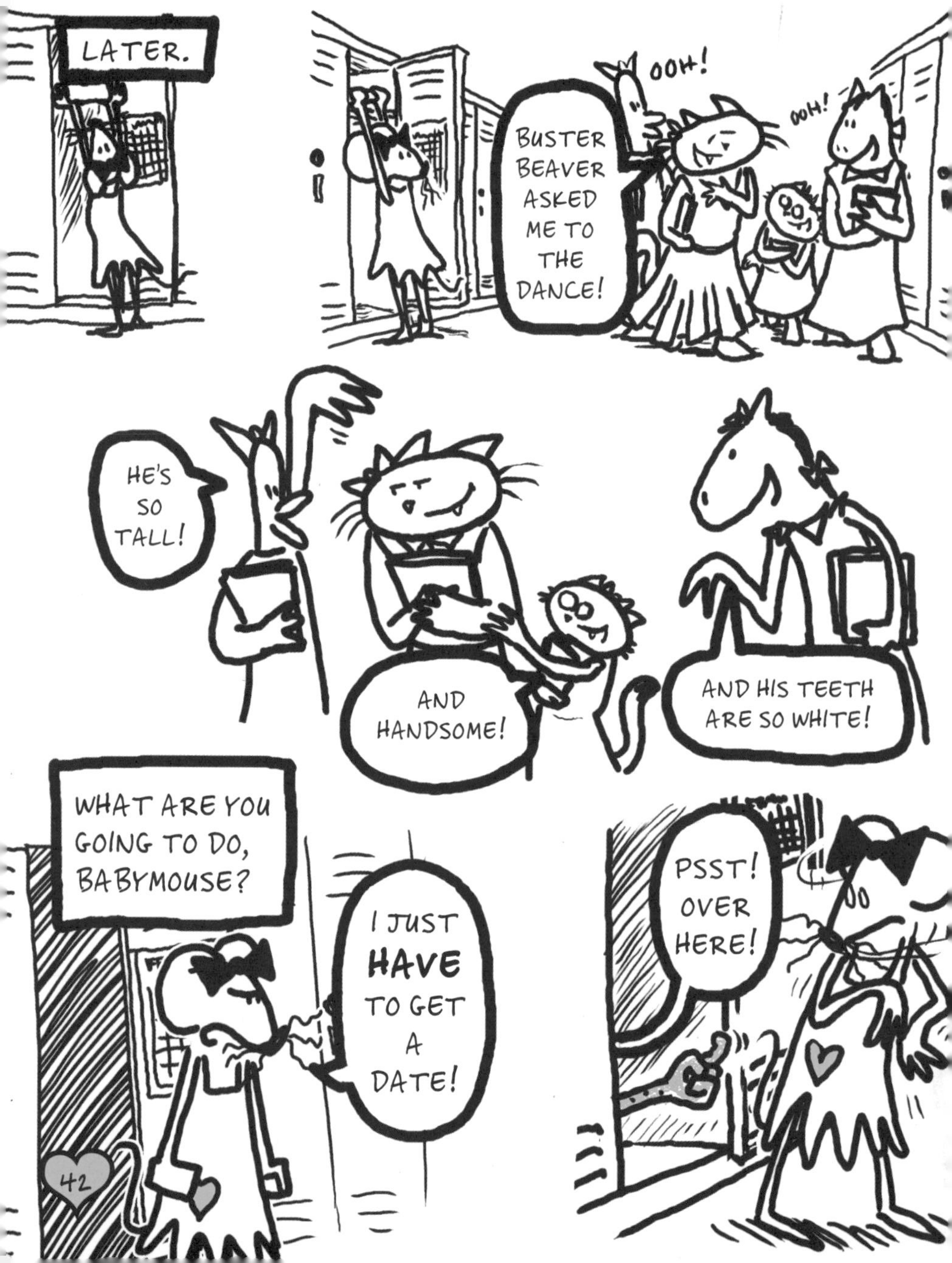
LATER.
BUSTER BEAVER ASKED ME TO THE DANCE!
OOH!
OOH!
HE'S SO TALL!
AND HANDSOME!
AND HIS TEETH ARE SO WHITE!
WHAT ARE YOU GOING TO DO, BABYMOUSE?
I JUST **HAVE** TO GET A DATE!
PSST! OVER HERE!

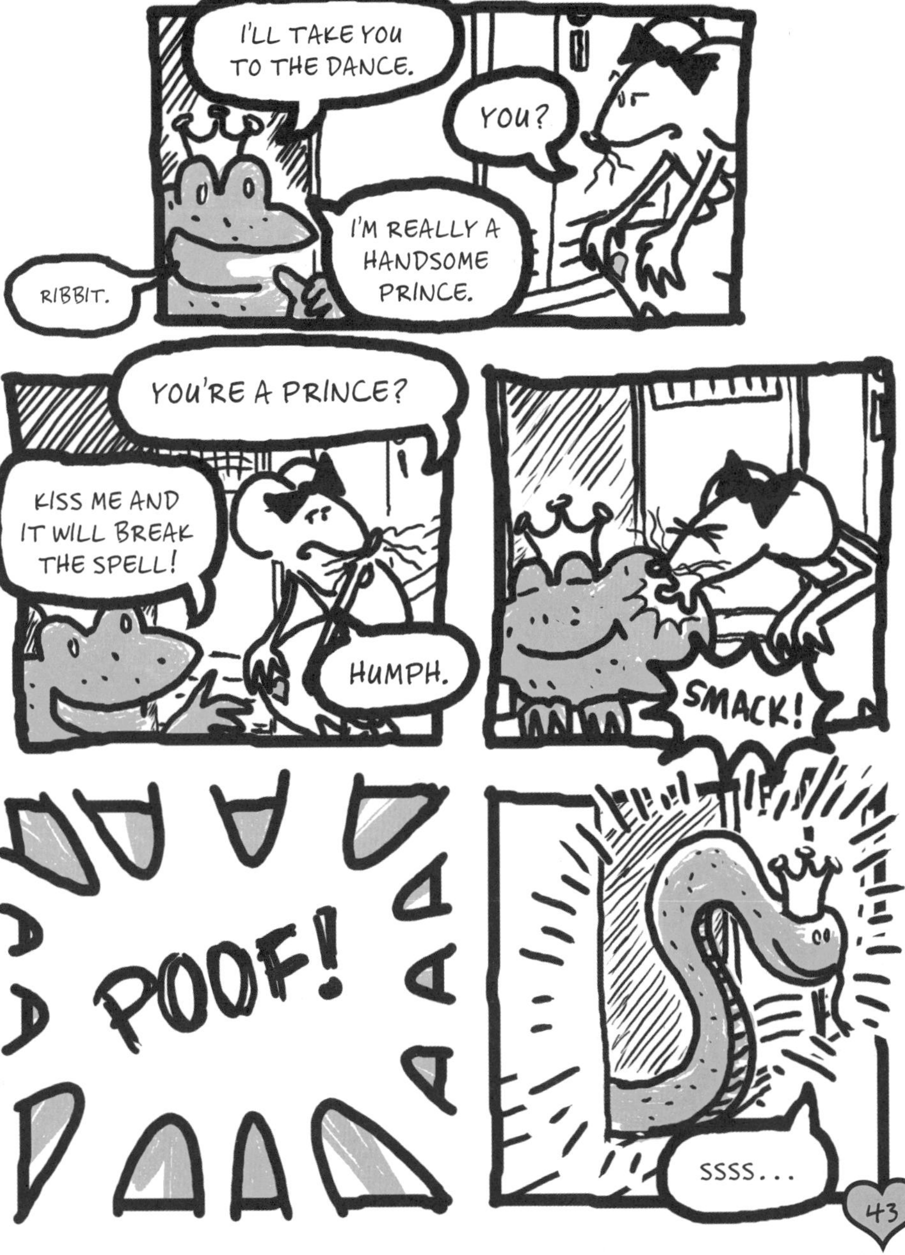
I'LL TAKE YOU TO THE DANCE.
YOU?
RIBBIT.
I'M REALLY A HANDSOME PRINCE.
YOU'RE A PRINCE?
KISS ME AND IT WILL BREAK THE SPELL!
HUMPH.
SMACK!
POOF!
SSSS...

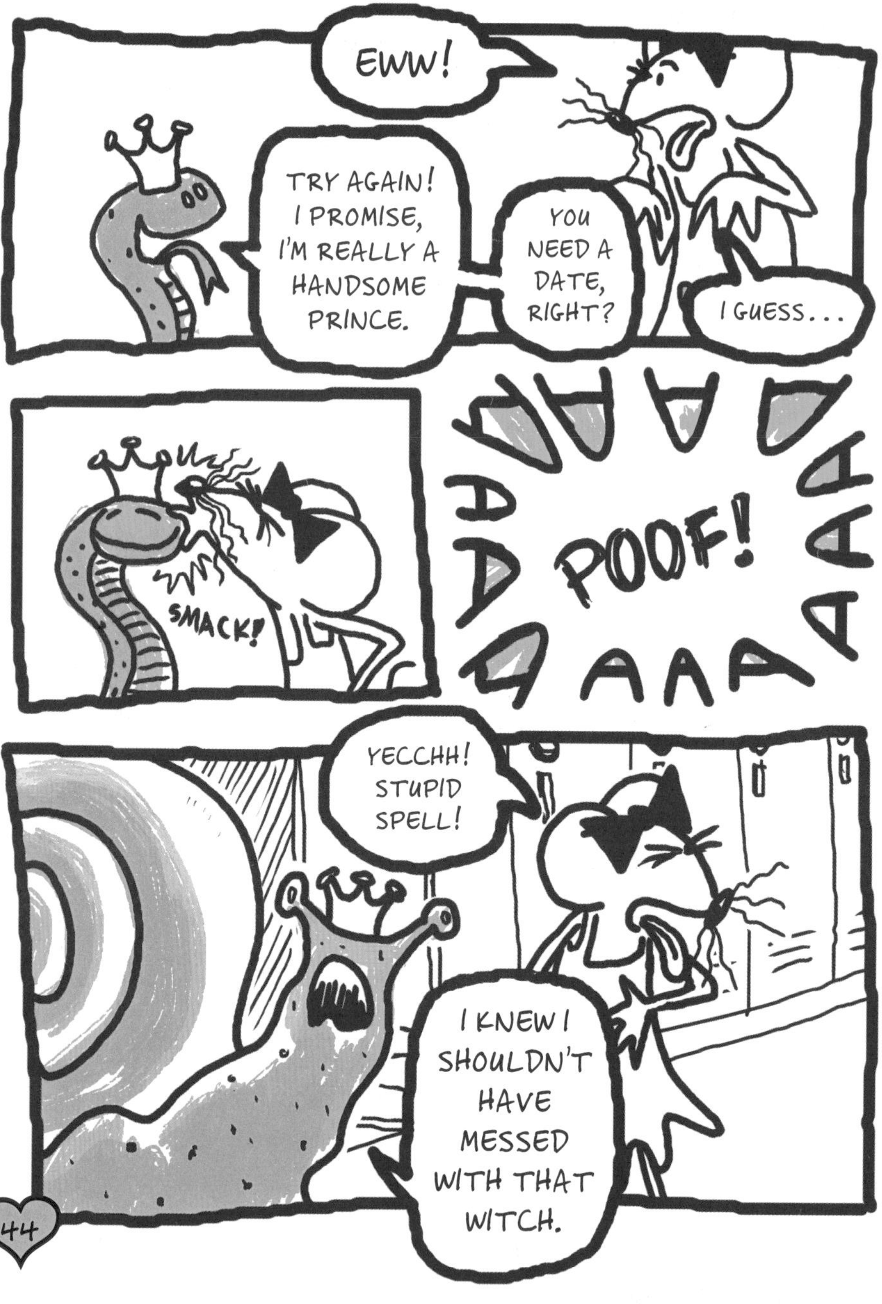
EWW!
TRY AGAIN! I PROMISE, I'M REALLY A HANDSOME PRINCE.
YOU NEED A DATE, RIGHT?
I GUESS...
SMACK!
POOF!
AAAAAAAAAAAAAAAAAA
YECCHH! STUPID SPELL!
I KNEW I SHOULDN'T HAVE MESSED WITH THAT WITCH.

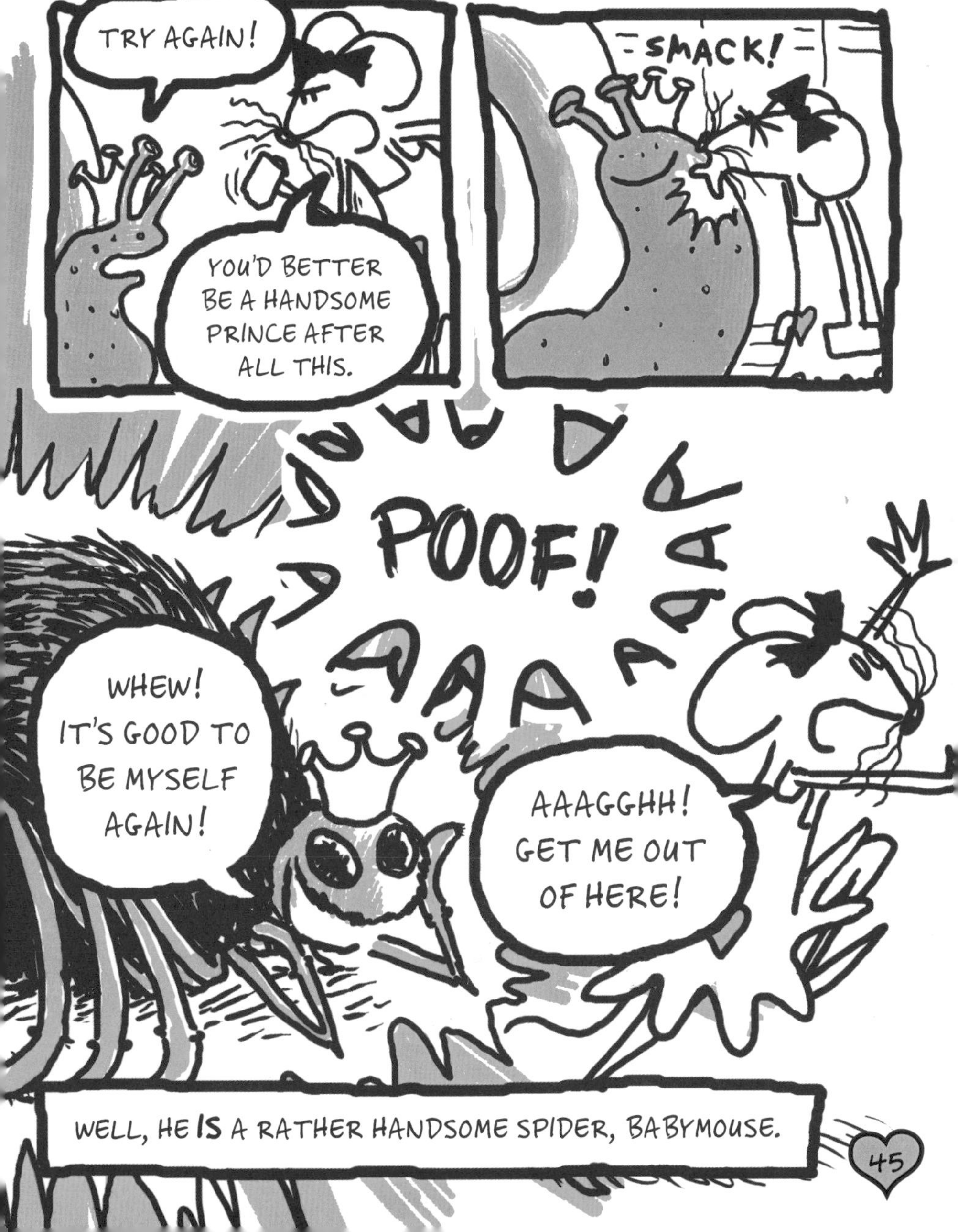
TRY AGAIN!
YOU'D BETTER BE A HANDSOME PRINCE AFTER ALL THIS.
SMACK!
POOF!
WHEW! IT'S GOOD TO BE MYSELF AGAIN!
AAAGGHH! GET ME OUT OF HERE!
WELL, HE IS A RATHER HANDSOME SPIDER, BABYMOUSE.

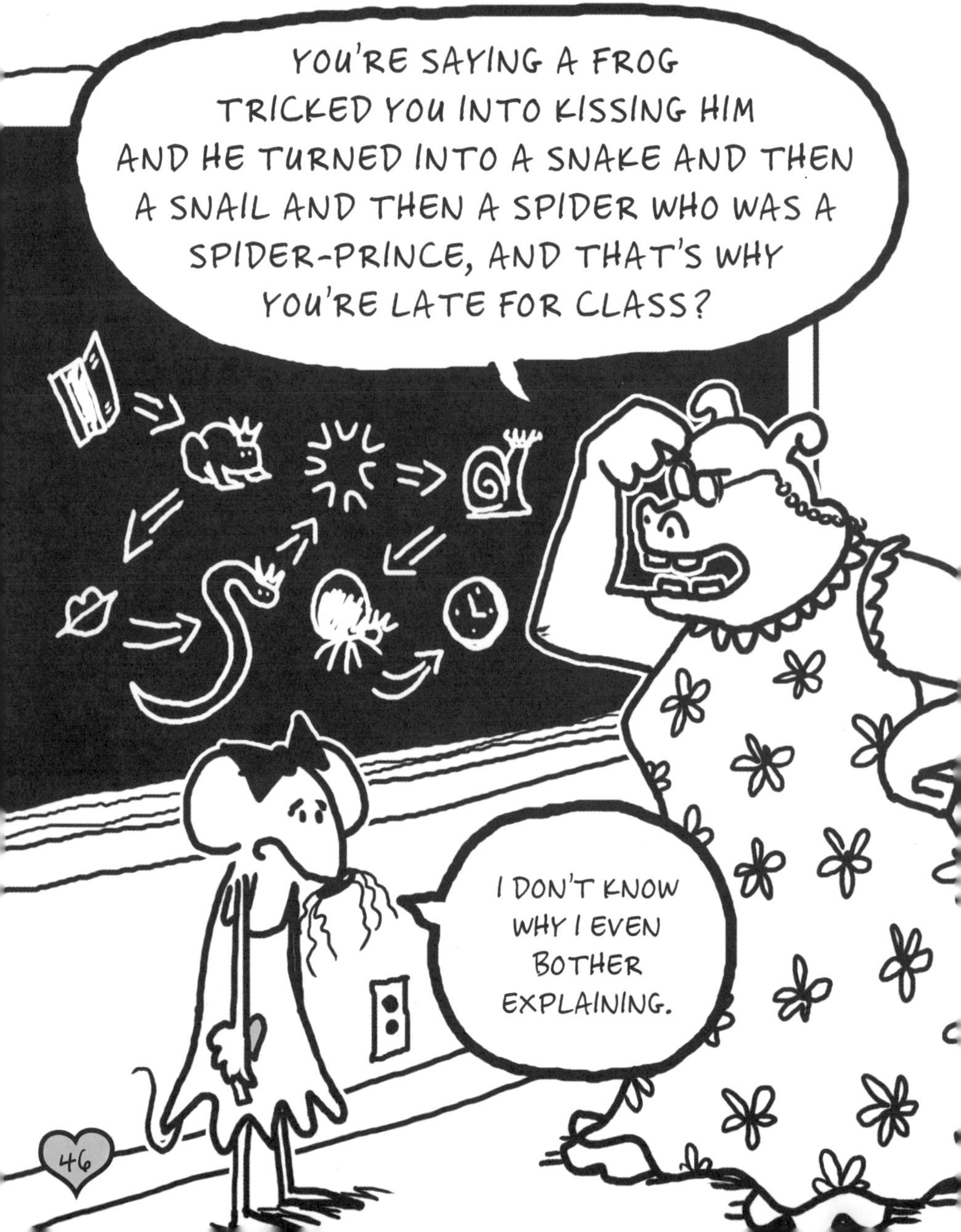
YOU'RE SAYING A FROG TRICKED YOU INTO KISSING HIM AND HE TURNED INTO A SNAKE AND THEN A SNAIL AND THEN A SPIDER WHO WAS A SPIDER-PRINCE, AND THAT'S WHY YOU'RE LATE FOR CLASS?
I DON'T KNOW WHY I EVEN BOTHER EXPLAINING.

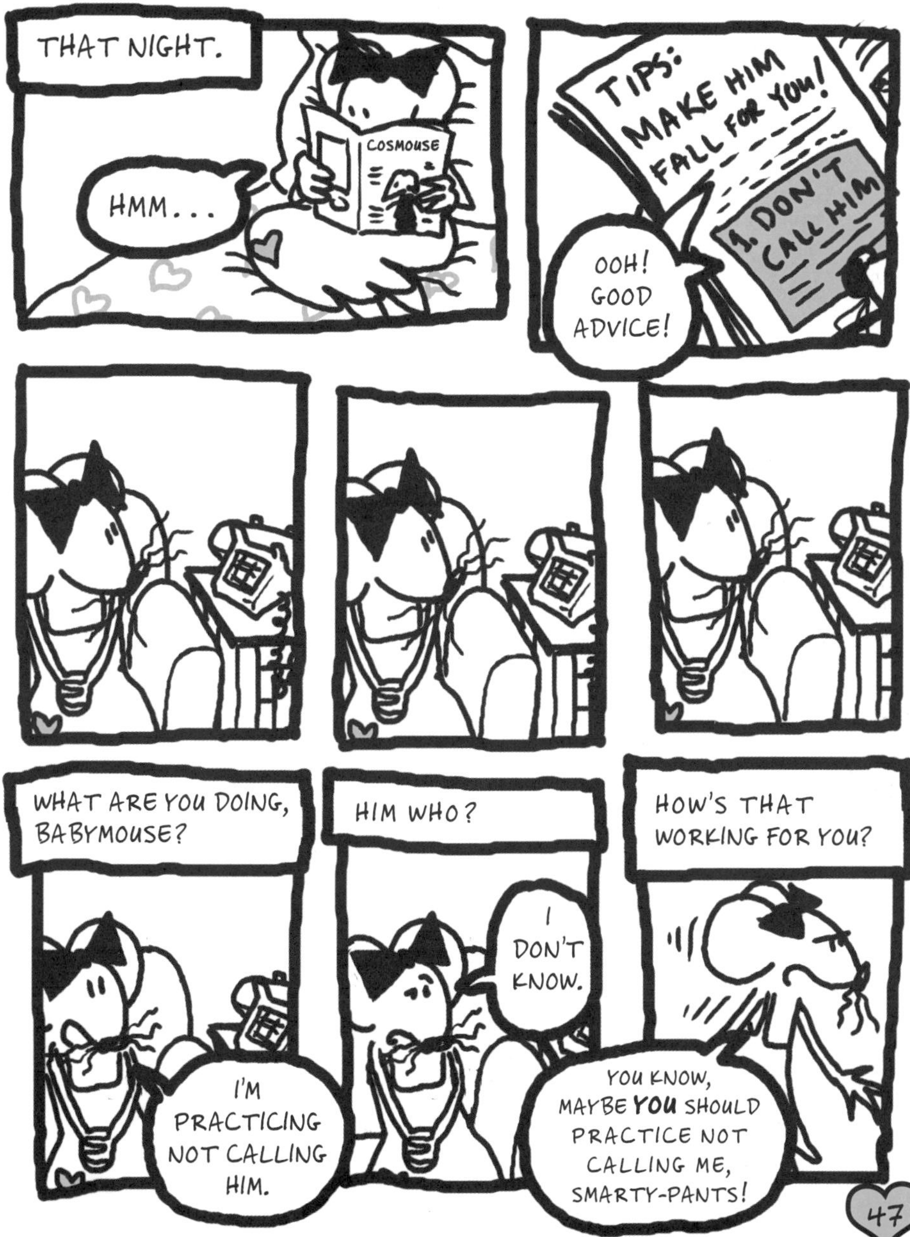
THAT NIGHT.
HMM...
COSMOUSE
TIPS: MAKE HIM FALL FOR YOU!
1. DON'T CALL HIM
OOH! GOOD ADVICE!
WHAT ARE YOU DOING, BABYMOUSE?
I'M PRACTICING NOT CALLING HIM.
HIM WHO?
I DON'T KNOW.
HOW'S THAT WORKING FOR YOU?
YOU KNOW, MAYBE **YOU** SHOULD PRACTICE NOT CALLING ME, SMARTY-PANTS!

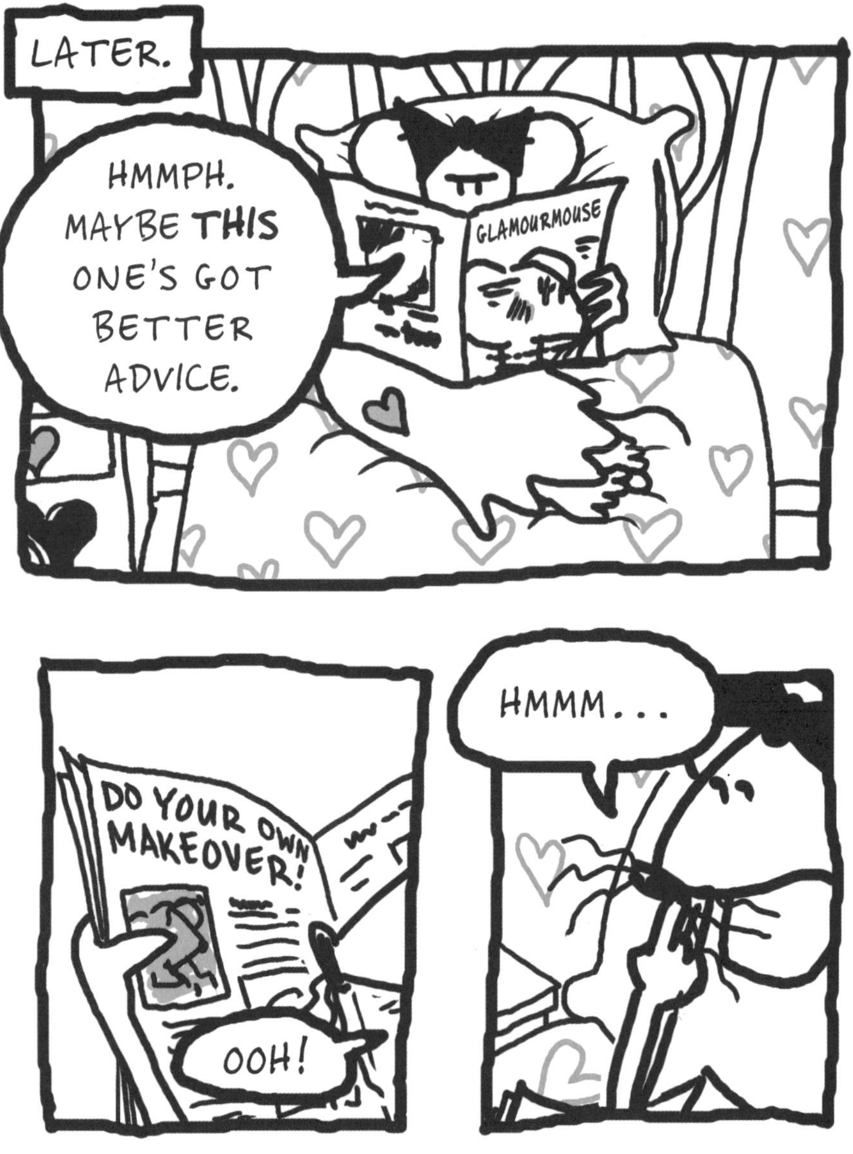
LATER.
HMMPH. MAYBE **THIS** ONE'S GOT BETTER ADVICE.
GLAMOURMOUSE
DO YOUR OWN MAKEOVER!
OOH!
HMMM...

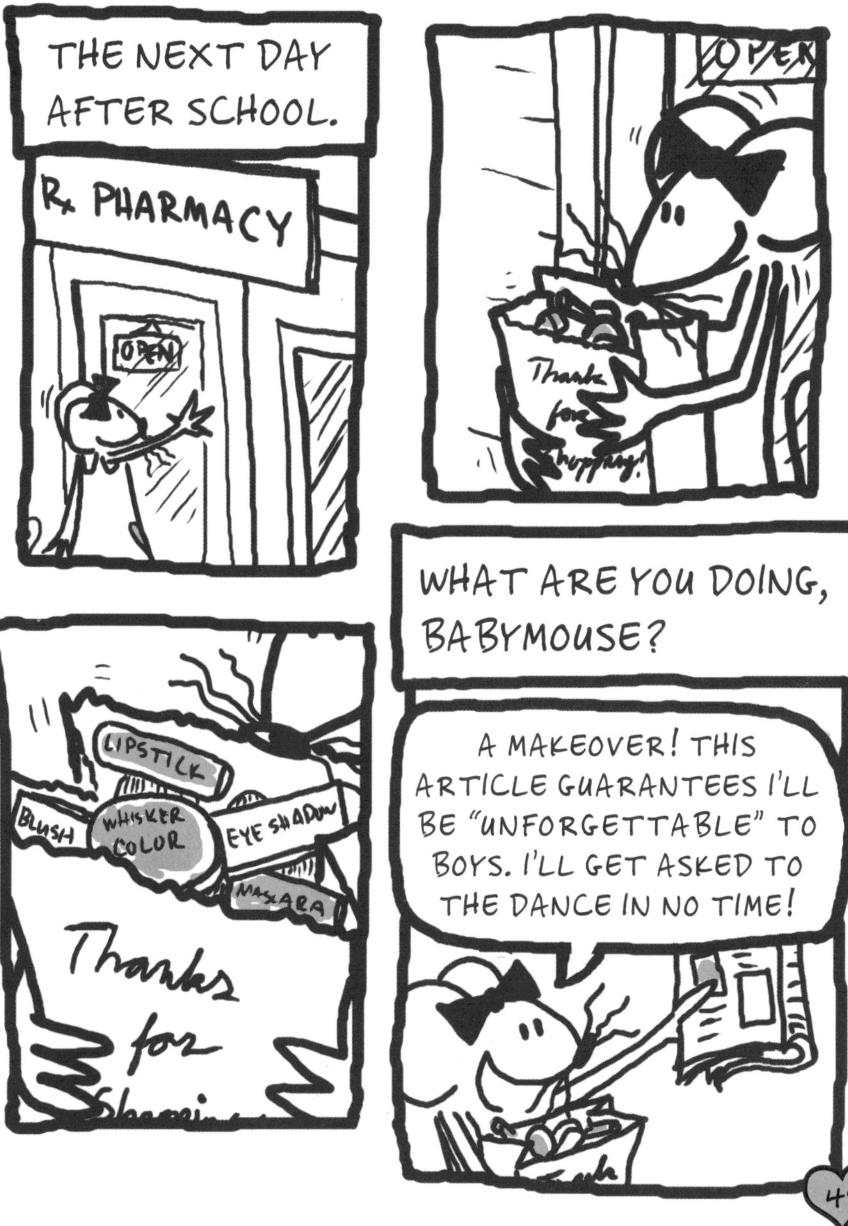
THE NEXT DAY AFTER SCHOOL.
Rx PHARMACY
OPEN
OPEN
Thanks for Shopping!
LIPSTICK
BLUSH
WHISKER COLOR
EYE SHADOW
MASCARA
Thanks for
WHAT ARE YOU DOING, BABYMOUSE?
A MAKEOVER! THIS ARTICLE GUARANTEES I'LL BE "UNFORGETTABLE" TO BOYS. I'LL GET ASKED TO THE DANCE IN NO TIME!

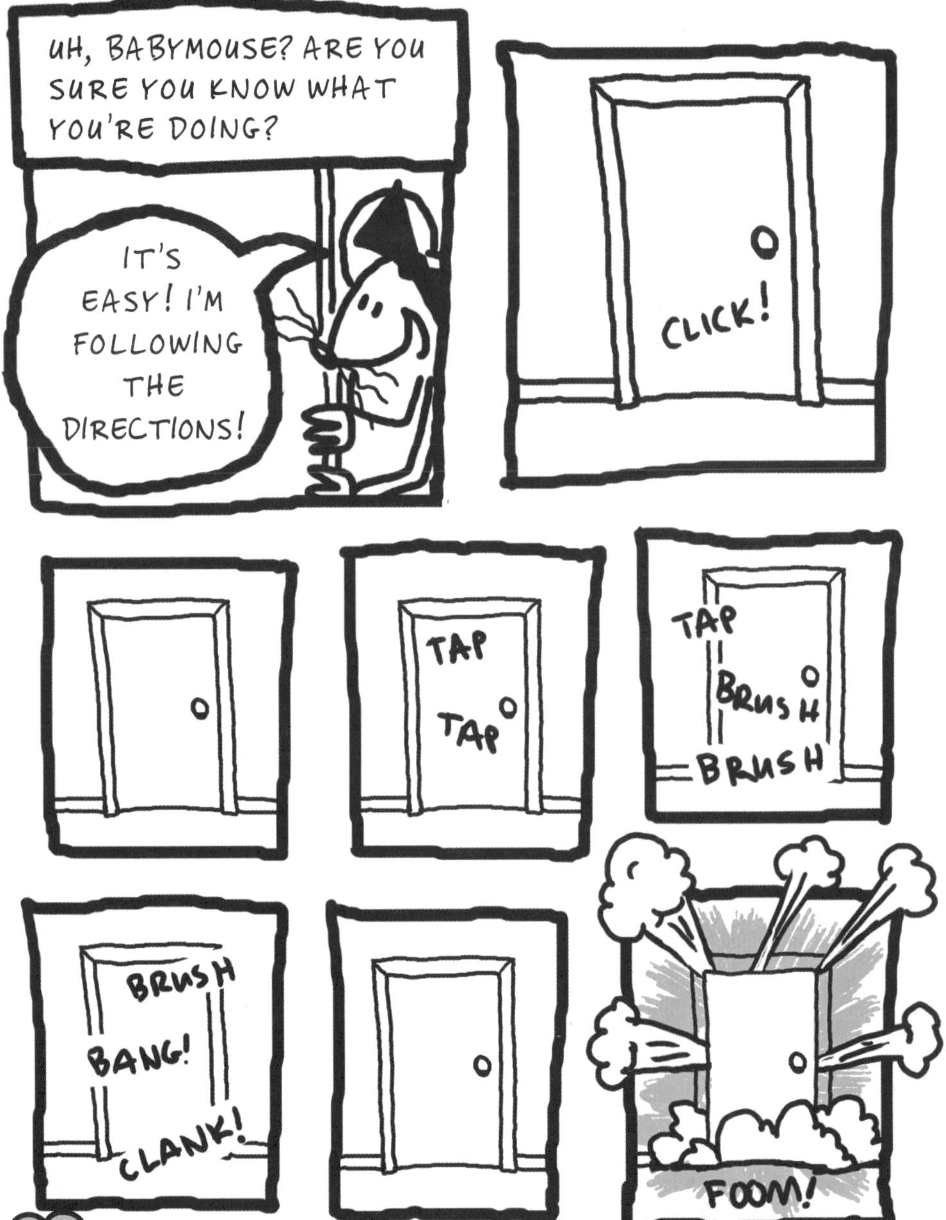
UH, BABYMOUSE? ARE YOU SURE YOU KNOW WHAT YOU'RE DOING?
IT'S EASY! I'M FOLLOWING THE DIRECTIONS!
CLICK!
TAP
TAP
TAP
BRUSH
BRUSH
BRUSH
BANG!
CLANK!
FOOM!

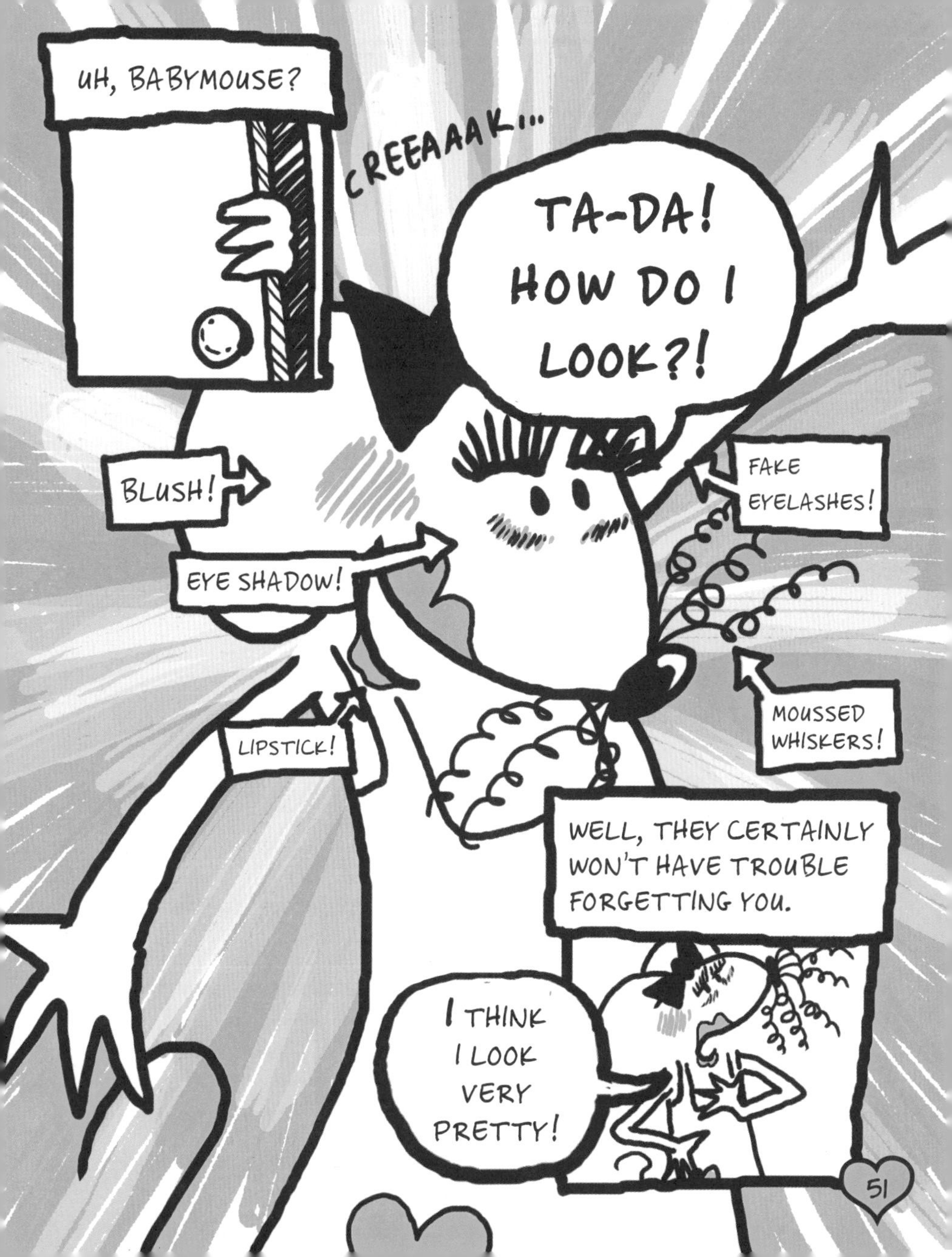

UH, BABYMOUSE?
CREEAAAK...
TA-DA! HOW DO I LOOK?!
BLUSH!
EYE SHADOW!
FAKE EYELASHES!
LIPSTICK!
MOUSSED WHISKERS!
WELL, THEY CERTAINLY WON'T HAVE TROUBLE FORGETTING YOU.
I THINK I LOOK VERY PRETTY!

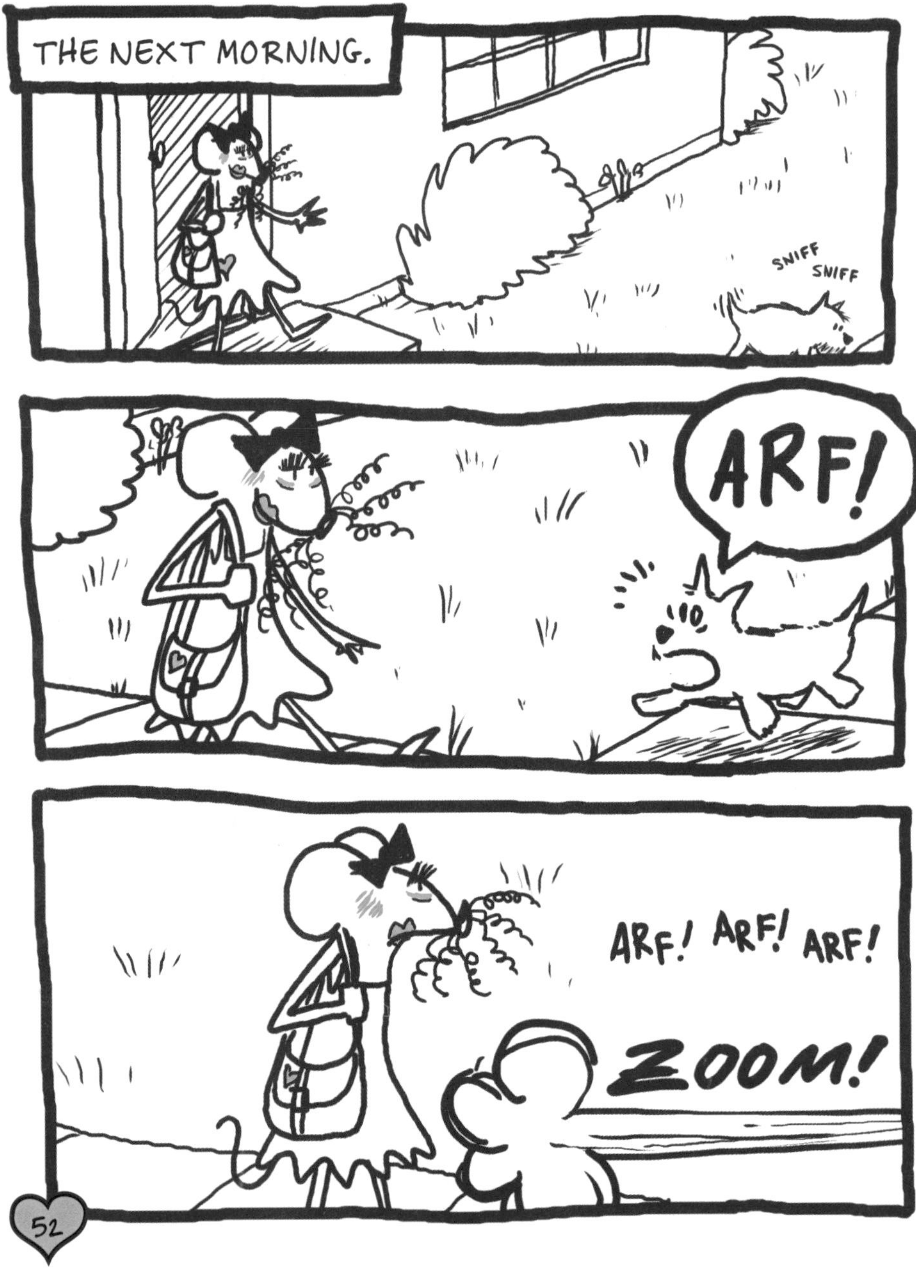
THE NEXT MORNING.
SNIFF SNIFF
ARF!
ARF! ARF! ARF!
ZOOM!

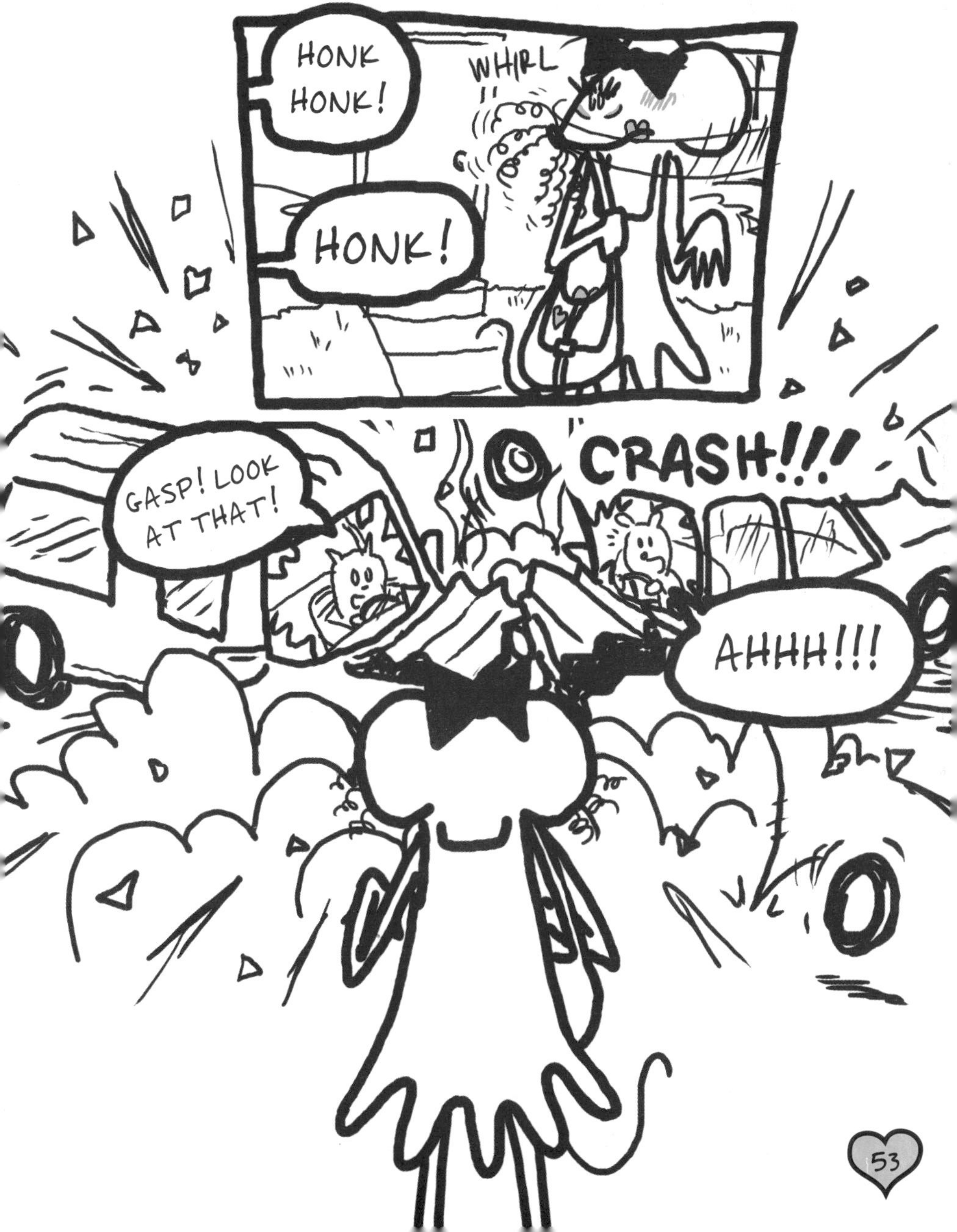
HONK
HONK!
WHIRL
HONK!
GASP! LOOK AT THAT!
CRASH!!!
AHHH!!!

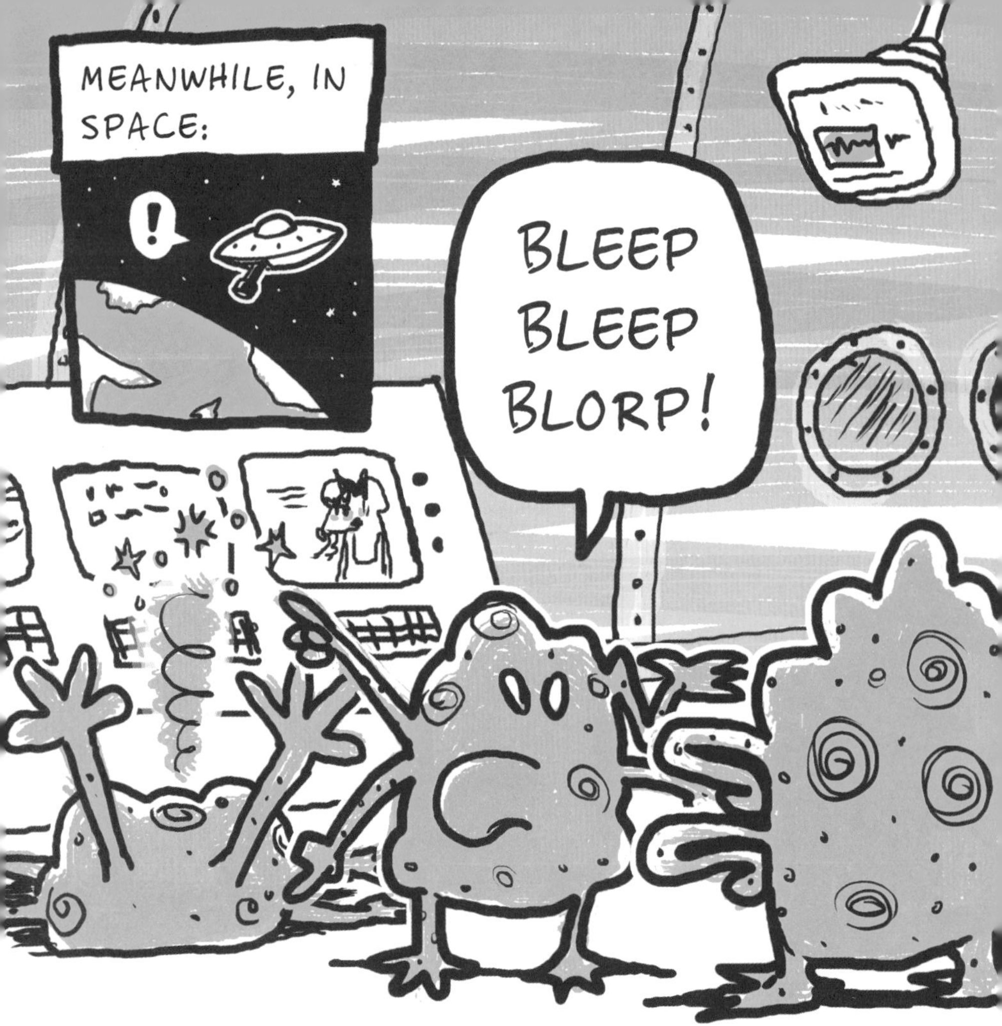
MEANWHILE, IN SPACE:
!
BLEEP BLEEP BLORP!

[I don't know, Commander—he was looking at something on Earth and he just fell over!]

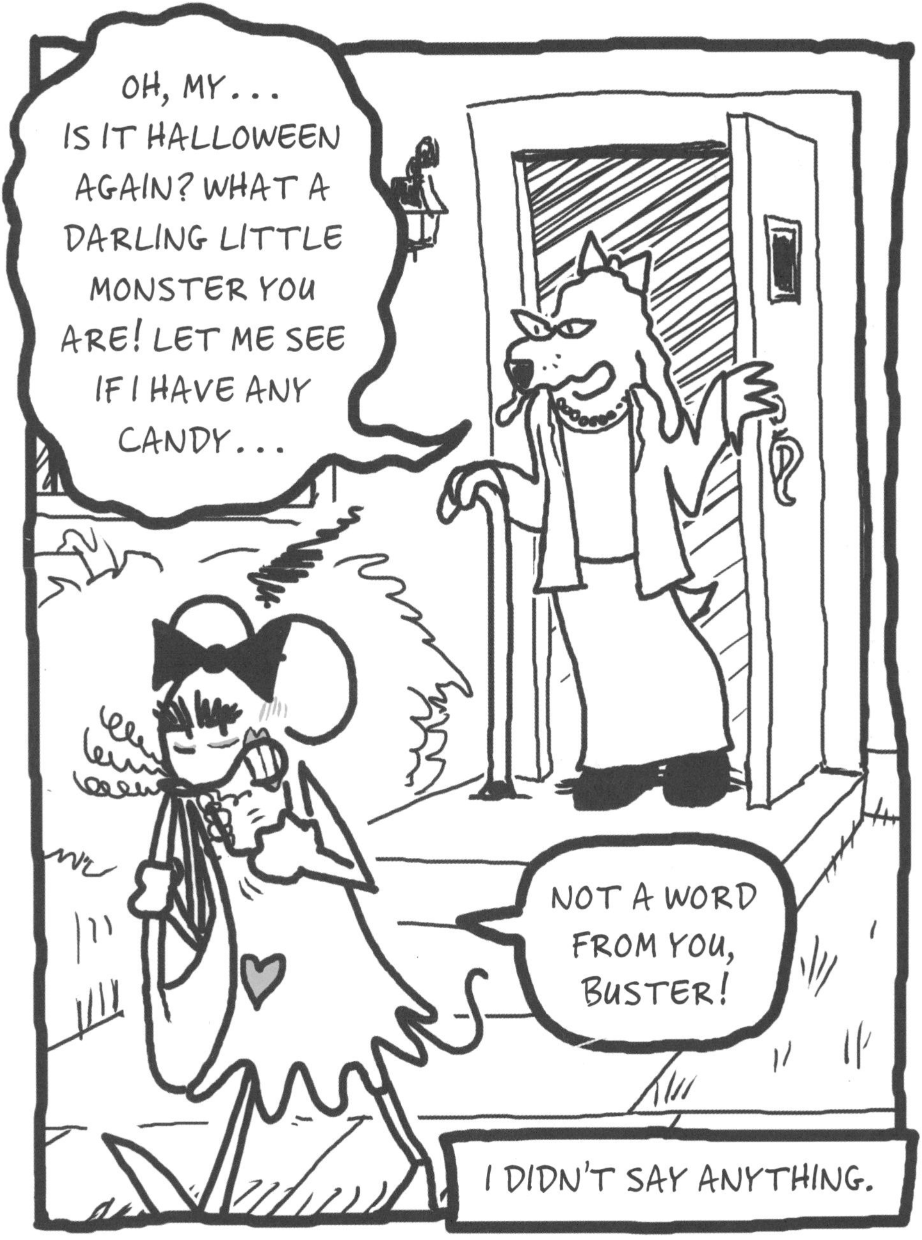
OH, MY . . . IS IT HALLOWEEN AGAIN? WHAT A DARLING LITTLE MONSTER YOU ARE! LET ME SEE IF I HAVE ANY CANDY . . .
NOT A WORD FROM YOU, BUSTER!
I DIDN'T SAY ANYTHING.

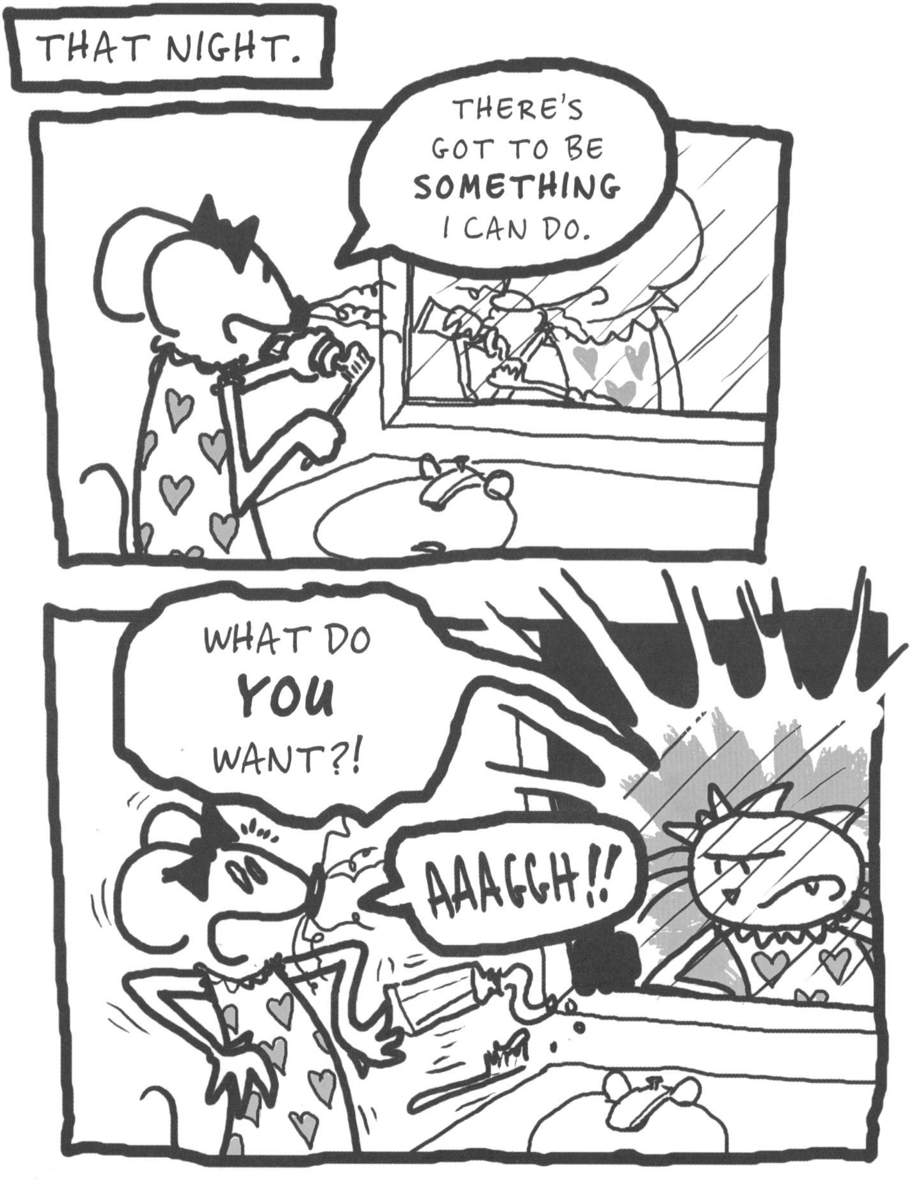
THAT NIGHT.
THERE'S GOT TO BE SOMETHING I CAN DO.
WHAT DO YOU WANT?!
AAAGGH!!

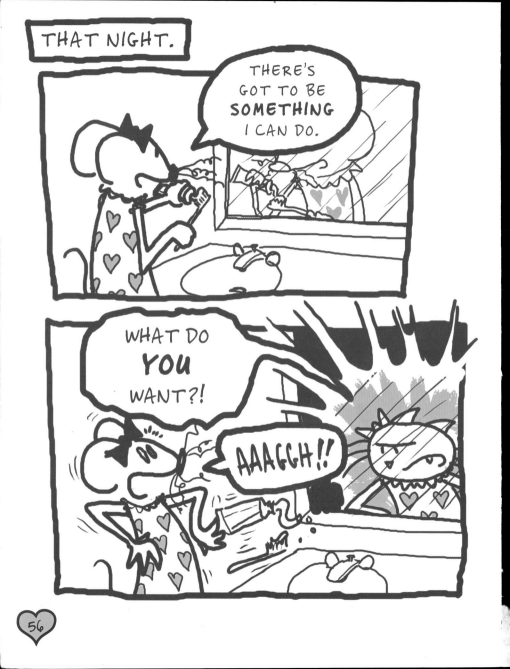

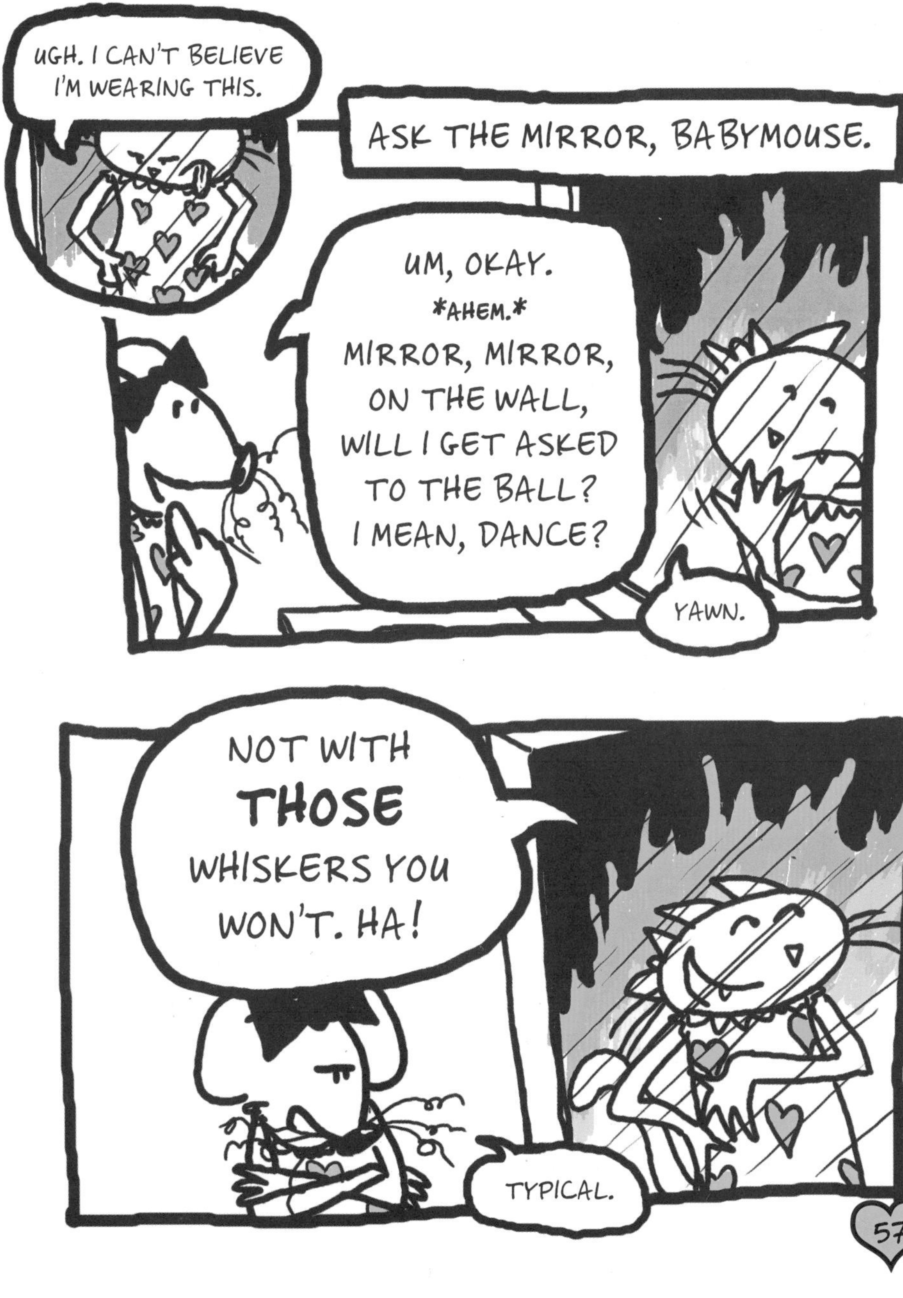
UGH. I CAN'T BELIEVE I'M WEARING THIS.
ASK THE MIRROR, BABYMOUSE.
UM, OKAY. *AHEM.* MIRROR, MIRROR, ON THE WALL, WILL I GET ASKED TO THE BALL? I MEAN, DANCE?
YAWN.
NOT WITH **THOSE** WHISKERS YOU WON'T. HA!
TYPICAL.

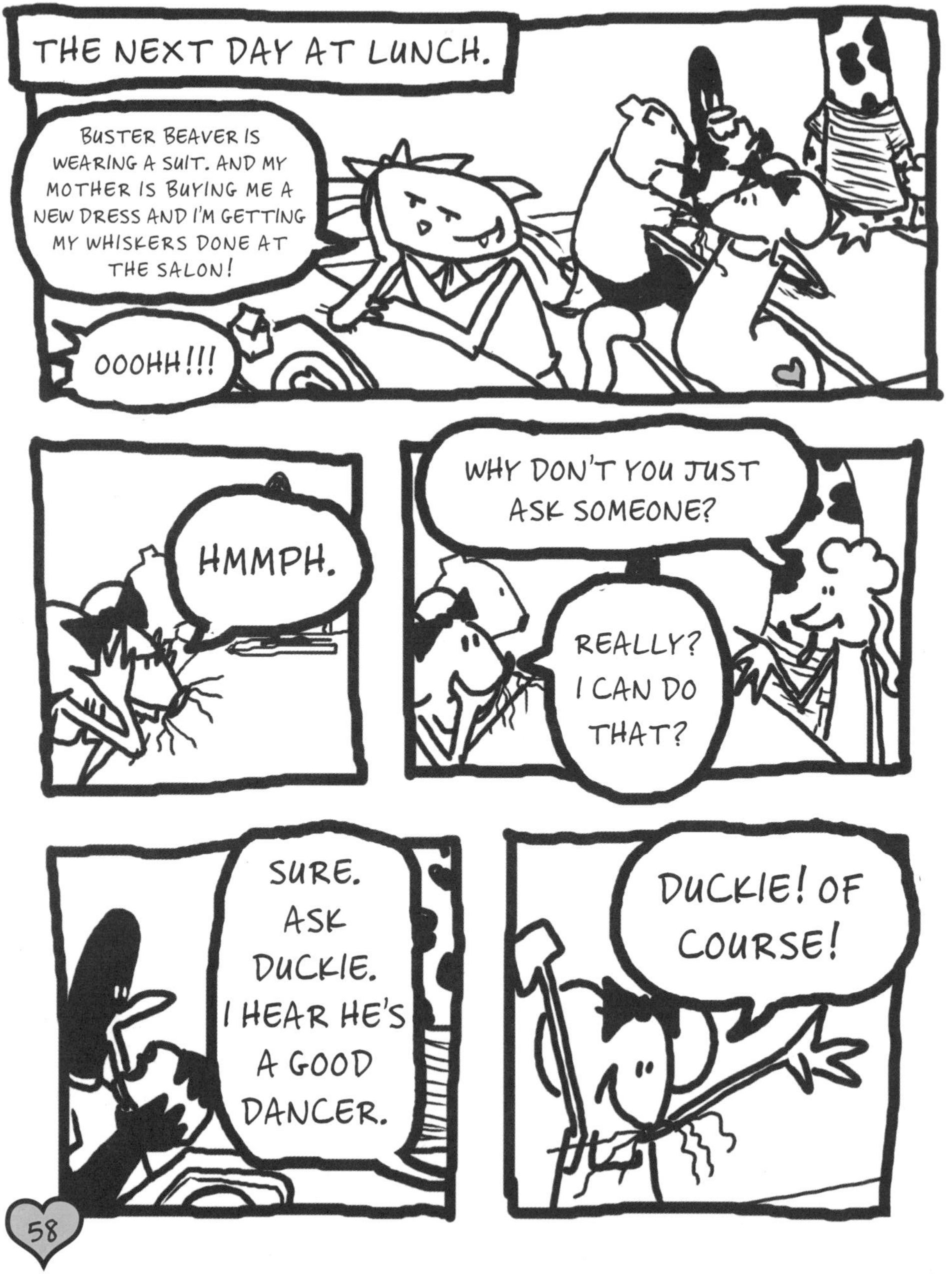
THE NEXT DAY AT LUNCH.
BUSTER BEAVER IS WEARING A SUIT. AND MY MOTHER IS BUYING ME A NEW DRESS AND I'M GETTING MY WHISKERS DONE AT THE SALON!
OOOHH!!!
HMMPH.
WHY DON'T YOU JUST ASK SOMEONE?
REALLY? I CAN DO THAT?
SURE. ASK DUCKIE. I HEAR HE'S A GOOD DANCER.
DUCKIE! OF COURSE!

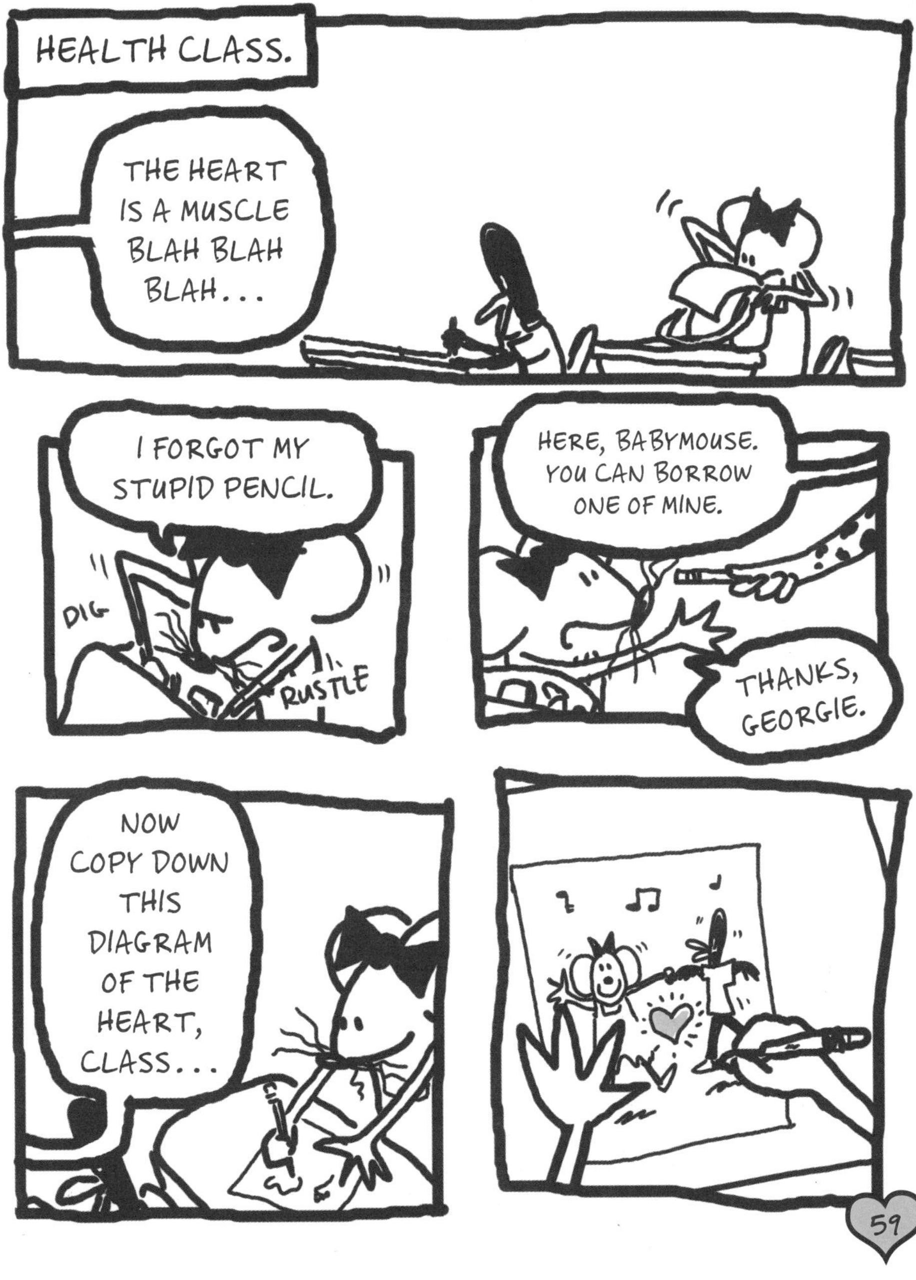
HEALTH CLASS.
THE HEART IS A MUSCLE BLAH BLAH BLAH...
I FORGOT MY STUPID PENCIL.
DIG
RUSTLE
HERE, BABYMOUSE. YOU CAN BORROW ONE OF MINE.
THANKS, GEORGIE.
NOW COPY DOWN THIS DIAGRAM OF THE HEART, CLASS...

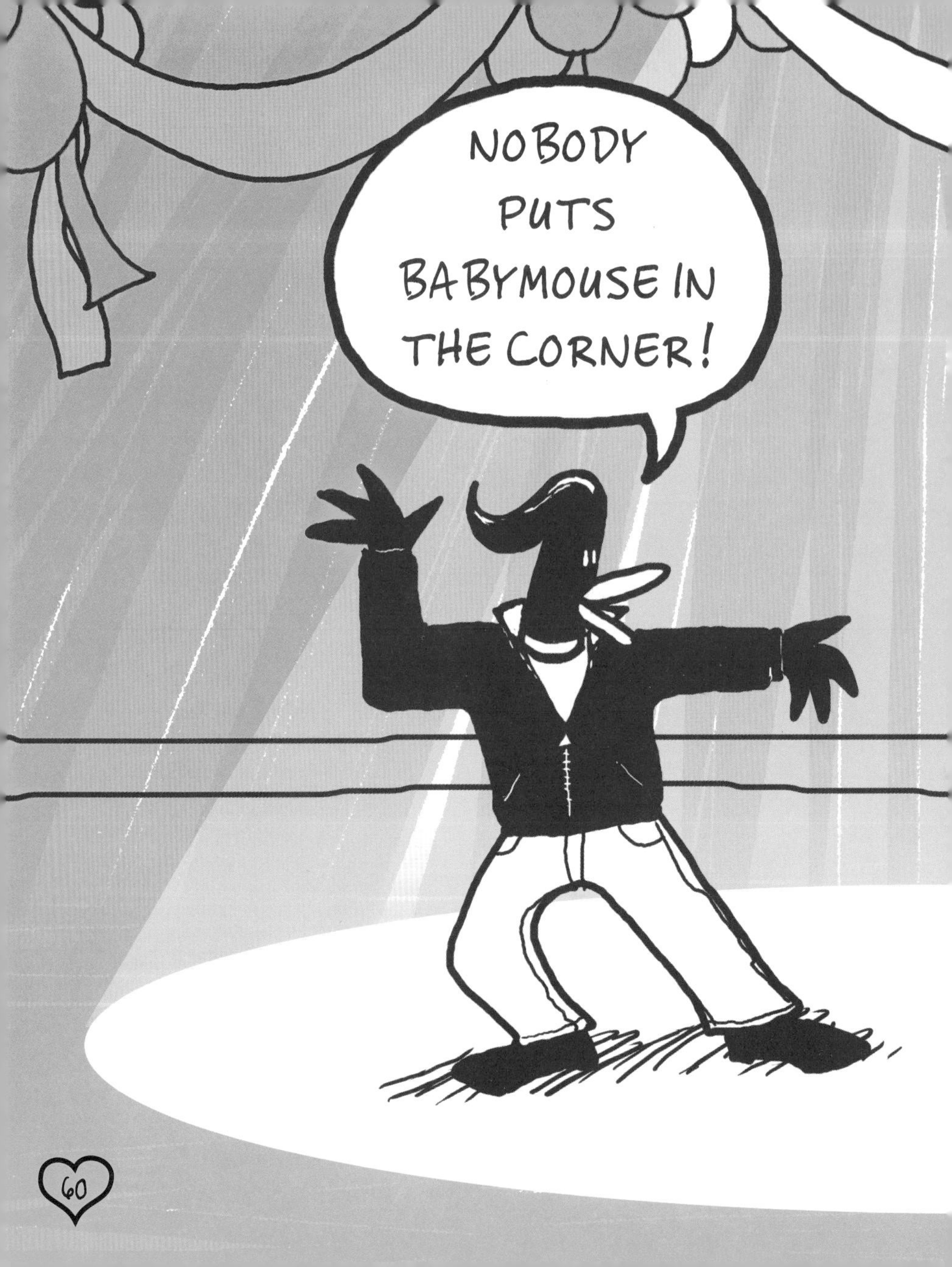
NOBODY PUTS BABYMOUSE IN THE CORNER!

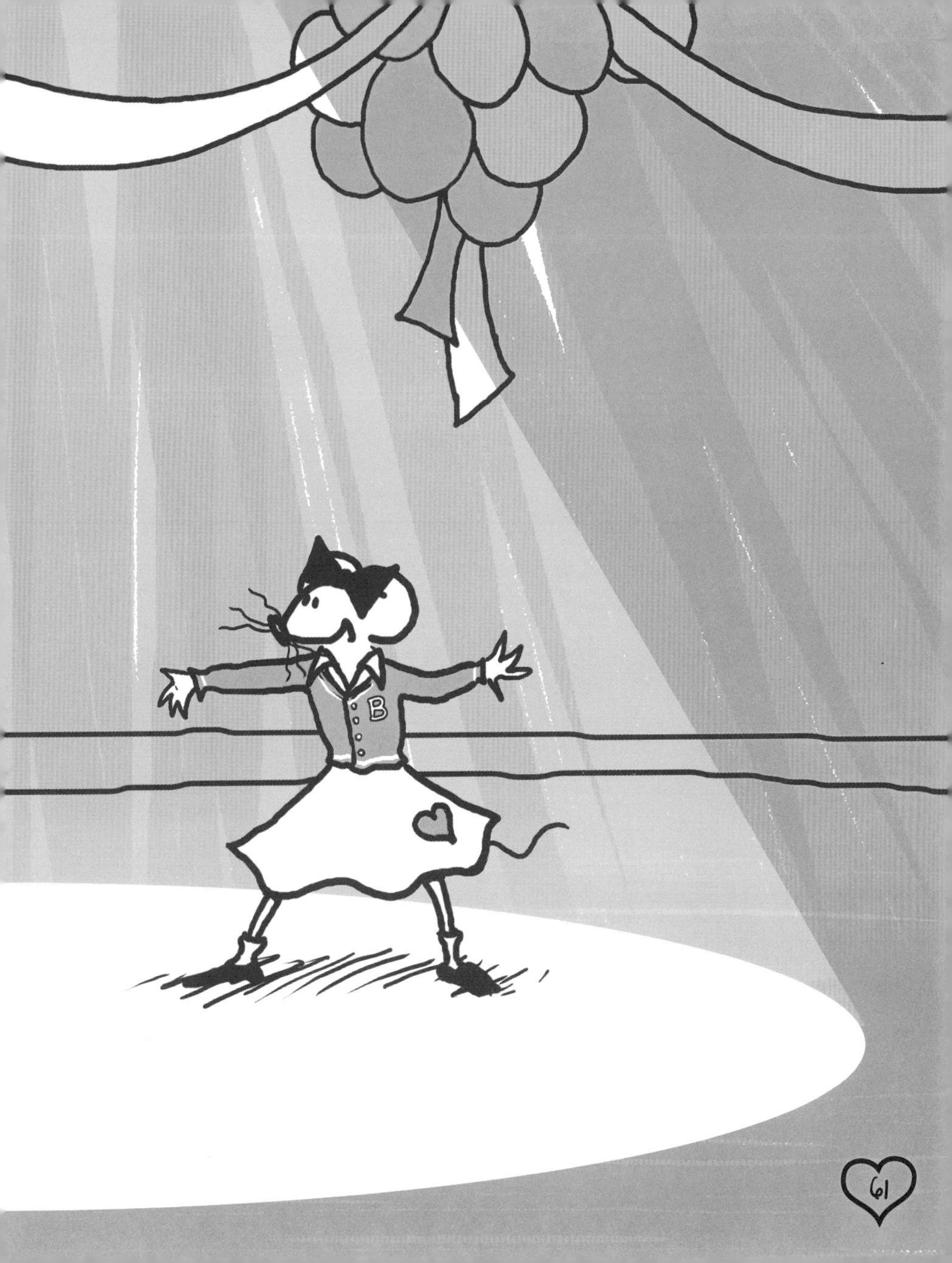
B

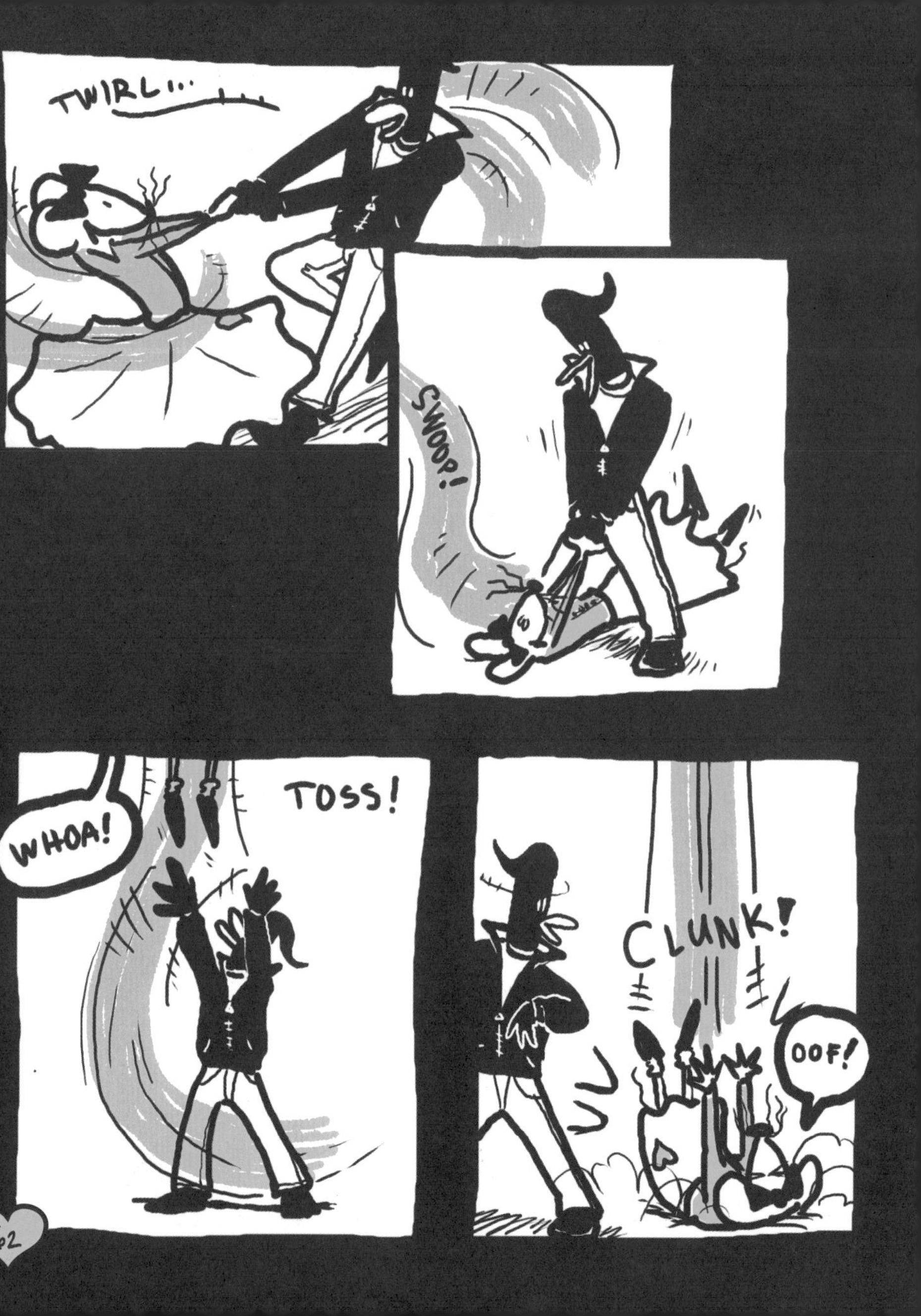
TWIRL...
SWOOP!
WHOA!
TOSS!
CLUNK!
OOF!

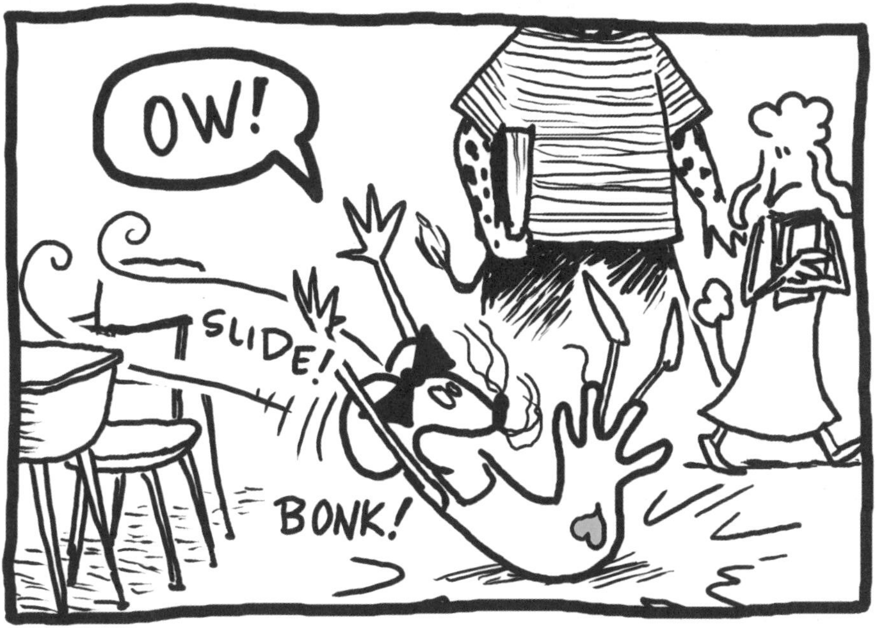
OW!
SLIDE!
BONK!

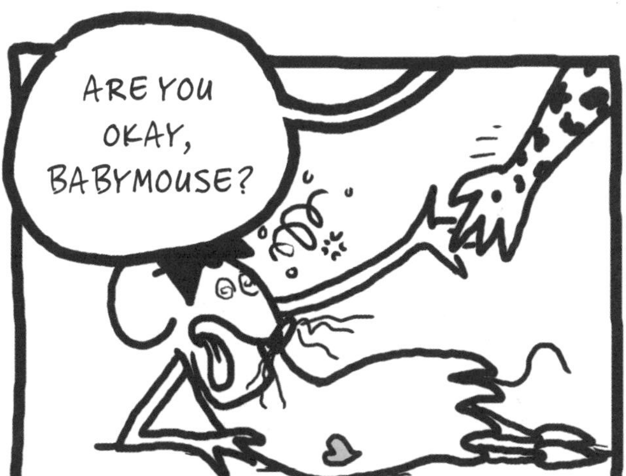
ARE YOU OKAY, BABYMOUSE?

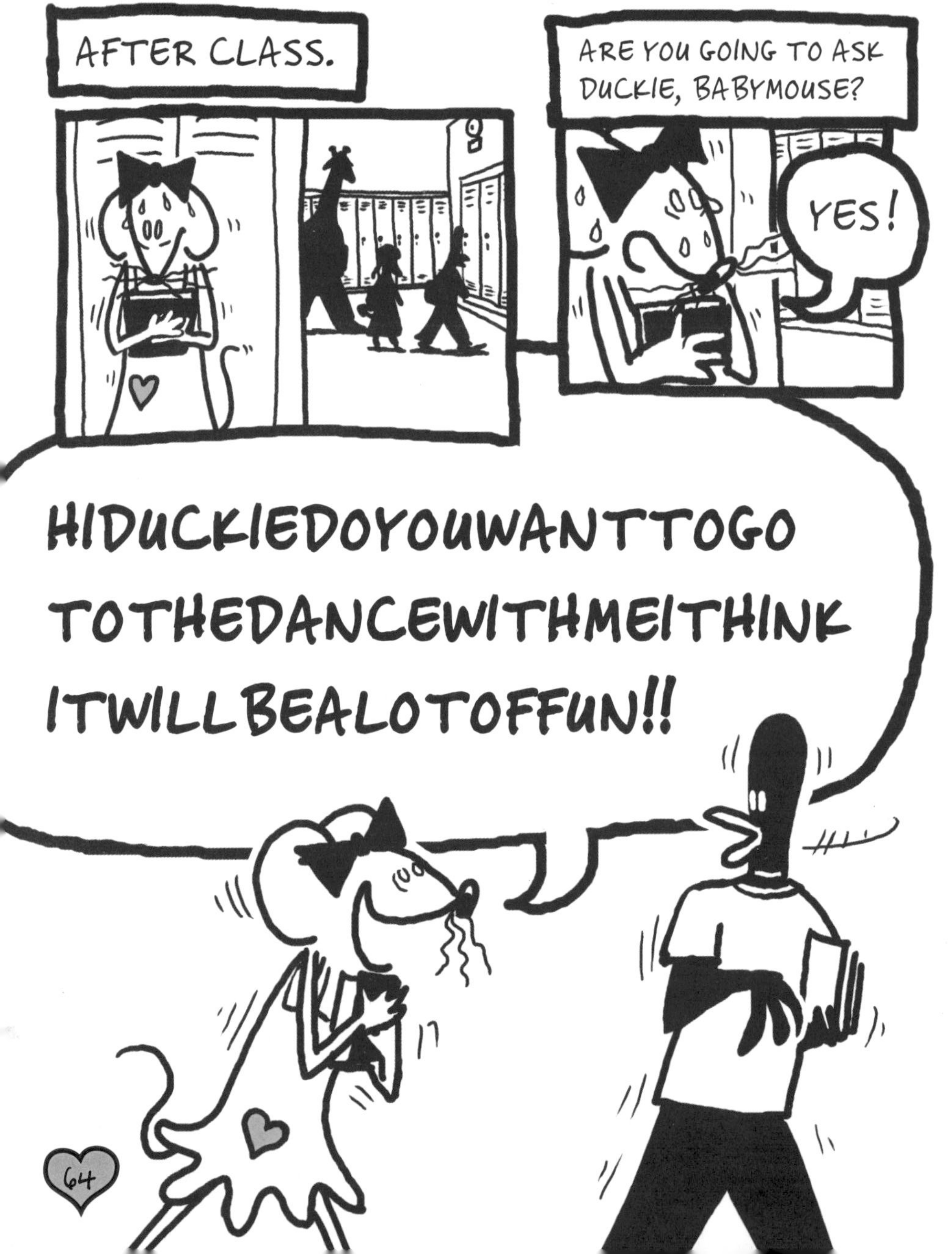

AFTER CLASS.
ARE YOU GOING TO ASK DUCKIE, BABYMOUSE?
YES!
HIDUCKIEDOYOUWANTTOGO TOTHEDANCEWITHMEITHINK ITWILLBEALOTOFFUN!!

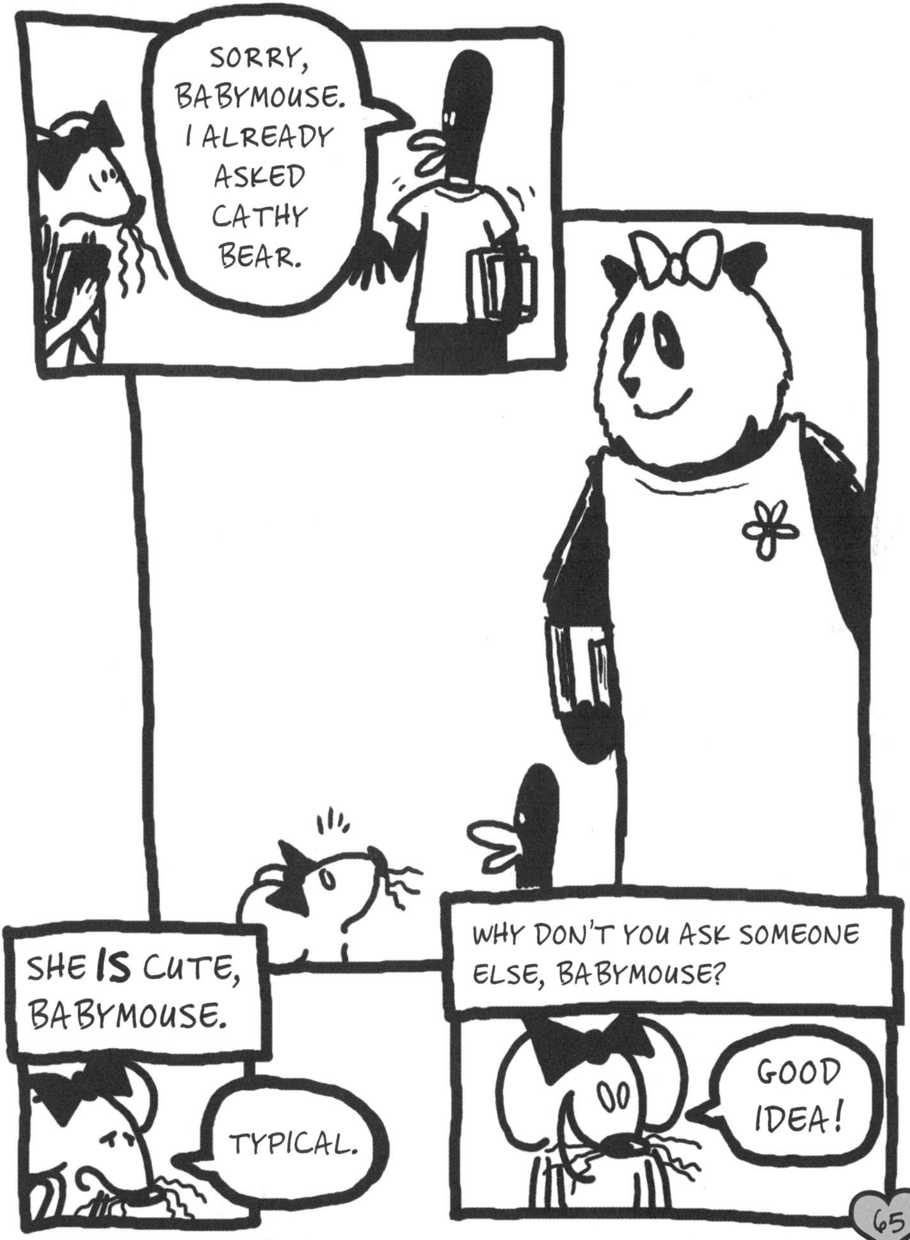
SORRY, BABYMOUSE. I ALREADY ASKED CATHY BEAR.
SHE IS CUTE, BABYMOUSE.
TYPICAL.
WHY DON'T YOU ASK SOMEONE ELSE, BABYMOUSE?
GOOD IDEA!

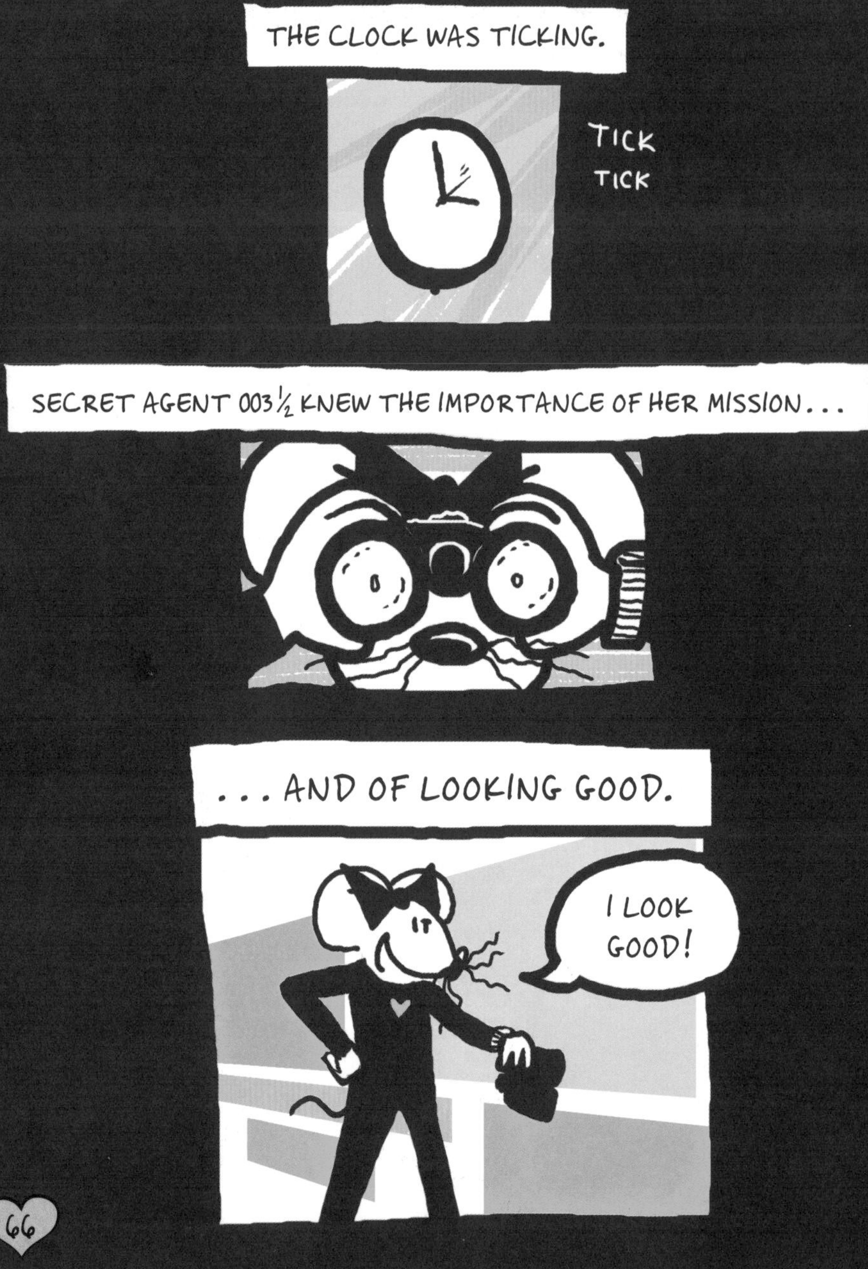
THE CLOCK WAS TICKING.
TICK
TICK
SECRET AGENT 003½ KNEW THE IMPORTANCE OF HER MISSION...
...AND OF LOOKING GOOD.
I LOOK GOOD!

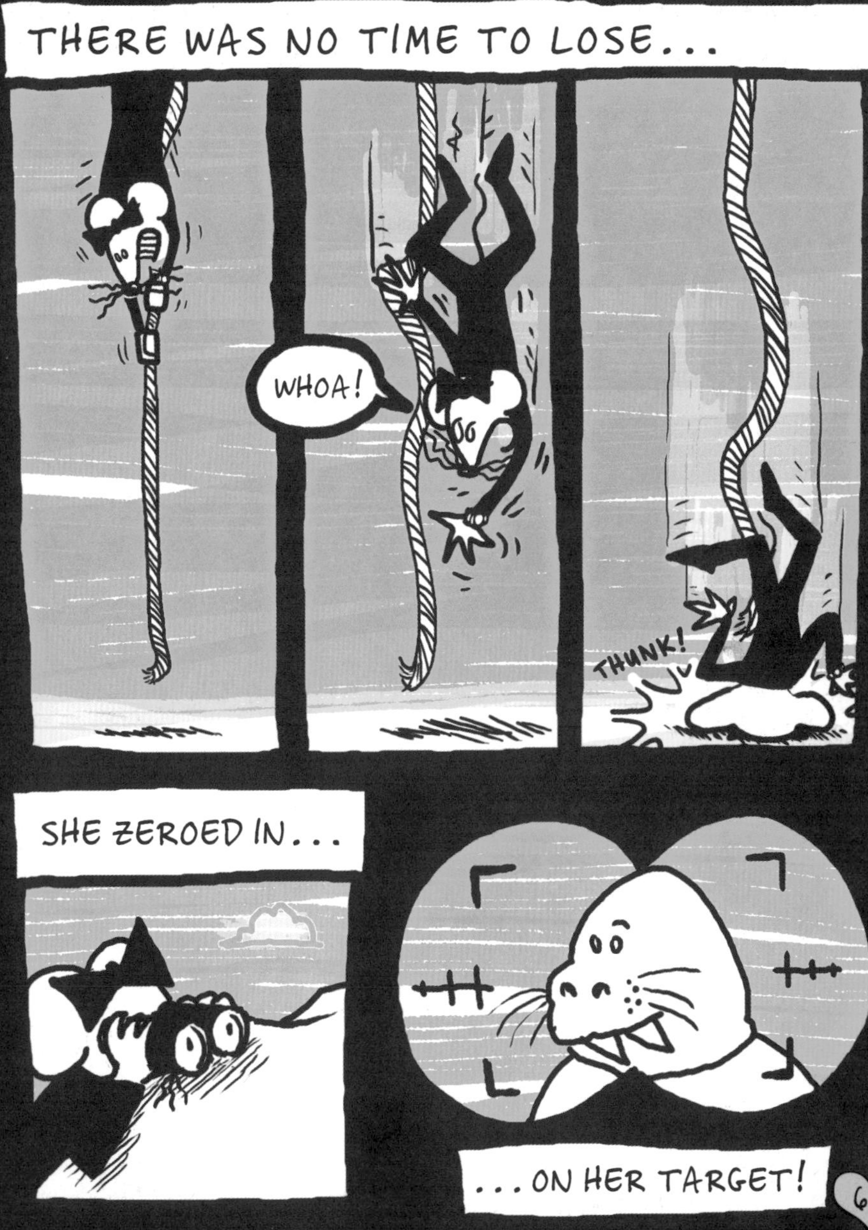
THERE WAS NO TIME TO LOSE...
WHOA!
THUNK!
SHE ZEROED IN...
...ON HER TARGET!

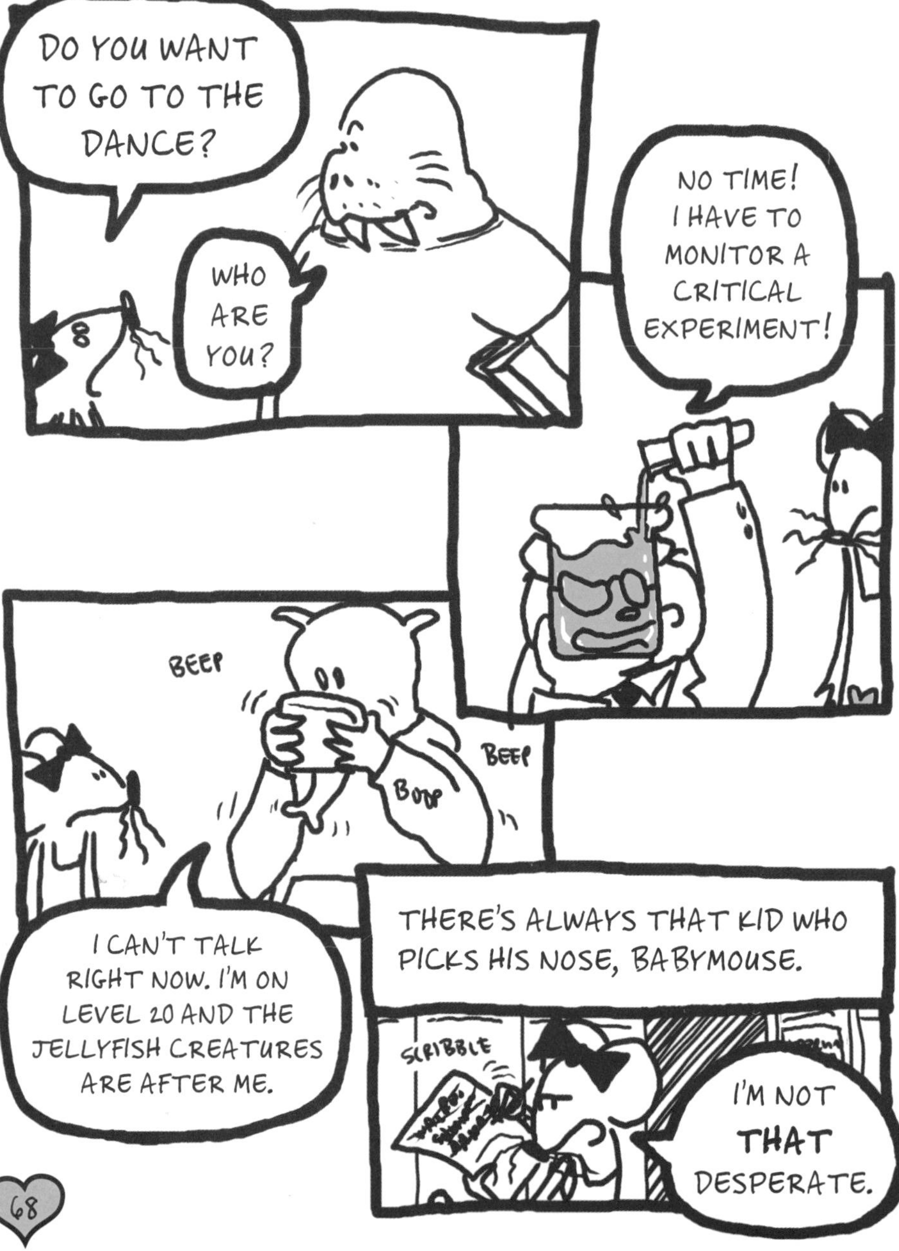
DO YOU WANT TO GO TO THE DANCE?
WHO ARE YOU?
NO TIME! I HAVE TO MONITOR A CRITICAL EXPERIMENT!
BEEP
BEEP
BOOP
I CAN'T TALK RIGHT NOW. I'M ON LEVEL 20 AND THE JELLYFISH CREATURES ARE AFTER ME.
THERE'S ALWAYS THAT KID WHO PICKS HIS NOSE, BABYMOUSE.
SCRIBBLE
I'M NOT **THAT** DESPERATE.

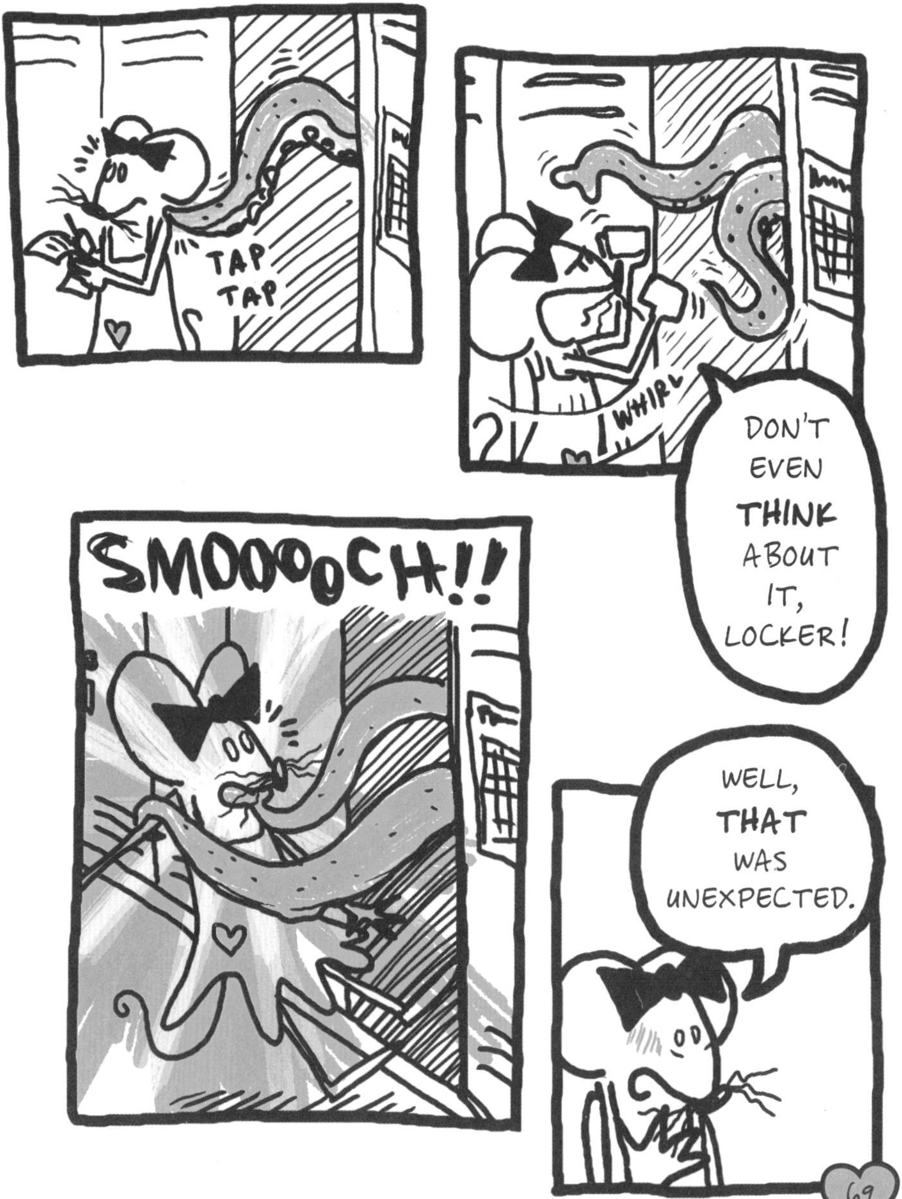
TAP TAP
WHIRL
DON'T EVEN **THINK** ABOUT IT, LOCKER!
SMOOOOCH!!
WELL, **THAT** WAS UNEXPECTED.

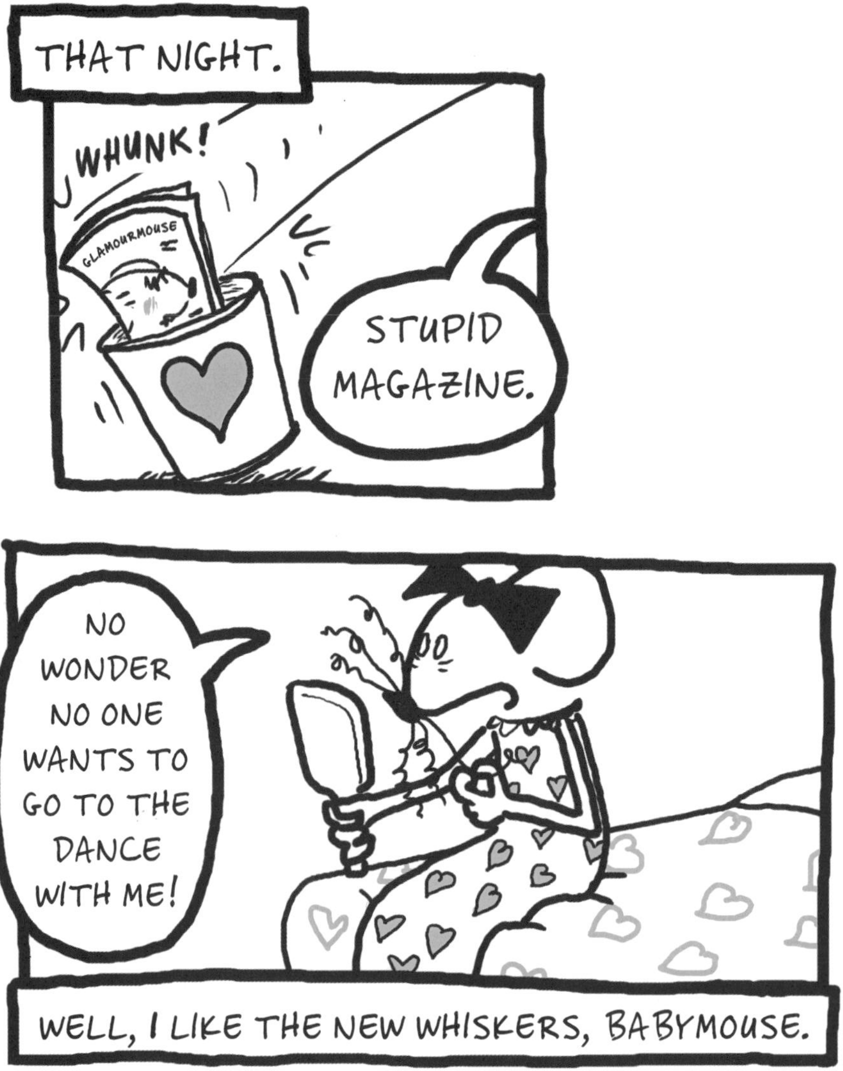
THAT NIGHT.
WHUNK!
GLAMOURMOUSE
STUPID MAGAZINE.
NO WONDER NO ONE WANTS TO GO TO THE DANCE WITH ME!
WELL, I LIKE THE NEW WHISKERS, BABYMOUSE.

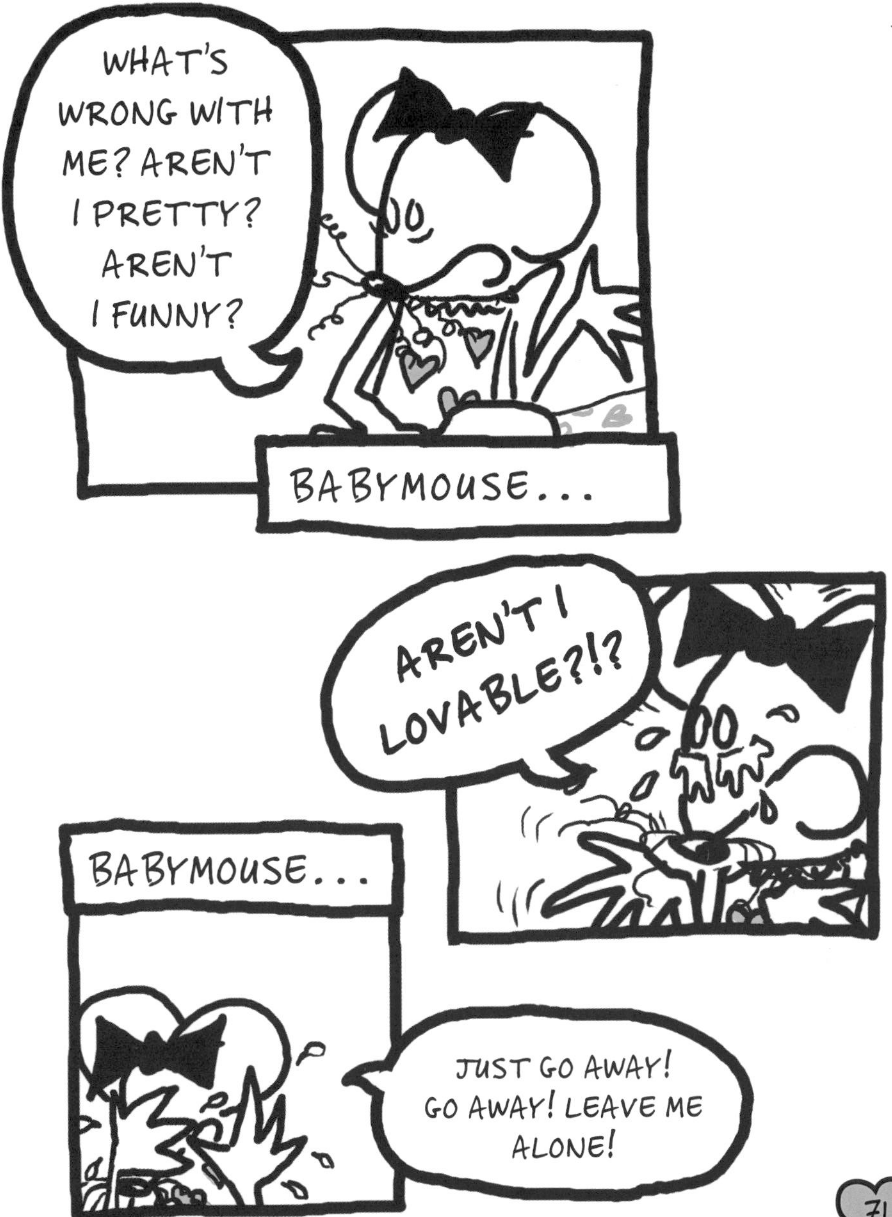
WHAT'S WRONG WITH ME? AREN'T I PRETTY? AREN'T I FUNNY?
BABYMOUSE...
AREN'T I LOVABLE?!?
BABYMOUSE...
JUST GO AWAY! GO AWAY! LEAVE ME ALONE!

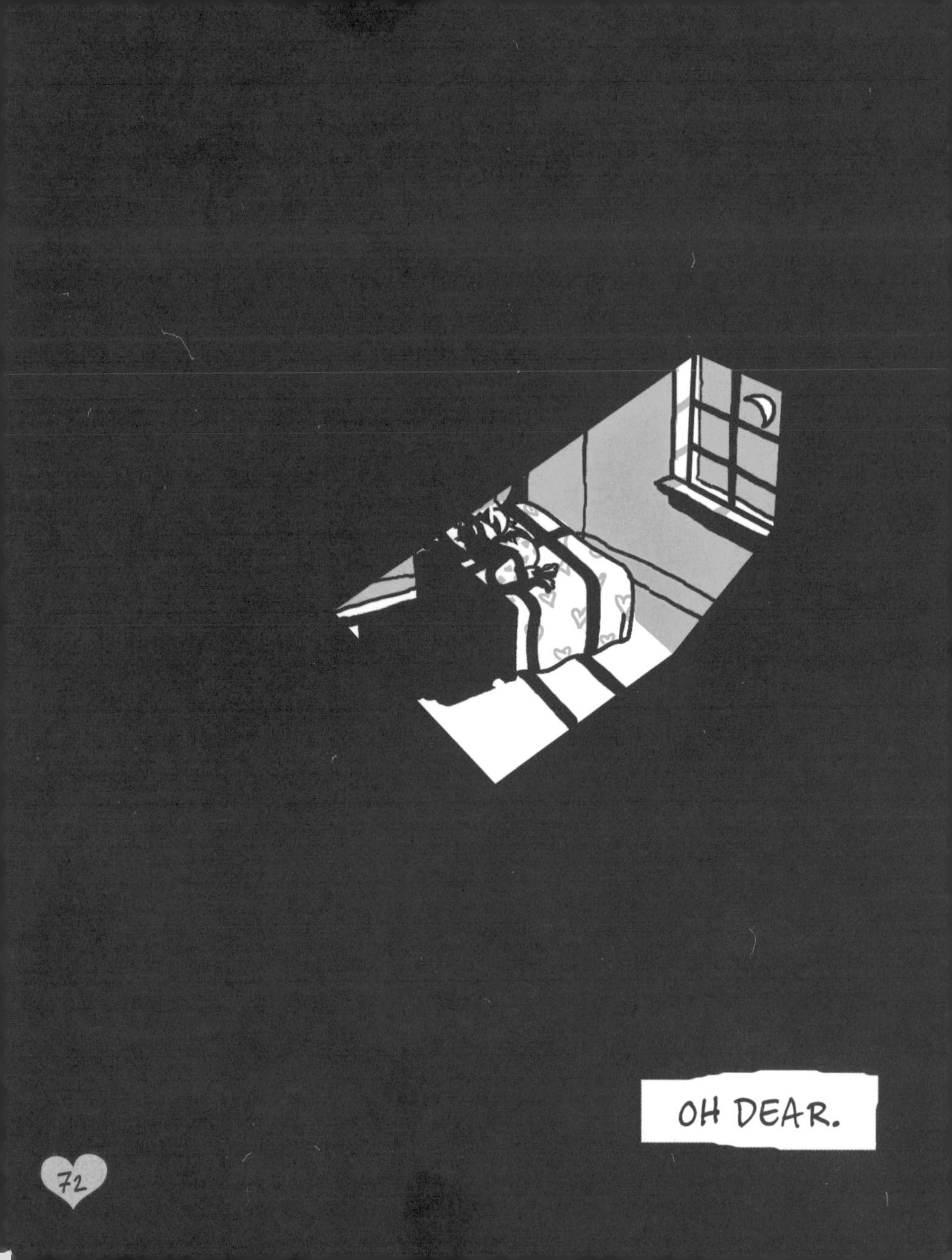
OH DEAR.

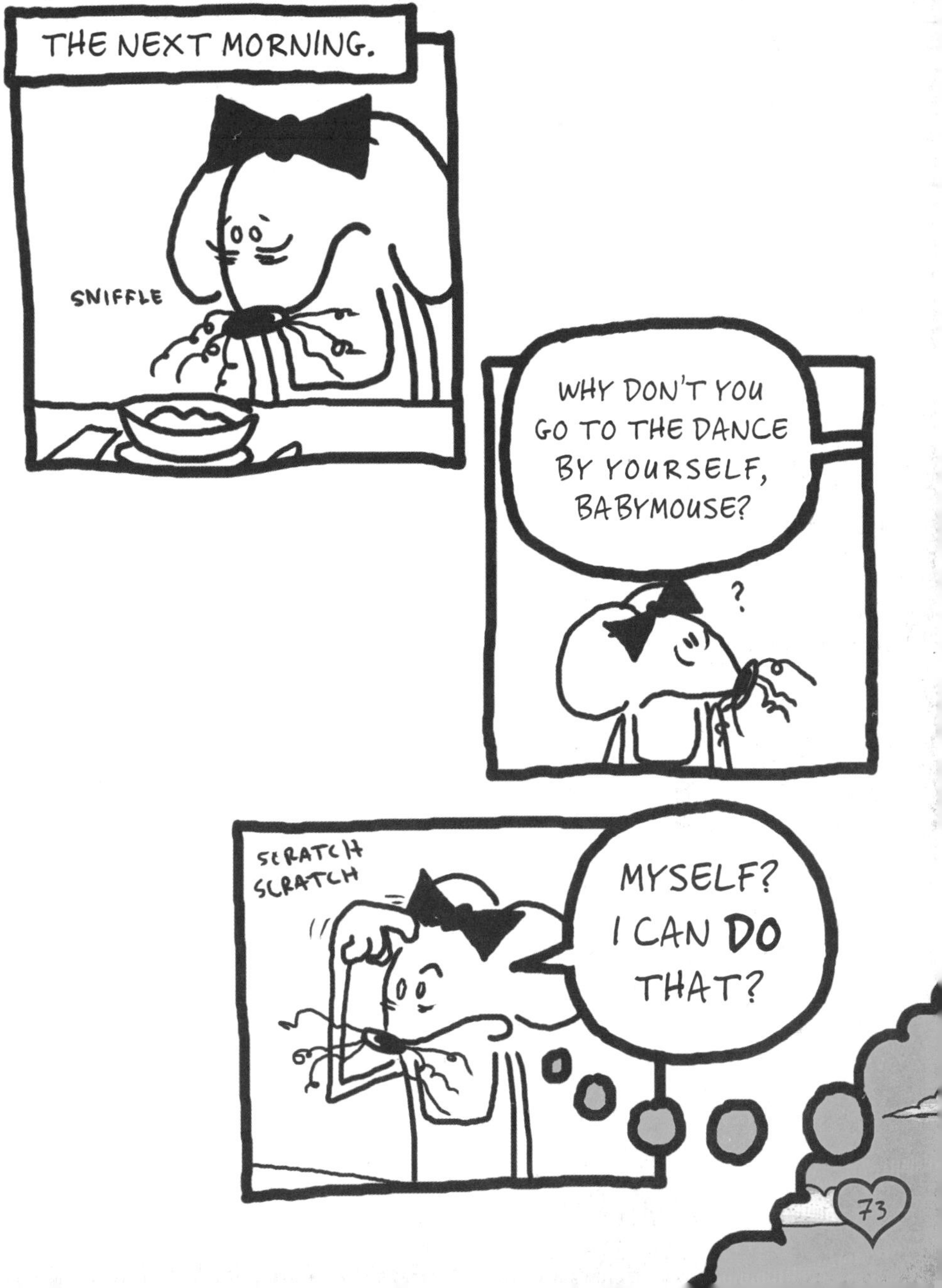

THE NEXT MORNING.
SNIFFLE
WHY DON'T YOU GO TO THE DANCE BY YOURSELF, BABYMOUSE?
?
SCRATCH SCRATCH
MYSELF? I CAN **DO** THAT?

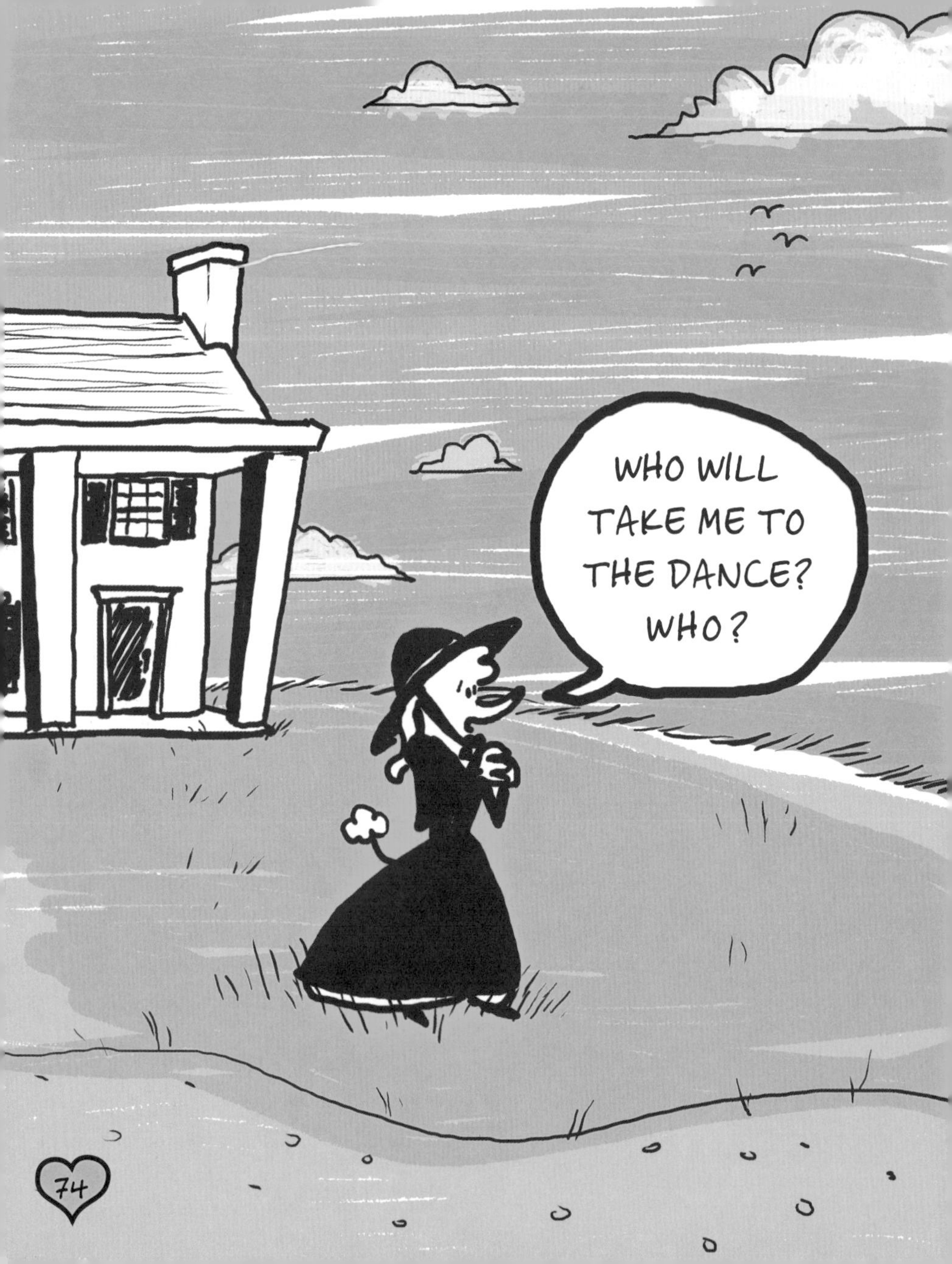
WHO WILL TAKE ME TO THE DANCE? WHO?

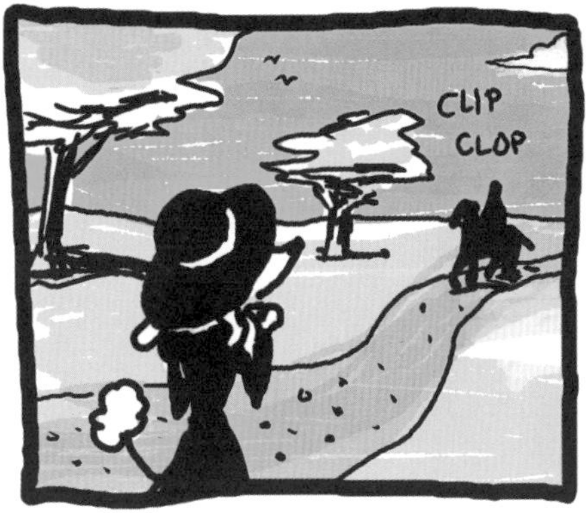
CLIP
CLOP

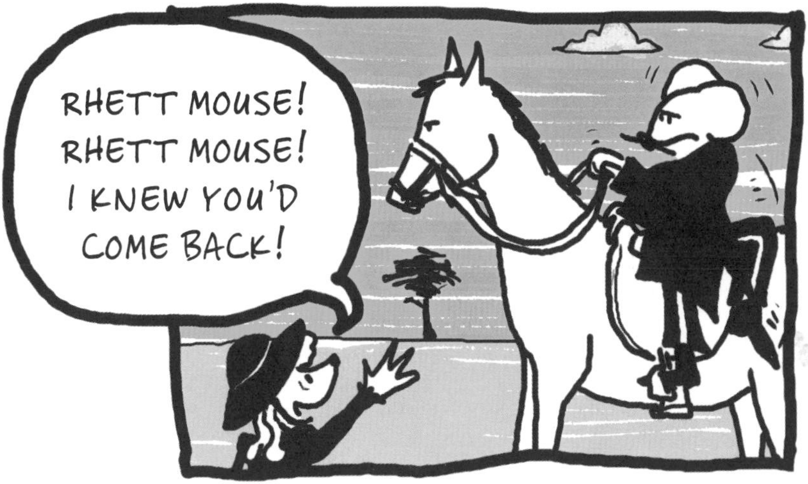
RHETT MOUSE! RHETT MOUSE! I KNEW YOU'D COME BACK!

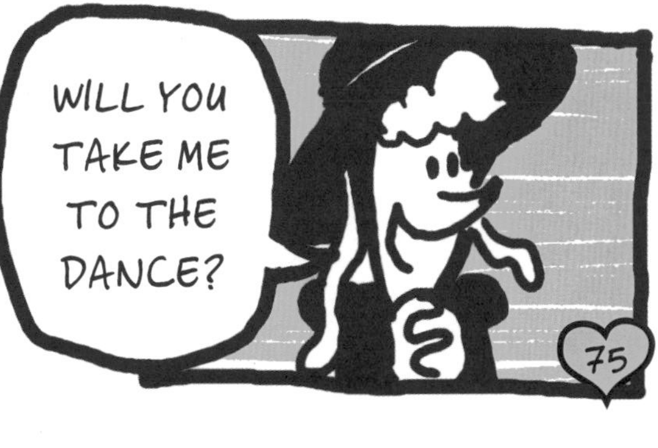
WILL YOU TAKE ME TO THE DANCE?

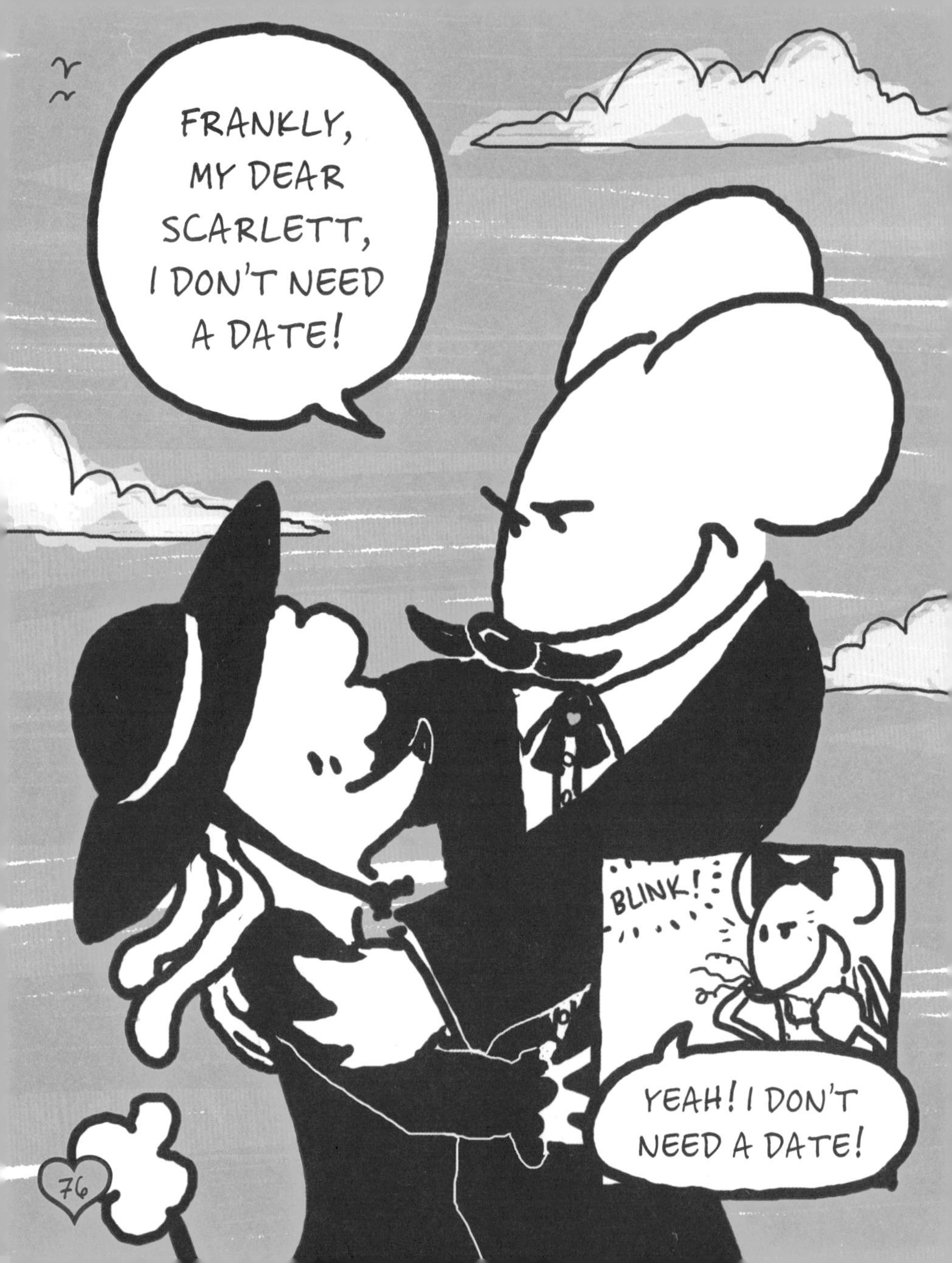
FRANKLY, MY DEAR SCARLETT, I DON'T NEED A DATE!
BLINK!
YEAH! I DON'T NEED A DATE!
76

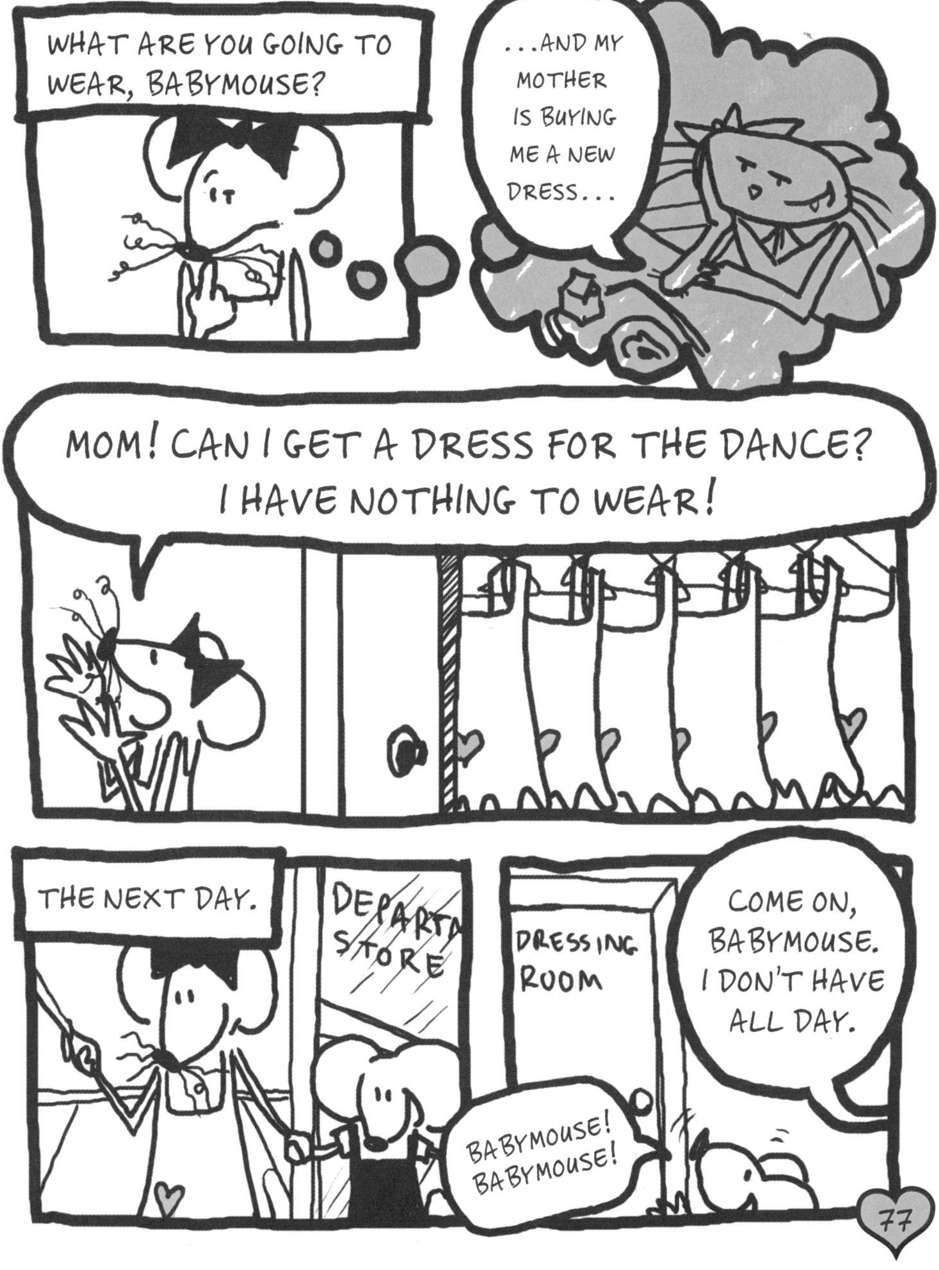

WHAT ARE YOU GOING TO WEAR, BABYMOUSE?
...AND MY MOTHER IS BUYING ME A NEW DRESS...
MOM! CAN I GET A DRESS FOR THE DANCE? I HAVE NOTHING TO WEAR!
THE NEXT DAY.
DEPARTM STORE
DRESSING ROOM
COME ON, BABYMOUSE. I DON'T HAVE ALL DAY.
BABYMOUSE! BABYMOUSE!

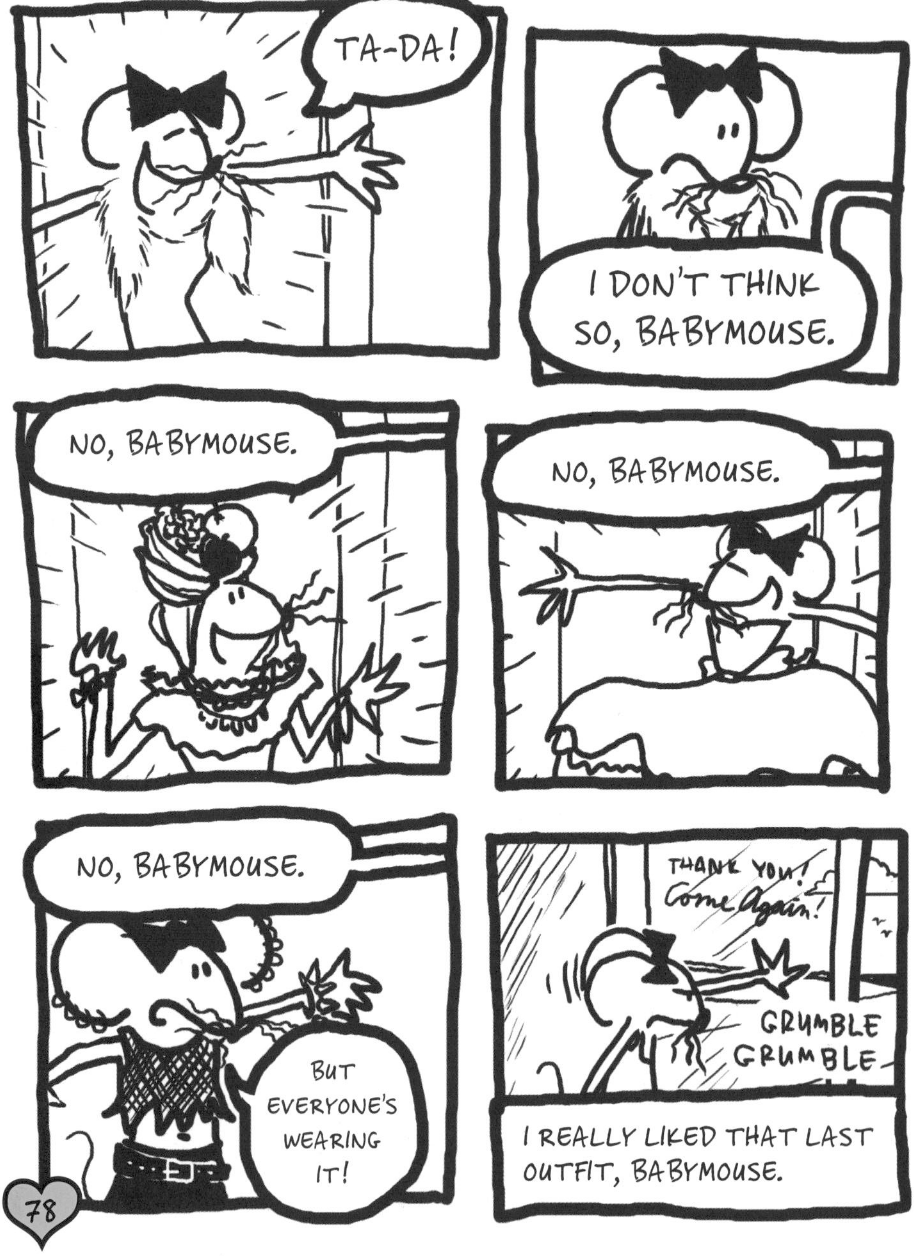
TA-DA!
I DON'T THINK SO, BABYMOUSE.
NO, BABYMOUSE.
NO, BABYMOUSE.
NO, BABYMOUSE.
BUT EVERYONE'S WEARING IT!
THANK YOU! Come Again!
GRUMBLE GRUMBLE
I REALLY LIKED THAT LAST OUTFIT, BABYMOUSE.

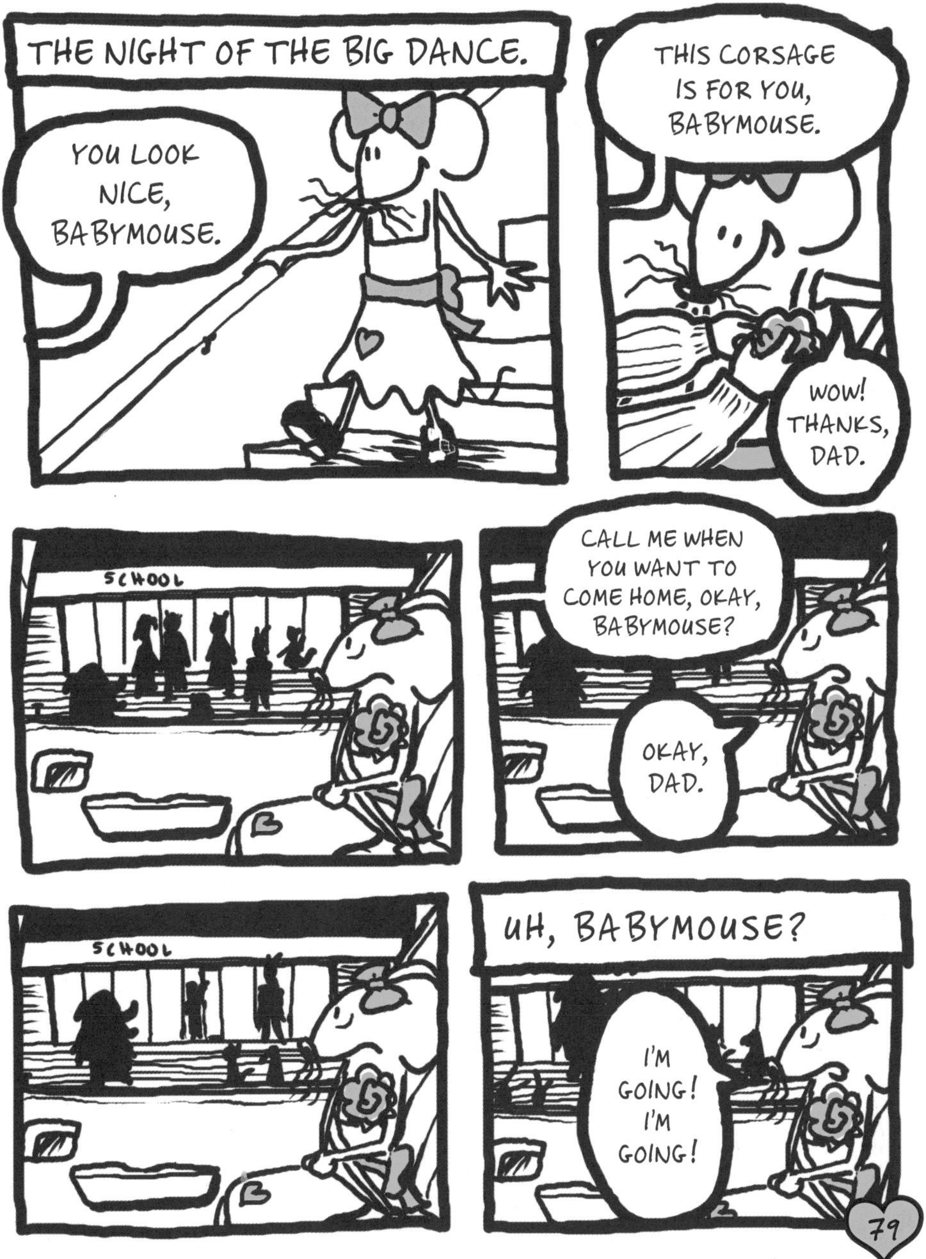
THE NIGHT OF THE BIG DANCE.
YOU LOOK NICE, BABYMOUSE.
THIS CORSAGE IS FOR YOU, BABYMOUSE.
WOW! THANKS, DAD.
SCHOOL
CALL ME WHEN YOU WANT TO COME HOME, OKAY, BABYMOUSE?
OKAY, DAD.
SCHOOL
UH, BABYMOUSE?
I'M GOING! I'M GOING!

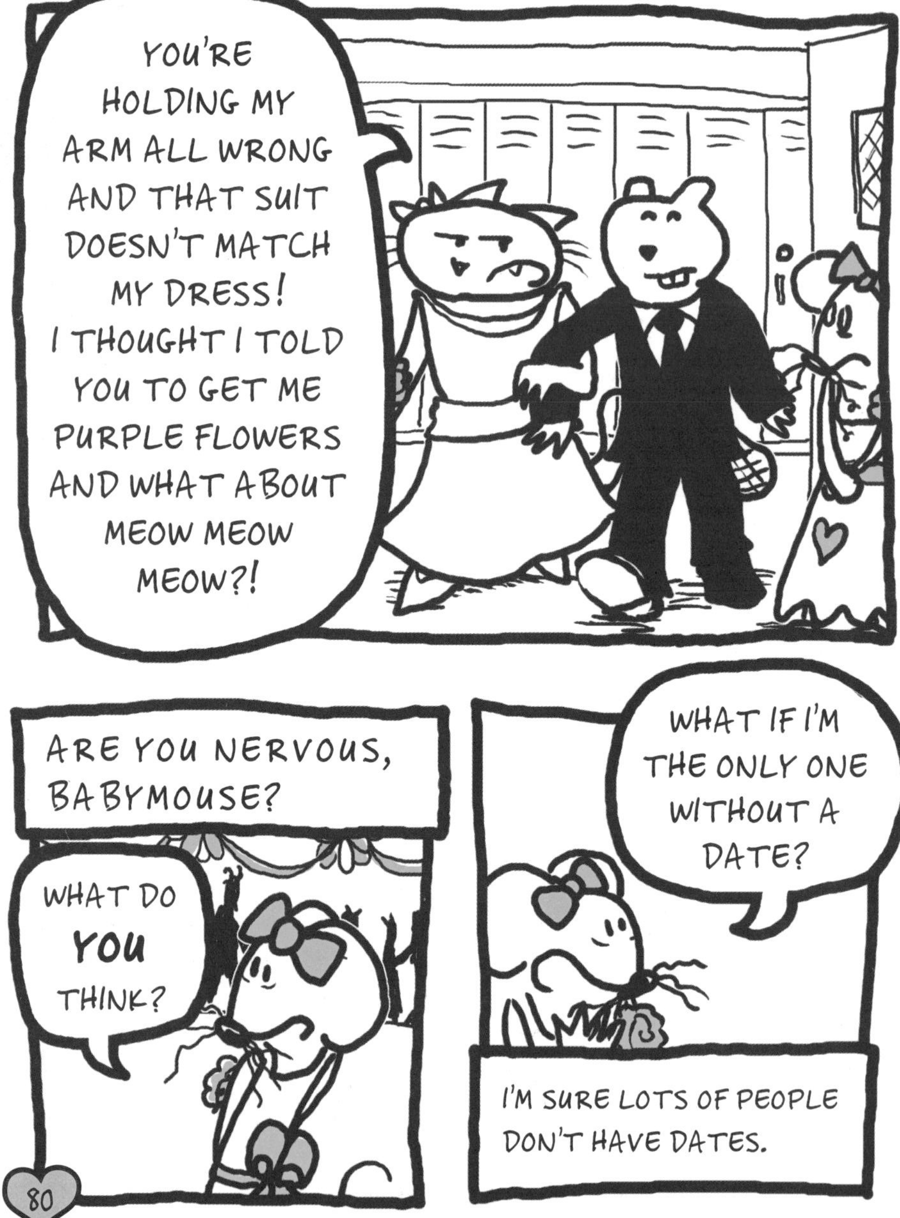
YOU'RE HOLDING MY ARM ALL WRONG AND THAT SUIT DOESN'T MATCH MY DRESS! I THOUGHT I TOLD YOU TO GET ME PURPLE FLOWERS AND WHAT ABOUT MEOW MEOW MEOW?!
ARE YOU NERVOUS, BABYMOUSE?
WHAT DO **YOU** THINK?
WHAT IF I'M THE ONLY ONE WITHOUT A DATE?
I'M SURE LOTS OF PEOPLE DON'T HAVE DATES.

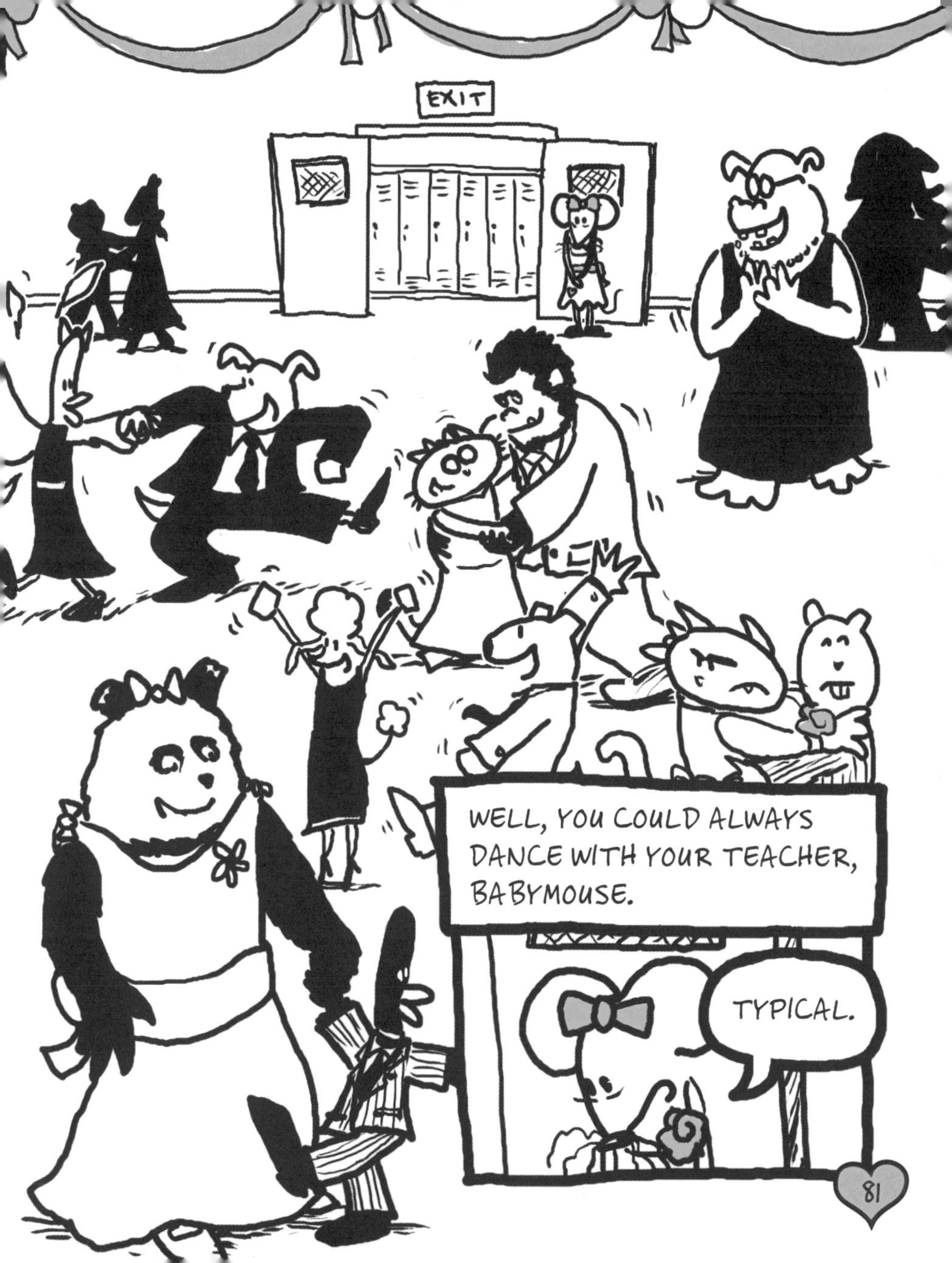
EXIT
WELL, YOU COULD ALWAYS DANCE WITH YOUR TEACHER, BABYMOUSE.
TYPICAL.

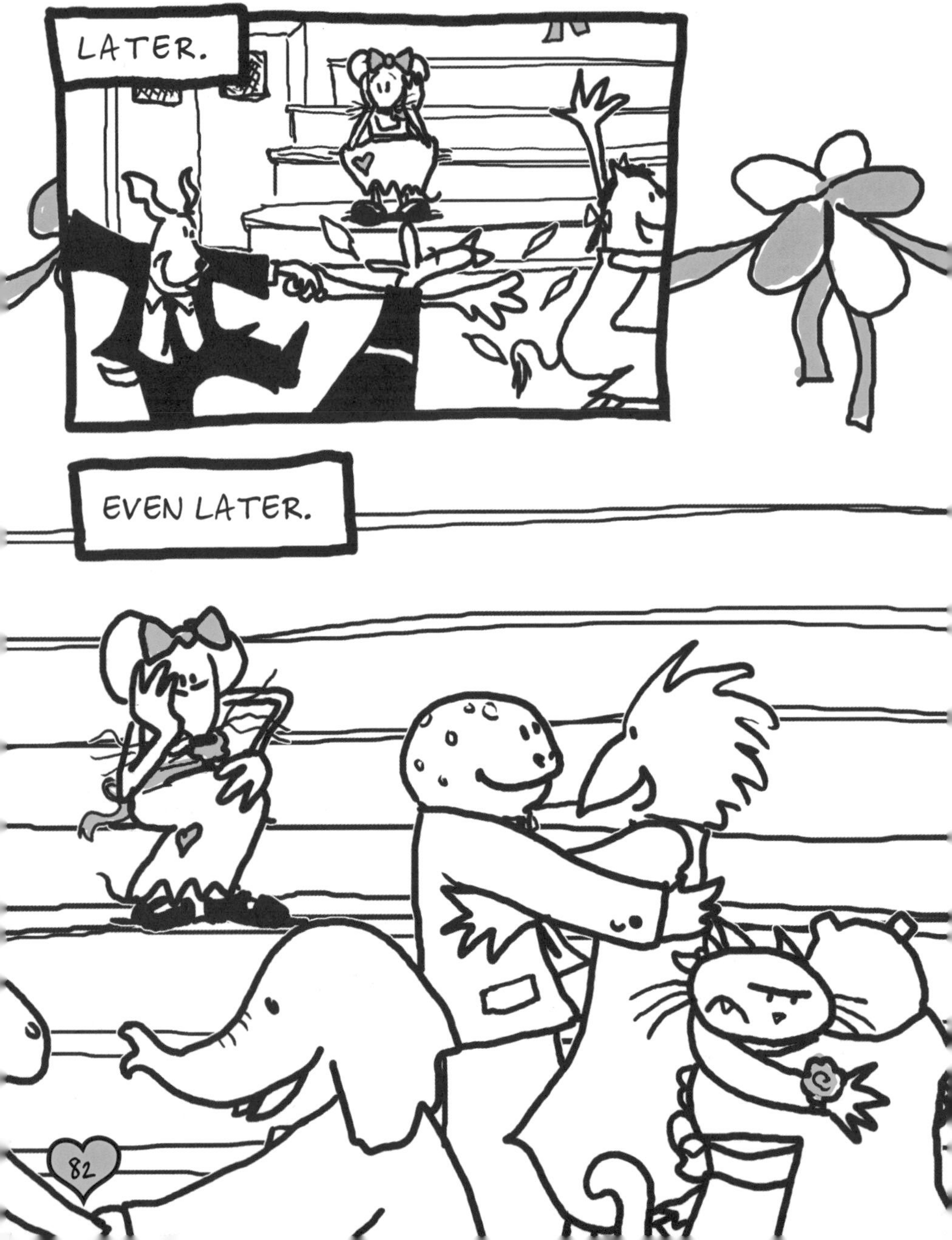
LATER.
EVEN LATER.

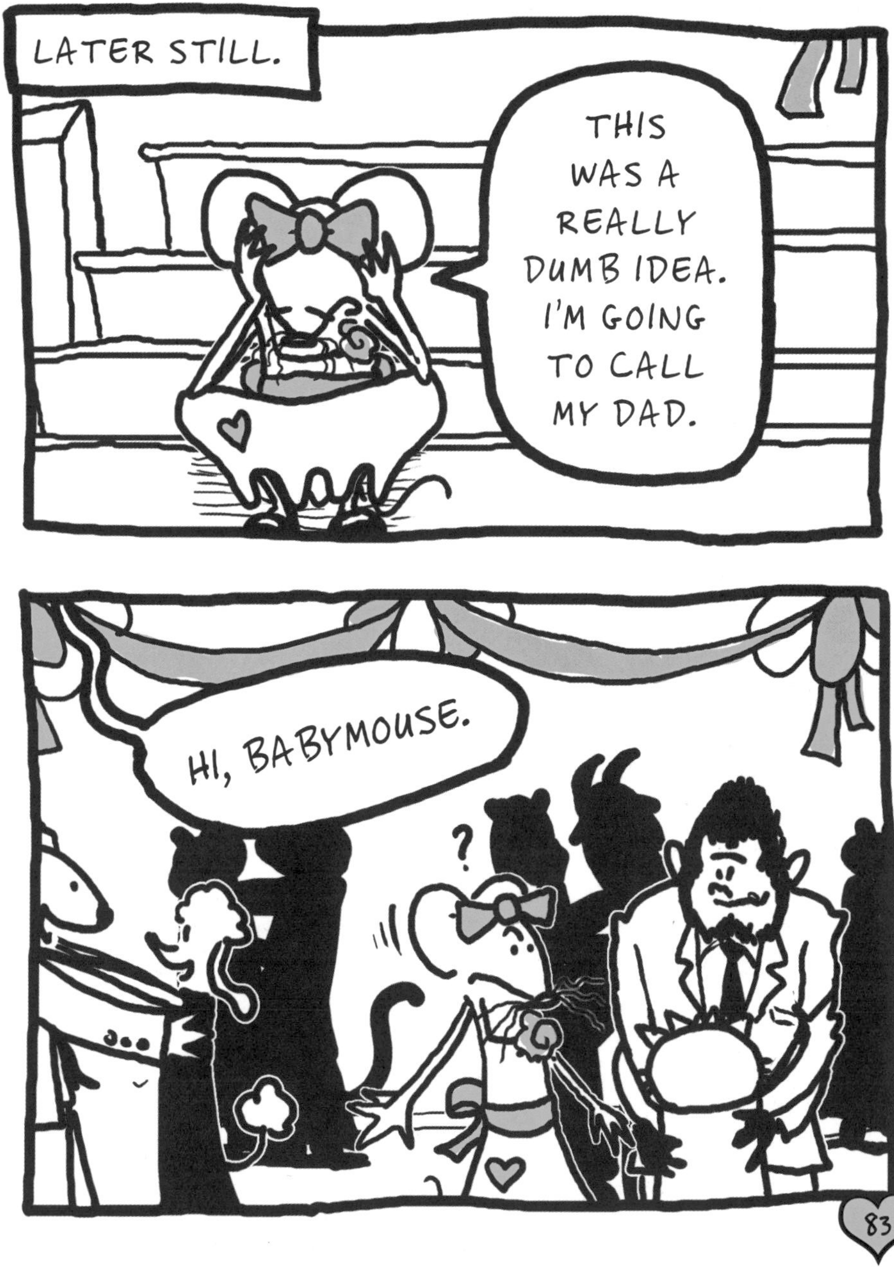
LATER STILL.
THIS WAS A REALLY DUMB IDEA. I'M GOING TO CALL MY DAD.
HI, BABYMOUSE.
?

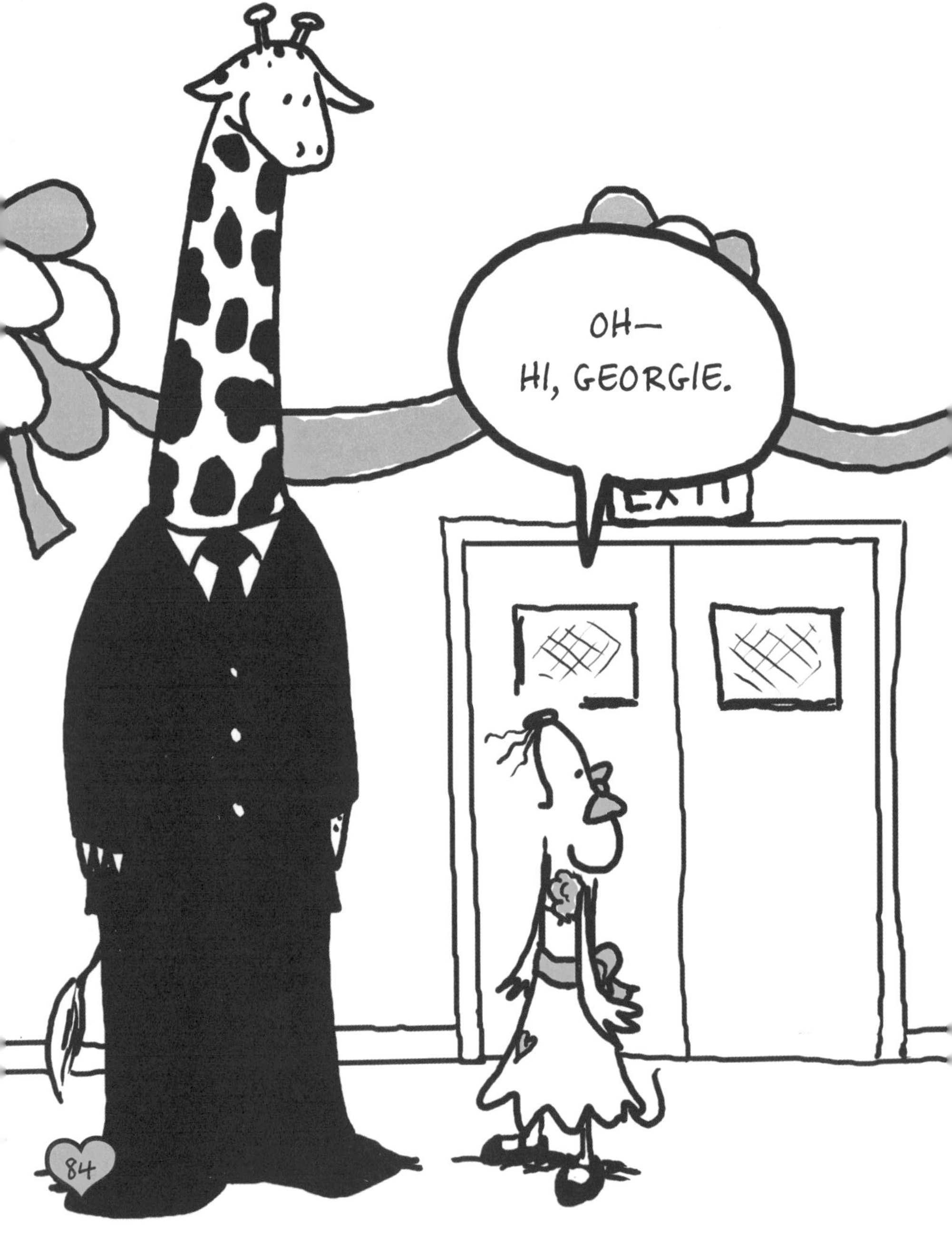
OH—
HI, GEORGIE.

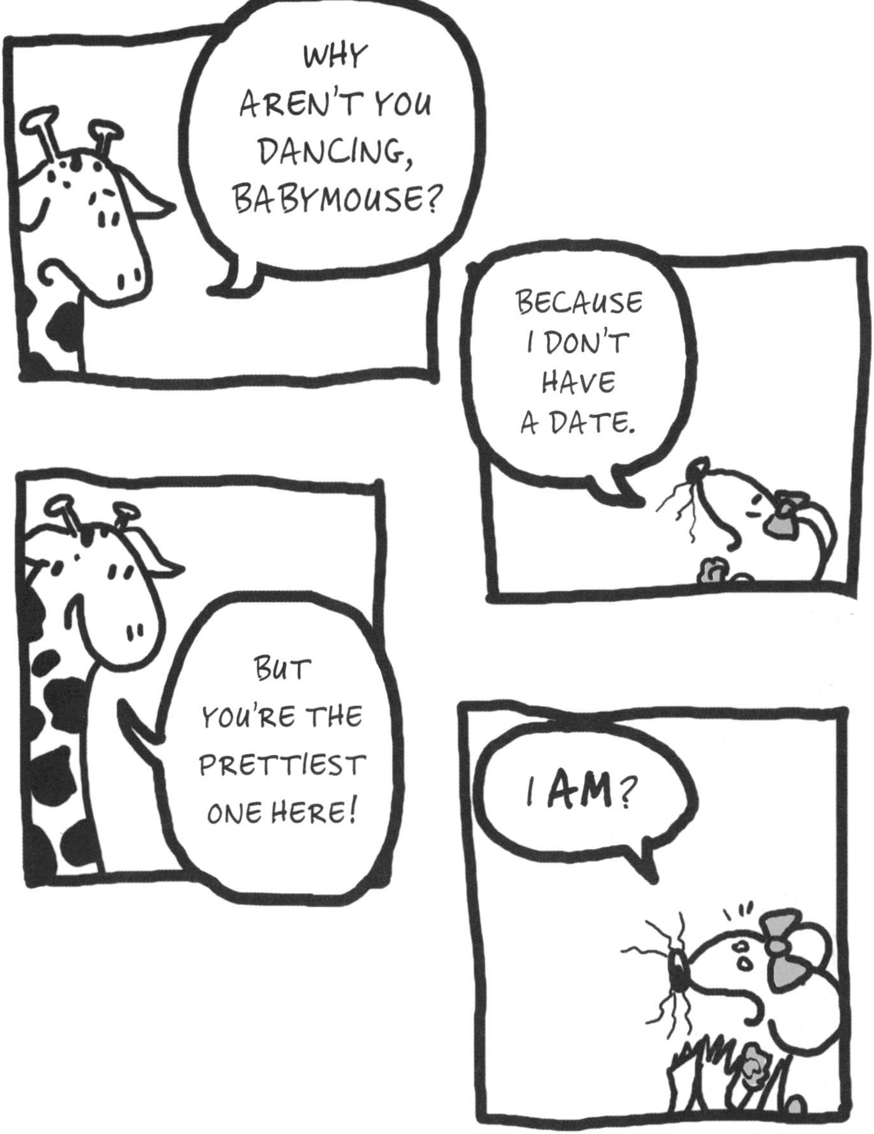
WHY AREN'T YOU DANCING, BABYMOUSE?
BECAUSE I DON'T HAVE A DATE.
BUT YOU'RE THE PRETTIEST ONE HERE!
I AM?

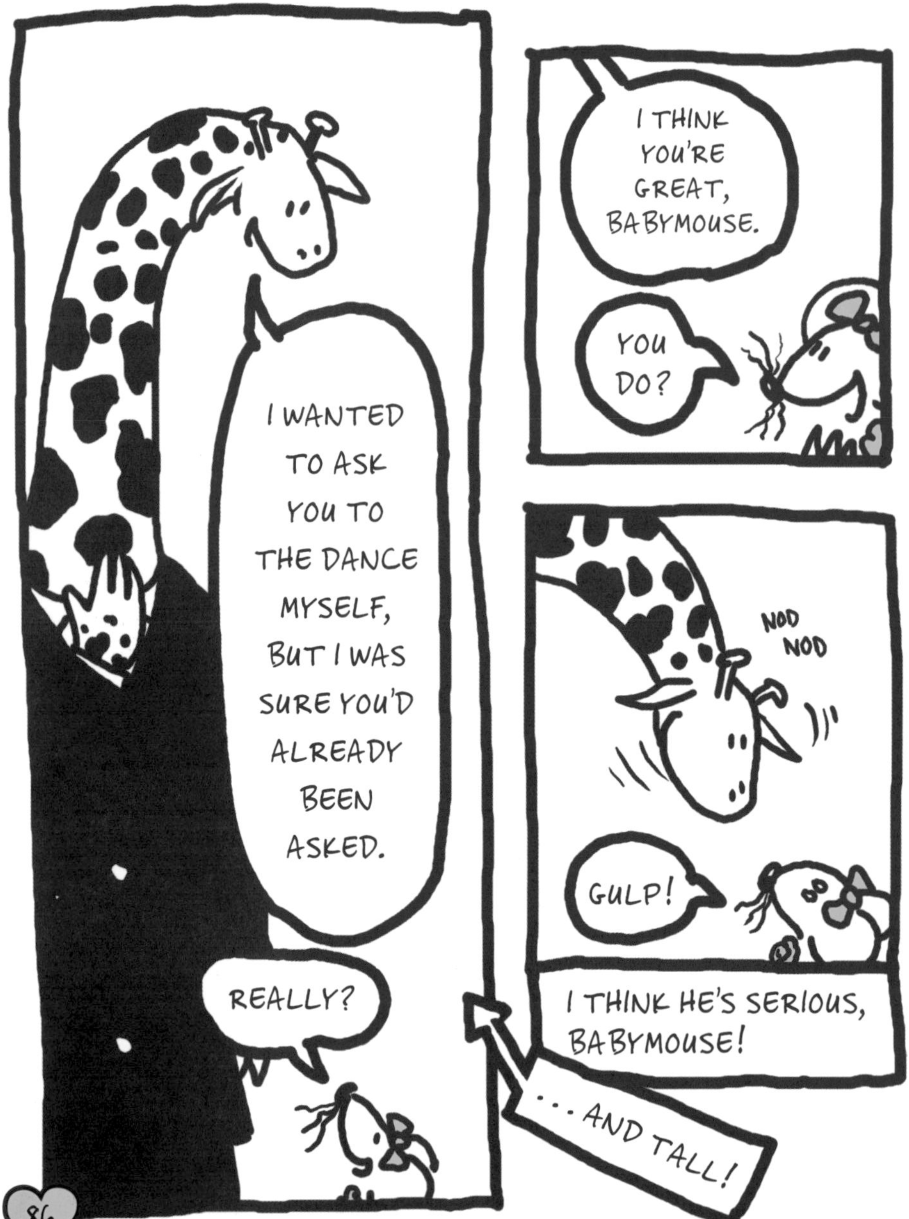
I WANTED TO ASK YOU TO THE DANCE MYSELF, BUT I WAS SURE YOU'D ALREADY BEEN ASKED.
REALLY?
I THINK YOU'RE GREAT, BABYMOUSE.
YOU DO?
NOD NOD
GULP!
I THINK HE'S SERIOUS, BABYMOUSE!
. . . AND TALL!

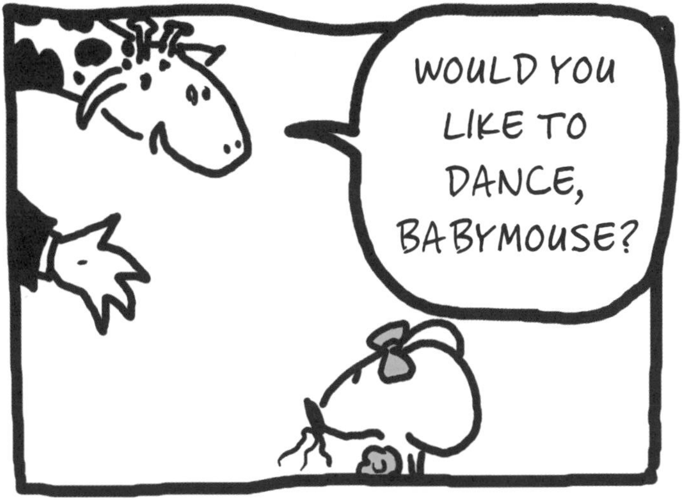
WOULD YOU LIKE TO DANCE, BABYMOUSE?

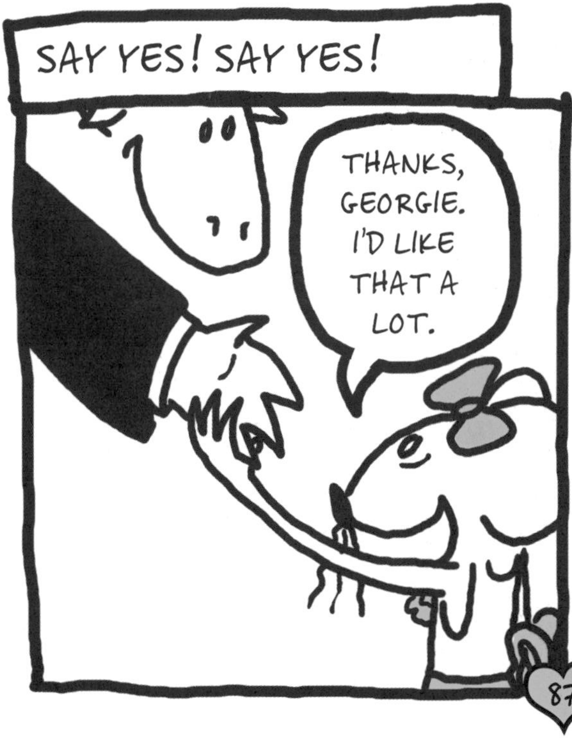
SAY YES! SAY YES!
THANKS, GEORGIE. I'D LIKE THAT A LOT.

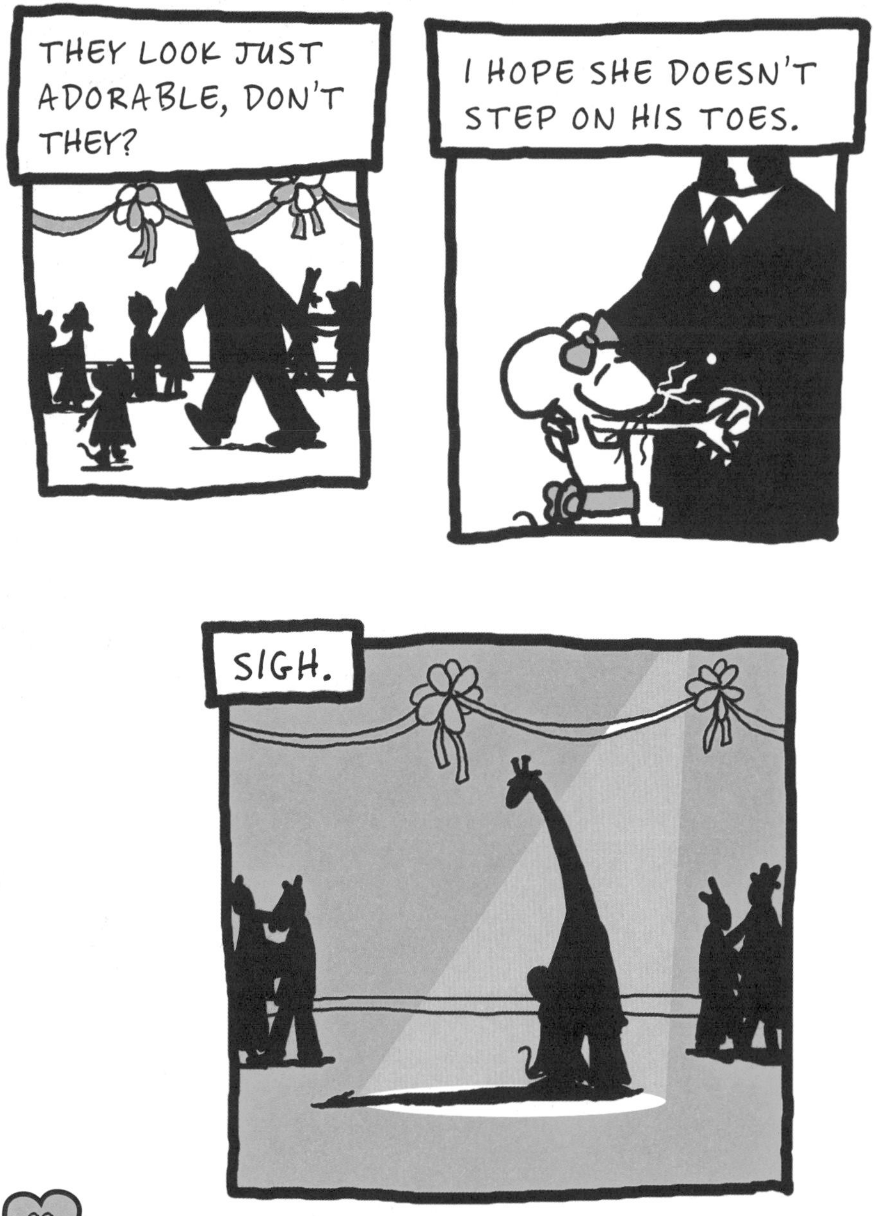
THEY LOOK JUST ADORABLE, DON'T THEY?
I HOPE SHE DOESN'T STEP ON HIS TOES.
SIGH.

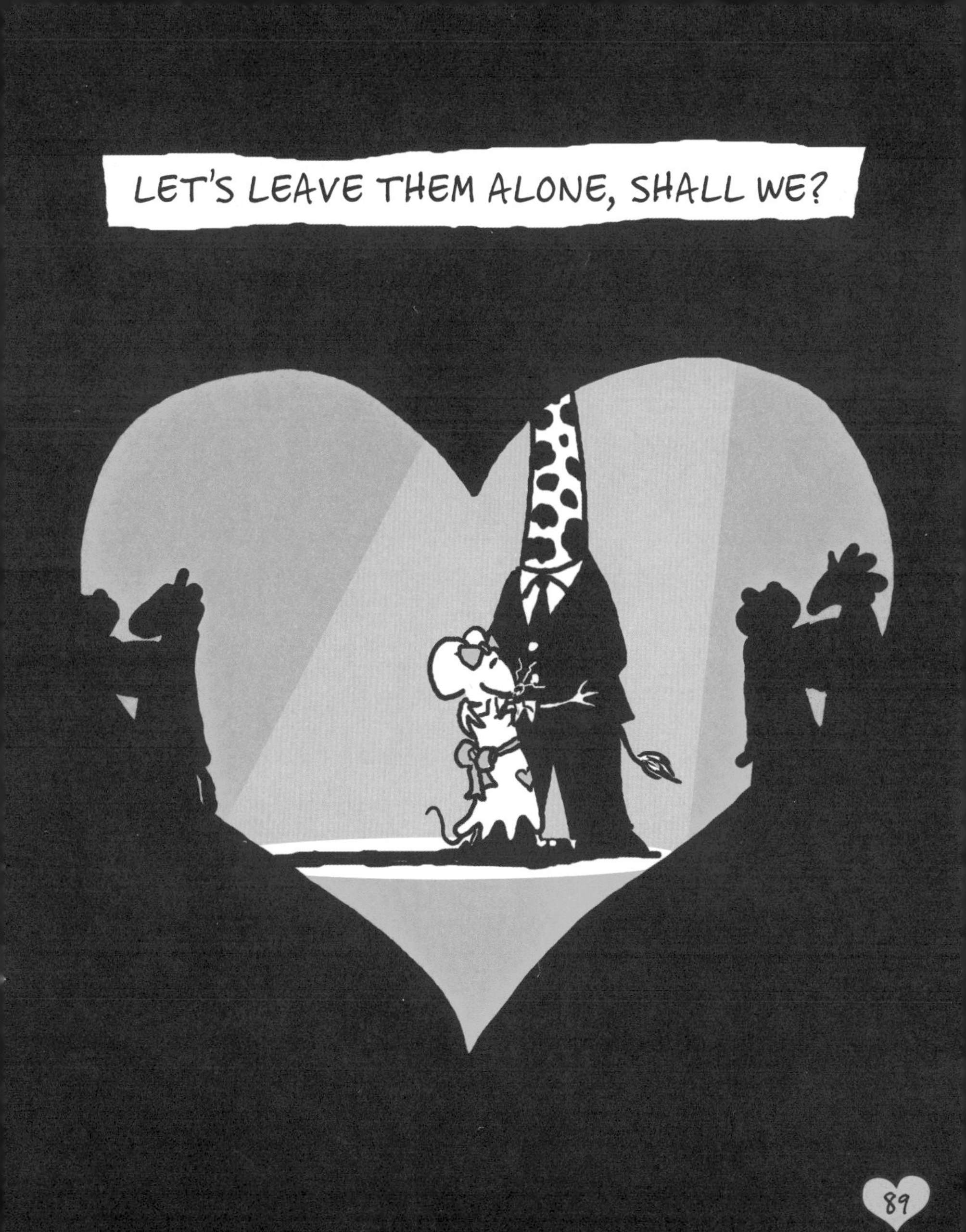
LET'S LEAVE THEM ALONE, SHALL WE?

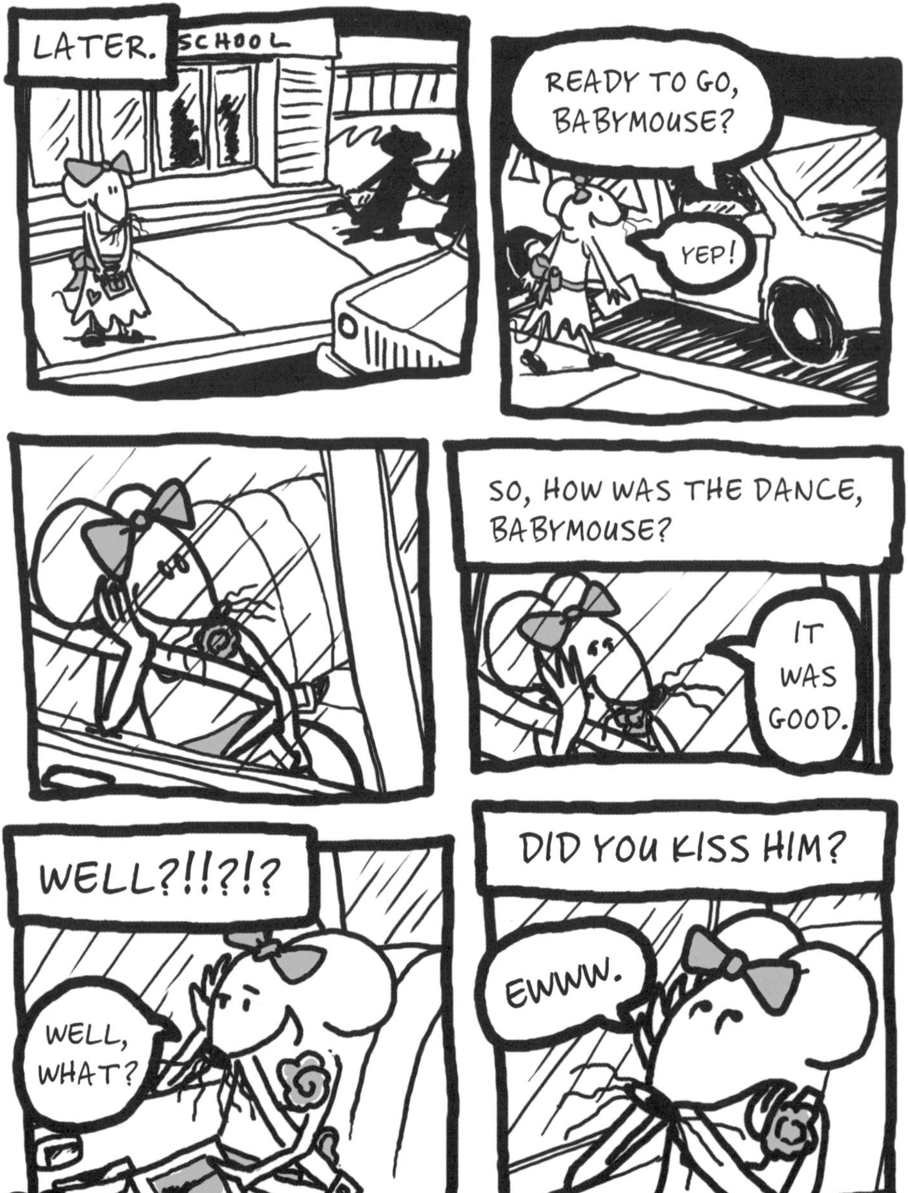
LATER.
SCHOOL
READY TO GO, BABYMOUSE?
YEP!
SO, HOW WAS THE DANCE, BABYMOUSE?
IT WAS GOOD.
WELL?!!?!?
WELL, WHAT?
DID YOU KISS HIM?
EWWW.

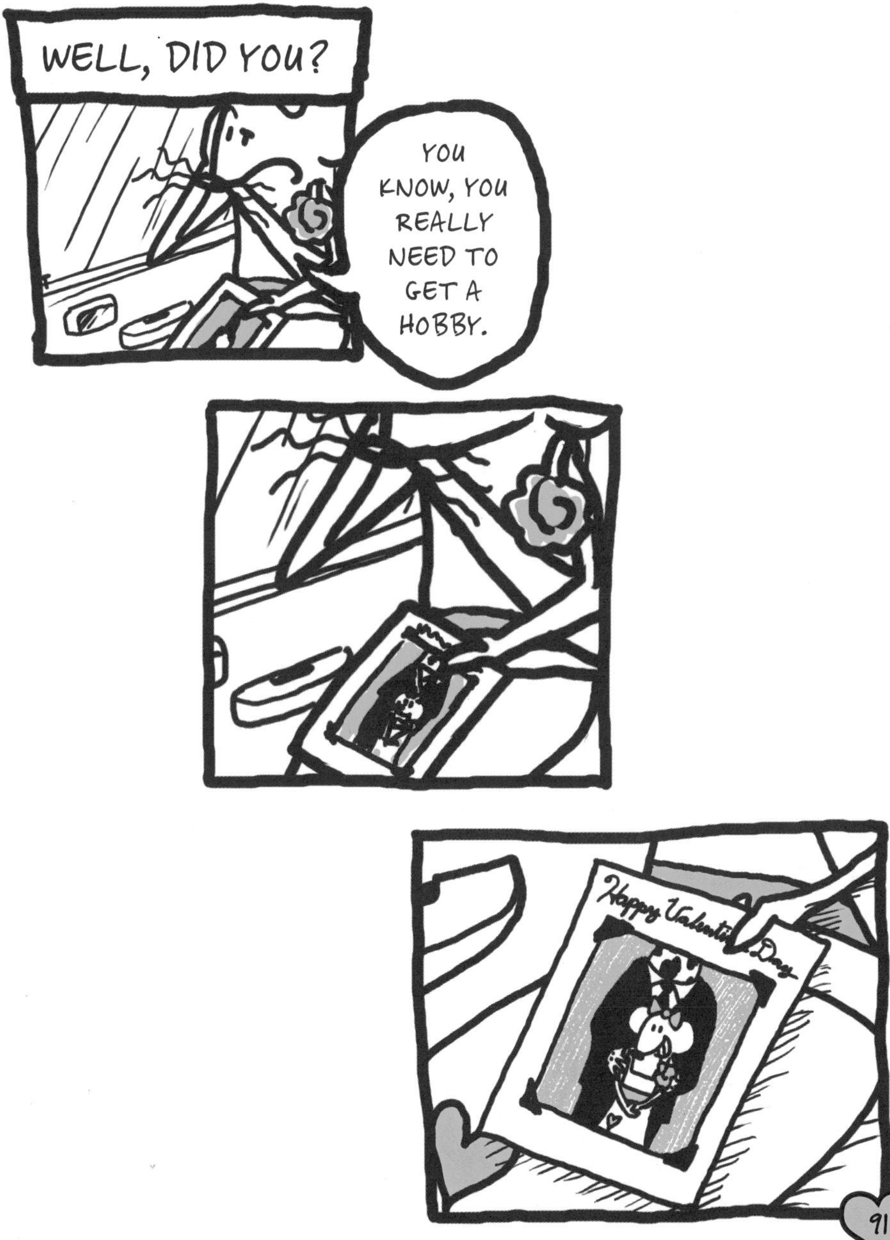
WELL, DID YOU?
YOU KNOW, YOU REALLY NEED TO GET A HOBBY.
Happy Valenti
Day

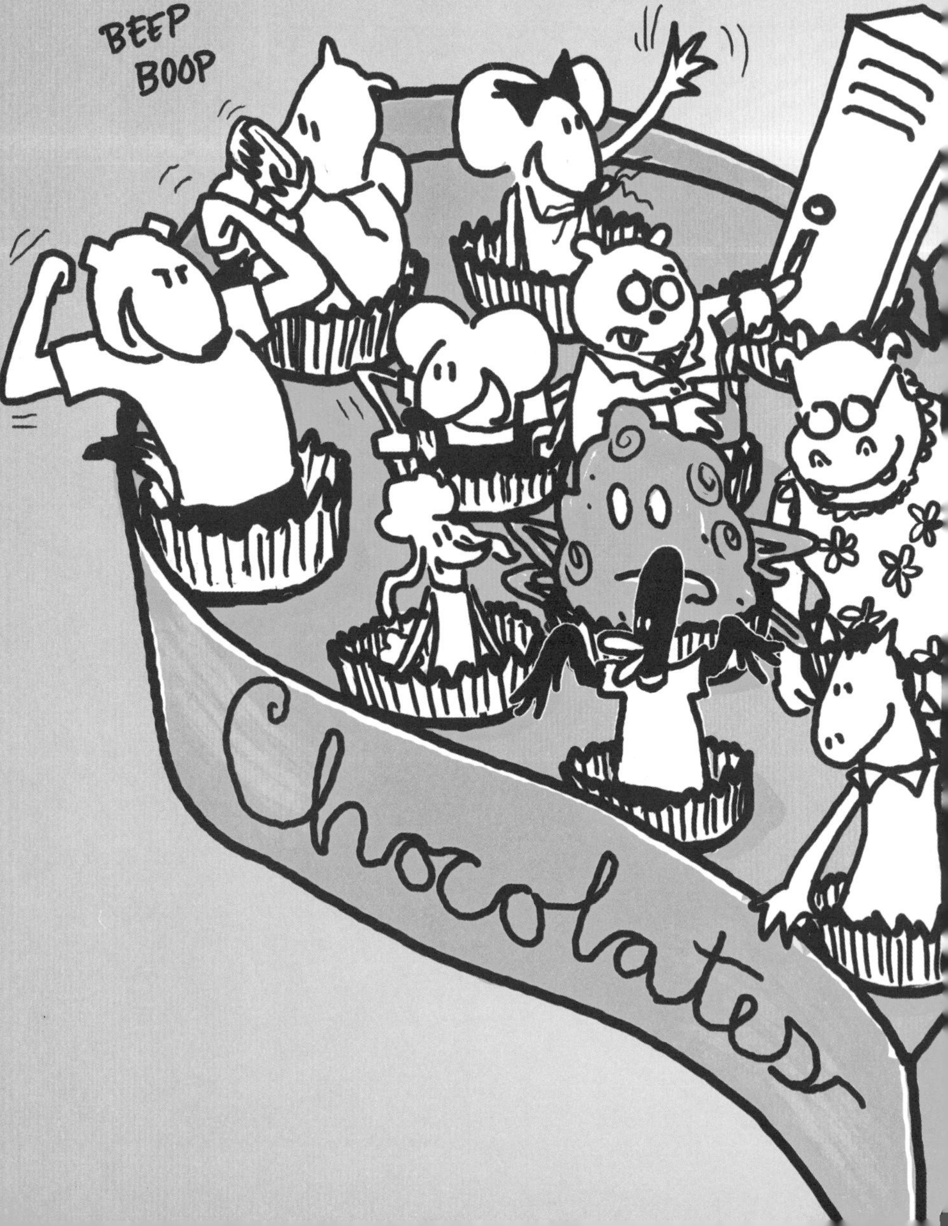
BEEP
BOOP
Chocolates

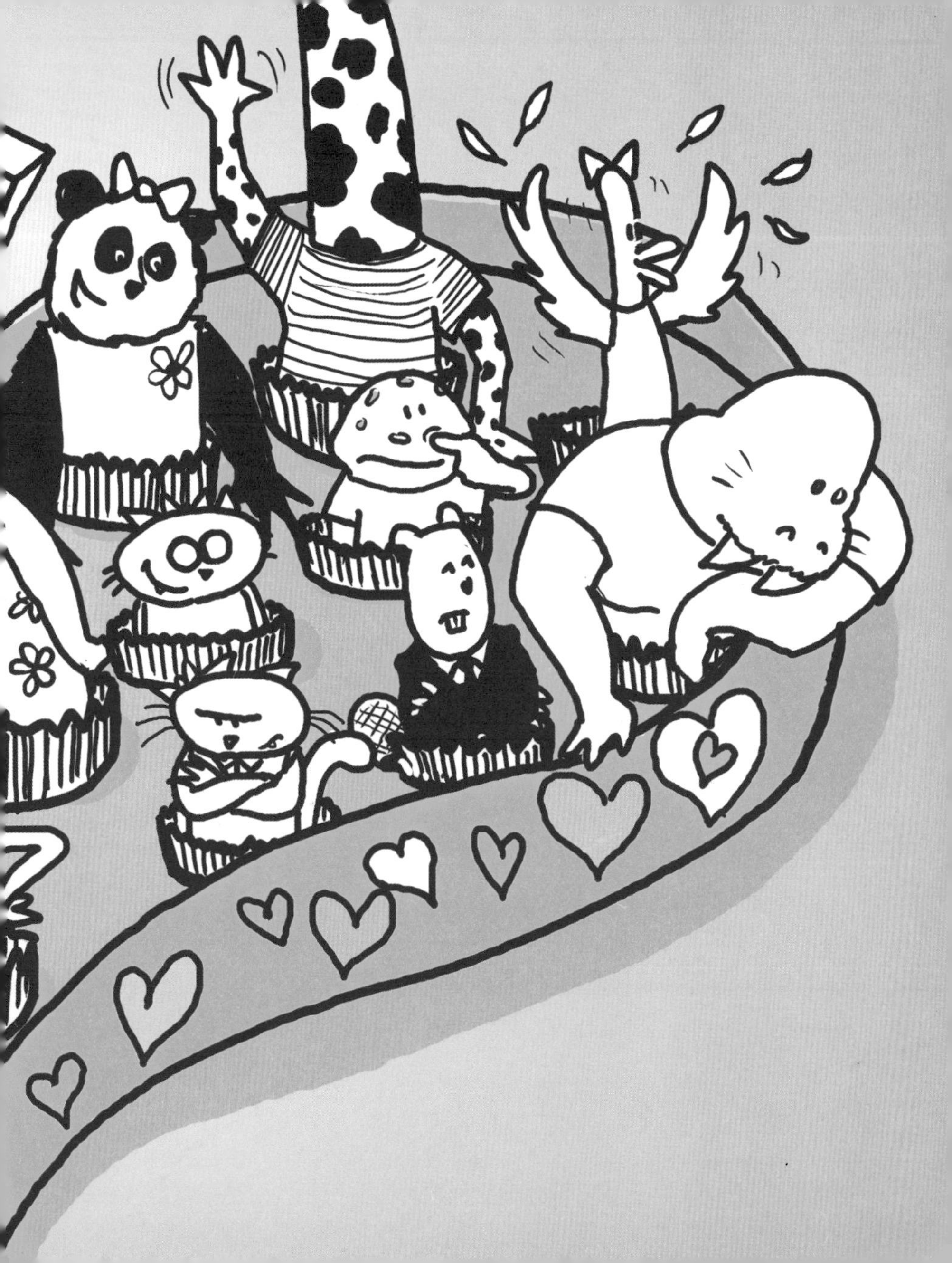